MW01174950

THE SWIFT REVENGE OF THE

GREEN GHOST

THE SWIFT REVENGE OF THE
GREEN GHOST

WRITTEN BY

JOHNSTON McCULLEY

INTRODUCTION BY

PETER POPLASKI

BOSTON

ALTUS PRESS

2012

PUBLISHING HISTORY
"The Green Ghost" originally appeared in THRILLING
DETECTIVE *(March 1934), "The Day of Settlement" originally
appeared in* THRILLING DETECTIVE *(May 1934), "Swift
Revenge" originally appeared in* THRILLING DETECTIVE
(June 1934), "The Green Ghost Stalks" originally appeared in
THRILLING DETECTIVE *(September 1934), "The Murder Note"
originally appeared in* THRILLING DETECTIVE *(January 1935),
"Deadly Peril" originally appeared in* THRILLING DETECTIVE
(June 1935), and "Bloodstained Bonds" originally appeared in
THRILLING DETECTIVE *(July 1935).*

TABLE OF

CONTENTS

PETER POPLASKI

I **n 1930 JOHNSTON McCULLEY** was living in Beverly Hills, California in a posh $85,000 home. Several months earlier, The Great Depression had suddenly seized the country by the scruff of its economic neck and had shaken it hard, several times. Even so, though the heavens had become heavy and dark for so many, it had not stopped people from going to the movies. So the view at this moment was still that of a sunny and blue cloudless California sky from where Johnston McCulley sat behind his typewriter, looking out at what may have been a Yucca tree in his own back yard. He was a forty-seven year old pulp magazine writer who had found his niche. Ten silent movies had been adapted over the past decade and a half from stories he had written for various pulp magazines that he was a frequent contributor to. Now, as this summer day was coming to an end, as Prohibition wore on, and as gangsters dominated the newspaper headlines along with unemployment figures, Johnston McCulley returned to one of the most important members of his little stock company of characters: the masked avenging hero, and he closed his eyes to daydream for a moment.

McCulley was a short, cocky, self-assured yarn spinner who had from behind his dark rimmed glasses, seen America as what was once termed a "tramp newspaperman." This was a label for many adventurous journeymen writers who traveled around finding temporary employment for uncertain periods of time on various daily or weekly journals as their skills were needed.

Then eventually, like a seasonal worker, they would be paid off and they moved on. Harold Ross, the man who founded *The New Yorker*, started his career running this sort of circuit out in Colorado, until he found his way to the top of the town. McCulley sold his skills and talent and gained considerable freedom as he jumped to and from the Peoria Times, over to the Portland *Oregonian*, up to the Seattle *Times*, down to the San Francisco *Examiner*, and then the Los Angeles *Herald-Express*, always moving on to greener pastures. It no doubt was a combination of ambition, his grandfather, a young wife, restlessness, and pretty girls that helped forge the youthful McCulley into to a prolific peddler of pulp prose for popular western and detective story magazines which were distributed on a weekly basis, blanketing every newsstand, book shop, and train depot in America since the beginning of the twentieth century.

McCulley's writing career began to take off in 1906 while he was living in Oregon. He had been published regionally there and then he took a chance and submitted a story to *Red Book* titled: "The Song of The Sand." It was immediately accepted for publication and appeared in the October issue. The twenty-three year-old writer's inspiration and luck continued as he managed to sell stories in quick succession to *Blue Book*, *Cosmopolitan*, and *Munsey's*. He was earning and learning. He tried writing a stage play. For *Railroad Man's Magazine* he created his earliest known continuing character: Richard Hughes–Railroad Detective that ran for six installments in 1908. In the same period he began selling longer serial stories to *The Argosy* like "The Land of Lost Hope." McCulley's more ambitious and longer pieces of fiction had an after taste of the best adventure classics. For instance, "Lost Hope" had a touch of H. Rider Haggard, and then "When the World Stood Still," (1909), seems to have a nod toward H.G. Wells. "King of Chaos." (1912), another *Argosy* novel, exhibits more than a passing wave to Anthony Hope and *The Prisoner of Zenda*. While still a feature writer for a mid-western newspaper in 1909, McCulley had waved around in the air a $300 check from

Munsey's he had just received that day to the great annoyance of his fellow reporters. He proclaimed that the real money was in writing for magazines and he crowed to the whole bullpen that he only took a newspaper job to get exercise. His colleagues seemed genuinely glad when he suddenly had to return to the west coast. Around 1910 McCulley jumped on the gimmick of using twin brothers or twin sisters or

Guy Williams and Johnston McCulley

the double: two look-a-like hero and villain characters he could play with and interchange to confuse and surprise the readers of his fiction. It was probably his over-use of this plot device that eventually led him to his future popular dual identity characters like his famous and iconic Zorro.

The winds of fortune seemed to favor Johnston McCulley. Surprisingly one day, for "Pennington's Choice," a *Cavalier* magazine story published in 1915, the writer received from his publisher Frank Munsey, news of the notification of receiving two telegrams from Anita Loos, a young lady who worked for D.W. Griffith in Hollywood. She wished to purchase the film rights to McCulley's pulp story for a studio who wanted to make a film starring Francis X. Bushman and Beverly Bayne. McCulley was delighted but unsure at this time how a lowbrow movie sale might affect his serious writing career and so he cautiously received his story credit as J.A. Culley. This is Johnston McCulley's earliest known movie sale, though in a later interview he bragged to have banged out fifty. A movie sale more than doubled the money he received at the time for a manuscript. The writer got $800 for an original serial to be published in *All-Story,* and then by contract, he split a $2,000 film rights fee with his publisher. There was also the added bonus of publicity. His name being thus attached to a film production insured that his credit would be appearing on the movie posters, in newspaper ads, and in reviews. Beginning here then is when McCulley's pulp stories became connected to the silent movies with the accent on action. "Unclaimed Goods" (1917), "The Brute Breaker" (1918), "A White Man's Chance" (1918), and "Broadway Bab" (1918), all appeared first in print and then a few months later on the silver screen with featured players Vivian Martin, Frank Mayo, J. Warren Kerrigan, and Ruth Roland portraying his lead characters to the great mass audience. The topper to all this success, a spike in his upward climb, was the moment when one of Hollywood's biggest stars, Douglas Fairbanks, bought the rights to "The Curse of Capistrano" (1919), and then hired McCulley to help adapt it into *The Mark of Zorro* (1920). The film was an outstanding success, keeping the struggling new United Artists Corporation alive while the film itself became something of a landmark in the history of silent cinema. Fairbanks received special praise in a note from D.W. Griffith for it. Thus both men, pulp writer and movie star, achieved with the masked Zorro something that changed and furthered their careers.

At first Fairbanks talked of a sequel and McCulley came up with "The Further Adventures of Zorro" (1922), but Doug changed his mind. Not wanting to repeat himself the producer/star considered something more medieval for which McCulley most likely penned "The Black Jarl" (1923), the writer's only medieval historical romance. *Robin Hood* (1922) turned out to be the blockbuster that Fairbanks chose to make, but still, the pirate elements from the proposed Zorro sequel would later turn up in *The Black Pirate* (1926). Douglas Fairbanks never wasted anything. McCulley realized that with the heavy promotional campaign Fairbanks demanded for *The Mark of Zorro,* masked characters and costume pictures could potentially come into vogue. So Johnston McCulley and his pen name, Harrington Strong, turned out every possible masked adventure character variant: The Thunderbolt, The Man in Purple, Madame Madcap, The Demon, The Scarlet Scourge, The Crimson Clown, all of whom with gun in hand appeared in print in a series of short stories, and multi-part serials in *Detective Story Magazine* throughout the Roaring Twenties. This deluge of masked adventure characters developed into the signature hallmark of McCulley's writing career. Also, since Fairbanks had found gold with Zorro, two earlier McCulley pulp stories with a Spanish California background: "Little Erolinda" and "Captain Fly-By-Night," both from 1916, were immediately sold to the movies and became The Kiss (1921) with Carmel Myers, and (without a title change) *Captain Fly-By-Night* (1922) was released as a starring vehicle for Johnnie Walker. Throughout the 1920s, the pulp stories of Johnston McCulley were translated into films. *Ride For Your Life* (1924) with Hoot Gibson, *The Ice Flood* (1926) with Viola Dana, *The Black Jack* with Buck Jones (1927), and *Saddle Mates* (1928) all contributed to the writer's continuing success.

Douglas Fairbanks returned to the Zorro character in his *Don Q, Son of Zorro* sequel of 1925, and he did an odd thing. Doug had acquired the film rights to *Don Q's Love Story*, a British pulp character with a Spanish locale that had been adapted for the London stage in 1920. Doug and Mary may have seen the production during their European honeymoon. He bought the rights to Don Q and later decided to combine this property with Zorro, since he already controlled the film rights to the bold masked renegade. This may have cut McCulley out of the loop on the project because even though as author McCulley still owned the literary rights to Zorro, he received no credit for his character in the second film or in any of its publicity. And he should have. Even though this is a lavish enjoyable Douglas Fairbanks spectacle, it is the sudden reappearance of the masked Zorro that speeds up the heavily laden melodrama, changing the film's tempo, switching it to a higher gear, and with great double exposures of Zorro/Doug fencing side by side with Don Q/Doug, this double dose of Doug playing father and son teamed up against the overwhelming numbers of Spanish soldiers drives the film to it's exciting climax. No wonder Douglas Fairbanks was every American boy's heroic ideal. McCulley also deserved some sort of mention in the credits of *The Black Pirate* for some of the original Zorro sequel bits that made it into this classic film. But he did not see any.

The success of Zorro guaranteed imitators. Fairbanks' Zorro inspired Rudolf Valentino to star in *The Eagle* in 1925, a masked Russian Cossack sort of Robin Hood. Richard Talmadge, a former stunt coordinator for the Fairbanks studio began starring in his own action films, and also in 1925, he fought drug smugglers in the *Prince of Pep* as an updated modern Zorro called The Black Flash (in France, the film was known as *Une Aventure a la Zorro*). Then there was cowboy star Tim McCoy, who with mask and sword had a go as an MGM Zorro type in *Beyond The Sierras* (1928).

In truth, the masked helper/stranger was a popular plot device that came out of dime novels and silent serials. *Deadwood Dick or The Black Rider of The Black Hills* was a masked outlaw who first appeared in his own dime-novel series in 1877. The Laughing Mask was a mysterious hooded helper rescuing Pearl White in *The Iron Claw* serial of 1916. With the Zorro character, McCulley thought it would be good theatre to let the audience in on the secret joke from the beginning, rather than at the end. For the audience to know that the weakest character was actually the strong hero made for good comedy. It was not used only for a surprising contrast, but also to give balance to the dangerous fast moving action scenes that come later in the story. This exciting transformation is part of playing make believe, of pretending to be someone else, of being opposite from who you really are, is the fundamental root of theatre that the silent movie comedians learned how to exploit to not only raise sympathy for their characters, but get big laughs. The fact that the great silent comedians like Fairbanks, Chaplin, Keaton, and Lloyd were physical enough to demonstrate this visually with their bodies and screen personas, also enabled them to leap to a world wide super star status that still keeps them all held in high esteem ninety years later. The influence of these men and their clever and hilarious films was immense. For example, a case could be made that the image of one of the most violent pulp heroes of the thirties, *The Spider–Master of Men* actually derives from the Harold Lloyd 1923 comedy *Dr. Jack,* wherein Harold, during one of the wackiest dark house chase sequences throws on a woman's cloak, a wig, a slouch hat, fangs and ambles about scaring the mansion's upper crust owners and their servants, who believe him to be a mad killer who has just escaped from prison. It's arguably, the first real visual appearance of The Spider! So a pulp story can inspire a movie and a movie can inspire a pulp magazine. It is all part of the growth of the entertainment industry. It is business, and yet, how the public comes to identify with and even love these imaginary characters who don't have to live a boring existence and who are able to solve everyone else's problems. So the success of the masked Zorro along with McCulley deliberately creating pulp magazine variations on the theme, and also combined with many cinema copycats, helped to establish a genre that inspired young cartoonists drawing comic books at the end of the 1930s. Amazingly, many of these characters became "intellectual properties" that are part of the costumed super-hero billion dollar industry of today. And yet eighty years earlier, there was just Johnston McCulley, daydreaming, with his fingers on the keys of his typewriter.

This time it was the Rollicking Rogue who emerged from the ether and took his form in words typed across a sheet of white paper. The new character was a figure in a yellow costume with a red sash and a shimmering yellow cape, a red skull cap mask with yellow devil's horns, a twisted leer painted to disguise his mouth (lipstick?) and a pistol in his hand. McCulley always had a sense of humor about these masked characters. The writer enjoyed creating someone who looked ridiculous, but who was also potentially deadly. His new dual identity character had to play weak, look funny, but could then be scary and strong. Chapter One was titled: "A Mocking Laugh" which no doubt echoed the mocking laugh that issued from the lips of Johnston McCulley as the writer visualized his latest "bent hero." (It sounded much like the mocking laugh that The Shadow would later laugh two years hence in that character's first appearance in print and then later on radio). The Rollicking Rogue was put through the paces of what would be at least two appearances in Clayton pulps' *All Star Detective Stories* (maybe there are more). McCulley used his basic plot formula, which usually began with a rich swindling financier being terrorized by a mysterious masked man demanding payment and personal vengeance. All of McCulley's heroes are letter writers who like to inform the victim as well as the police of their intentions. It was an open challenge. The evil greed of this businessman and his associates a decade before had not only destroyed the fortunes of a fine and upstanding family, but had also ruined their reputation. It was payback time. Curiously and causing great confusion was McCulley's later use in 1939 of this character's name for the title of a hardcover western novel with absolutely no connection to the earlier masked hero episodes.

Only just recently, McCulley had said goodbye to two earlier and popular long running masked confections: The Black Star and The Crimson Clown. McCulley had begun his run of The Black Star in 1916 in *Detective Story Weekly* using an alias, as John Mack Stone, to protect his real name if the story bombed. It didn't. He got fan mail from readers. His black hooded supercriminal with the star of black jet on his forehead to denote leadership, (who was in looks and character, very similar to the French Fantomas), had over the years plotted, robbed, blackmailed, gassed, and escaped through 16 novelettes, short stories, and several serials, and then many of the stories were collected in five hardcover reprint editions in Great Britain and the United States. The Crimson Clown in 1926, for 18 episodes in the same pulp magazine as The Black Star, by personal invitation, commenced fleecing all the weak rich bored society leaders who were brazen enough to display their jewels in public at wherever and whenever the social elite gathered. He called himself The Crimson Clown because of the special thin red silk outfit with hooded mask attached that he carefully wrapped around his torso under his silk dress shirt and then donned during the festivities in the shadowy recesses of a vacant corridor when he had a moment alone. The costume that concealed his dress suit with tails resembled a circus clown's but with a mournful hood and mask that never was in agreement with the brightly painted lurid covers that depicted the character looking like a white faced clown in red. The Crimson Clown also had two international hardcover reprint editions as well. Neither had movies made of them but perhaps one of their stories may have been adapted for publisher Street and Smith's early radio show.

Douglas Fairbanks announced remaking Zorro with sound. He had United Artists recall all prints of *The Mark of Zorro* from world distribution, perhaps in preparation for a new version. The King of Hollywood was fast approaching the age of fifty and with the coming of "talkies" the fun of movie making was fading for him. Sound had frozen cinema making the moving image static so that audiences could enjoy watching their favorite actors speak. His press secretaries threw out sound bites almost on a daily basis for the movie columns of America's newspapers. Although he never followed through with the idea, Fairbanks did say at various times that he was thinking of remaking Zorro with sound, then later, in color with sound, and finally, perhaps as a co-starring swashbuckler with his son, Douglas Fairbanks, Jr. The movies never happened, but Johnston McCulley thought he'd just better keep his hand in the game. He created The Rollicking Rogue for *All Star Detective Stories* in 1930, "Zorro Rides Again," a four-part serial for *Argosy* in 1931, (with a Zorro novelette every year through 1934 and a two-part serial in 1935), "Rogue of the Highway" starring the masked El Bribon for *Top-Notch* in 1932, the masked El Torbellino the Whirlwind for *Thrilling Adventures*, also in 1932, The Mongoose for *Detective Fiction Weekly* in 1933, The Green Ghost for *Thrilling Detective* in 1934, "Rangeland Justice," a hardcover novel he wrote in 1919 starring the masked Yellowjacket was reprinted in 1934, Walking Death for *Thrilling Western* in 1935. McCulley is also credited as "ghosting" a back from the dead masked character called The Bat for *Thrilling Detective*, also in 1934. McCulley was determined that one day Zorro, in one form or another, would return to the silver screen. It had been a smash hit for Douglas Fairbanks. Maybe it could be again for someone else. It was too good not to.

The Green Ghost was Johnston McCulley's only irish masked hero, and he wrote it with his usual sense of fun, dropping the "r" from "blarney" to name his character's secret identity and playing with the cliché of Irish cops. The snarl on Danny Blaney's lips beneath the green silk hooded mask he pulled over his head in the dark shadows of a back alley, was an expression not only of his "mick temper," but also an extension of the single-minded contempt he held for all gangdom, especially the crooks (and he knew who they were) who framed him for crimes he didn't commit and for the police officers, his own former colleagues, who had believed the set-up that had discredited him. It was pay back time for everybody. No one was excluded. It was as if McCulley had, in his own small way, gone over to the Warner Brothers Studio and adopted that dark edge that director William Wellman had given to his film *Public Enemy*. The Green Ghost was an Irish loner and he had been a good cop in the concrete urban jungle, still, his seven adventures of delivering comeuppance to criminals follow the rigid McCulley formula of all the writer's other masked avengers of the modern big city scene. Perhaps it was his living near the Hollywood movie studios that caused McCulley to give The Rollicking Rogue such a crazy yellow costume with cape and devil's horns, but by late 1931, an *Argosy* writer's profile reported the writer living in New York City. It stated McCulley worked out of an apartment on the eleventh floor of a hotel in Manhattan, and described the writer looking down at the people in the street and up over into the windows of the nearby buildings across the way, imagining plot ideas for his next story. Was this the way Johnston McCulley had come to realize The Green Ghost? Had McCulley lost his Beverly Hills home to the Great Depression?

From 1929 to 1933 Johnston McCulley appears to have had no movie sales from his fiction. But it seems he attempted to connect with the fast ever-growing medium of radio in 1933. According to his incomplete biographical information he wrote ten radio plays and worked with some production group. Then from late 1934 and on, Monogram and Republic Studios began buying McCulley western pulp stories for their B-movie production units. They started with his 1923 "The King of Cactusville" (from *Western Story Magazine* which had then been reprinted in 1924 in hardcover as *The Ranger's Code*). The studio adapted it into *The Outlaw Deputy* for Tim McCoy in 1935. Perhaps the experiment with radio and the interest shown by Hollywood studios in his backlog of western stories written for pulp magazines that could be used for B-movies distracted McCulley from continuing and writing endings for The Rollicking Rogue, The Whirlwind, The Mongoose, and The Green Ghost, because after several installments over a couple of years these masked characters just stop. Was the reason the writer's commuting from Los Angeles to New York and back again?

In 1934 Douglas Fairbanks retired from the screen after starring in *The Private Life of Don Juan,* which was filmed in England. Almost immediately, new sound versions of his silent screen blockbusters were remade beginning with *The Three Musketeers* in 1935. A new version of Zorro was not far behind. Since Zorro had been the hinge of his career, Doug had mentioned the idea of remaking Zorro in sound and in color. McCulley, selling his pulp stories to Monogram Pictures, managed to persuade the newly formed Republic Studios to take a chance on a new Zorro film. This project was titled "The Return of

Zorro" and the green light was given to writer-director Wells Root to make it, adding in the on-screen credits: "based on an idea by Johnston McCulley." The new 1936 film was retitled *The Bold Caballero* and starred Robert Livingston as the all-talking and singing Don Diego and a grim hooded silent Zorro in color. Fairbanks still controlled film rights to *The Mark of Zorro* and so Republic had to approach the character in a different way and with a different look. The studio also made a serial: *The Vigilantes Are Coming* with Livingston again in mask, this time as The Black Eagle, a Zorro clone, in the same year. RKO studios had earlier jumped in with *The Far Frontier*, a western serial starring the young Lon Chaney Jr. as The Black Ghost. Columbia Pictures filmed *The Spider's Web*, perhaps the best serial adaptation of a pulp magazine character. Republic Pictures continued with a modern updated Zorro serial that starred singer John Carroll in *Zorro Rides Again*. It is not known how much McCulley contributed to this project, but his "Tainted Caballero" *Argosy* serial was made as *Rose of the Rio Grande* by Monogram with the same actor singing "Ride, Amigos Ride" and playing the hero El Puma (later, it would be remade as the Cisco Kid film *South of The Rio Grande* in 1945). His name does not seem to appear in four out the five Zorro serials Republic Pictures made in the 1930s and '40s. He should at least receive credit as the Zorro character's creator.

Over at Twentieth Century Fox, Darrel F. Zanuck saw Zorro as a musical. He had plans to cast Lawrence Tibbitt, the Metropolitan Opera baritone star of *The Rogue Song* in the Don Diego/Zorro double role but when the film musical *Metropole* starring the singer bombed at the box office, Zanuck scraped the project including Zorro's big song "My Saddle Is My Throne." He went back to the original pulp and Fairbanks silent classic and worked on the script for two years. Since Fairbanks was still alive and controlled the film rights to *The Mark of Zorro*, the project was titled *The Californian*. Tyrone Power was cast in the lead and Zanuck hired Rouben Mamoulian to direct, even agreeing to an unusual director's cut contractual deal. With

Fairbanks' untimely death, 20th Century Fox managed to obtain the film rights from Doug's estate and retitled their film. Thus, Johnston McCulley and *The Mark of Zorro* hit the theatres in November of 1940 to great acclaim although critics made the observation that Power was no Fairbanks. And it can be said that the only thing missing from the film is a dueling scene with Zorro himself in action. Still, it was another great success and it inspired another 5-part *Argosy* serial "The Sign of Zorro" out of McCulley.

By 1940 there were scores of masked avengers out in plain view thanks to the Sunday comics (The Phantom), pulps (The Shadow, The Spider, The Phantom Detective, The Black Bat), radio (The Lone Ranger, The Green Hornet), movie serials (The Black Ghost, The Black Eagle, The Spider, The Lone Ranger, The Green Hornet, The Copperhead), and comic books (The Masked Avenger, The Sandman, Batman, The Spirit). Even W. C. Fields dressed up as The Masked Bandit to get a kiss from Mae West who he thinks he is married to in *My Little Chickadee*. The masked costumed character was becoming part of what would become the super-hero genre. This market niche turned out to be a gold mine thanks to media and the love of the fans, both young and old. And television was still in the future. When it did come along, Zorro and Johnston McCulley would score big yet again.

The Rollicking Rogue and the Green Ghost live in the smelly pages of old pulp magazines, but now the reprinting of their collected adventures in editions like this one will bring them back to life for an audience who seeks out hard to find examples of Depression Period entertainment. This book also shines a light highlighting a part of the mysterious McCulley and his writing career. The Rollicking Rogue and The Green Ghost are but two of a crowd of at least 16 masked adventure characters. One day in Hollywood, in March, 1956, Johnston McCulley blithely inscribed a recent British hardcover edition of his 1940 *Argosy* serial "The Devils Doubloons" to visitors writing, "Just to let them know I am not *"hombre de un libro."* Well no, actually he had over fifty hardcover books published, mostly reprinting collected pulp character series and westerns. McCulley wasn't a "hombre of one movie" either. There are at least 29 movies that give him some sort of writing credit. His pulp stories were bought and filmed by all the Hollywood studios: Paramount, United Artists, Universal, MGM, Republic, Columbia, Monogram, Puritan, 20th Century Fox, and Disney. So beyond Zorro, who was this writer of a thousand pulp stories? Behind the mask, who was Johnston McCulley? A piece of that puzzle lies within these pages.

PETER POPLASKI
August 20, 2012
St. Hippolyte du Fort, France.

(This introduction was written from material complied by Peter Poplaski from his 20 year project: Zorro–The Myth, The Mask and The Image*)*.

THE GREEN GHOST

CHAPTER 1

SIX FEET FROM THE mouth of the alley, it was pitch dark. At the edge of the darkness, Danny Blaney waited. He was keyed to a high nervous pitch. Crouching against the wall of the apartment house, he watched carefully. In his right hand, he held a blackjack.

"Snoopy" Carns was the first to appear. A distant tower clock had just struck two when Blaney saw Snoopy slip furtively to the mouth of the alley. He glanced in both directions, then darted into the darkness. Blaney gripped his blackjack and crouched closer to the wall.

Snoopy Carns had to pass within a few feet of him to get to the side door which opened into the basement of the apartment house. Danny Blaney knew the exact path he would have to take. He did not need a light to accomplish his purpose.

Shuffling steps, scarcely heard, came along the pavement of the alley.

"Carns!" Blaney spoke the name softly.

Snoopy Carns stopped abruptly. Blaney knew he was trying to peer into the darkness, and that he could see nothing.

"Who is it?" Carns' words were mere whispers.

"Here!"

Blaney crept forward cautiously, extending his left hand. It brushed against Snoopy's shoulder. And suddenly it thrust Snoopy back against the wall—and then Blaney struck with the blackjack.

1

Max Ganler himself opened the door, expecting his friends. "Wh—what—?"

The blow fell true. Snoopy Carns had started an ejaculation of surprise, but it ended in a gurgle. Blaney caught his sagging body and lowered it to the ground.

Now, Blaney worked swiftly. He searched the pockets of Snoopy's clothes, but did not find what he sought. He ripped open waistcoat and shirt, and an instant later had in his possession a money belt, its compartments filled with jewels.

Blaney stuffed the jewels into his own pockets, and tossed the money belt away. Then he bound Snoopy's wrists behind his back, and fastened his ankles together using cords that were as strong as wire. He gagged Snoopy with a gag previously prepared, and rolled him over against the wall.

Crouching against the wall again, Blaney waited. In less than ten minutes, Bill Sorsten appeared. He, too, stopped at the mouth of the alley to glance up and down the street, then slipped back into the darkness.

Bill Sorsten was not like Carns. Bill Sorsten was a thug, a master in the art of rough-and-tumble fighting. Rendering him helpless would be a more difficult job.

Blaney stepped out from the wall and waited. Bill Sorsten

lurched toward him through the black night.

"Bill!" Blaney hissed the word.

Sorsten did not reply. He was too cautions, too suspicious for that. He stopped suddenly, was silent and motionless, waiting for the unknown in the darkness to speak again, so he could locate him exactly.

But Blaney did not speak. He scarcely breathed. He did not move enough to cause his clothing to rustle. There, within only a few feet of each other, the pair stood, each trying to locate the other.

Blaney sensed that Bill Sorsten stepped closer to the wall. In a lull in the wind that swept through the alley, he heard a man's deep breath. Then a sleeve brushed against his sleeve.

Blaney whirled and grappled with the man. Bill Sorsten grunted a curse. The blackjack fell, but glanced off a shoulder. Sorsten cursed again, aloud.

Once more Blaney struck, and the blow brought a cry of pain. Bill Sorsten was trying to put up a fight. Blaney evaded a bearlike hug that probably would have been his undoing. He struck again, and this time the blackjack cracked against the side of Bill Sorsten's head. Blaney lowered him to the ground and worked swiftly to get his wrists tied securely. He fastened the ankles, also, and then began going through Bill Sorsten's pockets. In a chamois bag fastened in Sorsten's left armpit, he found more jewels.

BLANEY TOOK them, returned a few to one of Sorsten's pockets, and retained the others. Then he crouched against the wall again and waited. Presently, Sorsten moaned. Snoopy Carns had been gurgling for some little time, showing that he had regained consciousness. Blaney heard both of them squirming and twisting. Both were conscious and aware of their bonds.

"Sorsten, can you hear?" Blaney asked.

"Who is it? What's happened?"

"It's the Green Ghost, Sorsten!"

CHAPTER II

THERE WAS SILENCE FOR a moment, save for the rustling of the wind as it swept through the alley. Then Sorsten spoke in a tense voice:

"The Green Ghost! Who are you? What's this mean, anyhow? You'll be put on the spot for this!"

"Yeah? How can you put on the spot a man you don't know?"

"Maybe I do know you."

"If I thought you did, Sorsten, I'd stick the muzzle of my automatic in your ear, and pull the trigger. But you don't know— you can't."

"What's your game?"

"I hate crooks, Sorsten. I know a lot about 'em. I'm out to wreck 'em, and their plans, and turn 'em in."

"Workin' for the cops, huh?"

"I hate the cops, too. That's enough—I'm not giving out a lot of information. I sent a note to Max Ganler, told him I'd be after him next."

"He thought it was somebody's joke."

"It's no joke, Sorsten. You pulled off a neat jewel job at the Carstairs house a short time ago, didn't you, Sorsten? I knew all about it in advance. I know who was on the job. It was big, and it'll be a sensation. Max Ganler's done it again. But the fool cops wouldn't be able to pin it on him."

"Whoever you are, you're crazy!" Bill Sorsten said. "I ain't seen Max Ganler for ages."

"You just said you knew about my note."

"I was told about that. I was just comin' to see Max now."

"Why sneak in to the alley entrance?" Blaney asked.

"Max don't like to have some of us go through the lobby late at night."

"You're not fooling me a bit, Sorsten. Max was on that big job himself tonight. So was Snoopy Carns. I tapped Snoopy on his head, and he's over there against the wall. Gagged him so he couldn't yell and warn you when you came into the alley."

"I say you're crazy! I'll bet Max has been home all this evenin'. I know he was intendin' to have a little party. It's his girl's birthday—Lily Ratch's. That's why I waited so late to come and see him.

"If it's any of your business, I wanted to borrow a little jack off him.

"I just took a lot of jewels from you, Sorsten. You could have peddled them to a fence, if you needed jack. But you were bringing them to Max Ganler, so he can handle 'em. I got some off Snoopy, too. You were carrying home the swag. Max wouldn't run the risk of packing them himself."

"WHO ARE you? How'd you know? What's the percentage in your racket?" Sorsten asked.

"I'm the Green Ghost, and that's enough to you. I know a lot of things. Knew you were going to pull off that Carstairs job. And I'm going to turn you in for it! About percentage—I keep some of the swag for expenses, and give the rest to charity."

"I'm tellin' you—" Sorsten began.

"Tell me nothing!"

"Untie me, and let me go. You've got the loot."

"Can't think of it, Sorsten. Howl for the cops, if you like. Somebody may hear you and call 'em, and then you'd have a lot of explaining to do."

"You goin' to leave Carns and me here, tied up?"

"You've guessed it, Sorsten. Somebody will happen along and pick you up, I imagine."

"But what's the idea? What've I ever done to you?"

"If I told you too much, you might guess my identity," Blaney said. "Good-by, Sorsten!"

Blaney backed away through the darkness. It swallowed him. Silently he crept along the wall of the apartment house toward the basement door.

He knew that Bill Sorsten would get loose soon, and free Snoopy Carns, and that they would hurry into the building and carry news of this double outrage to Max Ganler, the boss crook the cops were unable to catch.

But that was exactly as Danny Blaney wanted it.

CHAPTER III

BLANEY HAD TAKEN A bunch of keys from Snoopy Carns' pocket. Now he hurried to the little basement door, tried the keys, and found that the third he tried did the work. He went through the door and locked it behind him.

An instant later, he was creeping quietly along a basement hall, alert, ready to dodge to cover if he heard anybody coming.

He got to a service stairs and up to the first floor, went unseen along a hall to a rear stairway, and began ascending. Max Ganler's apartment, his objective, was on the fourth floor.

Almost directly across the hall from the entrance door of Ganler's apartment was a supply closet. Blaney got in among the mops and brooms. He unbuttoned coat and vest, and from around his body took a garment made of thin green silk. Slipped over his head, it became a hood that came down to his shoulders, and had slits for eyes. He drew on a pair of thin green gloves. His suit was of inconspicuous black, not unlike thousands of other suits in the city. His shirt was dark, his tie black, his shoes black and of ordinary pattern.

WITH THE hood enveloping his head and throat, the gloves shielding his hands, Danny Blaney had no fear of being identified. In size and general build he was not unlike thousands of other men.

Inside the closet, where it was hot and stifling, he waited. He had ceased being Danny Blaney for the time; he was the

7

Green Ghost, the man who hated the crooks, who was out to run them down, but not particularly to aid the police, since he hated them also.

Danny Blaney had been on the Force. He had been an honest and conscientious officer. He had been framed by crooks, and his shield taken from him. Though he had not been tried for crime, the world had judged him guilty. Crooks had wrecked his career, because he had been too active in giving testimony against some of their leaders. And his comrades had believed!

So, Danny Blaney became the Green Ghost. It was a perilous role he played. Once he was suspected, it would become more perilous. He pretended that he had inherited some money. He owned a corner cigar store, and ran it with the assistance of three clerks. That was good cover.

Now he heard a burst of laughter, and opened the closet door a crack. The front door of Max Ganler's apartment had been opened, and Max stood framed in it—a short, squat, swarthy man with a twisted smile and the eyes of a killer.

Max Ganler was sending another man on an errand.

"Get those cigarettes! Be sure to mention I'm howling because I'm out, and that we've been having a party here since nine last night. Make it thick. And hurry back!" The other hurried toward the elevator. Max Ganler closed the door of the apartment. Blaney closed the door of the closet.

But he opened it a crack again not more than ten minutes later, when he heard somebody hurrying along the hall. Snoopy Carns and Bill Sorsten were there. They had got free of their bonds, as Blaney had expected they would.

They rang, and were admitted immediately. Inside the Max Ganler apartment, the sounds of merriment ceased suddenly. Blaney could visualize the scene—Carns and Sorsten telling what had happened to them in the alley, and Max Ganler at the point of murdering them.

IN THE near distance, an elevator door clanged. Blaney glanced through the door again. The man Ganler had sent for cigarettes was coming back.

As he passed the door of the closet, Blaney jerked it open and struck once with the blackjack. He caught the slumping form and pulled it inside. Working swiftly, he affixed a gag, and used the thin, tough cords to bind the man's wrists and ankles.

Breathing heavily, he stood against the door, listening. Nobody was in the hall. Blaney slipped out, and to the door of Max Ganler's apartment. He had stowed the blackjack away. Now he held an automatic pistol.

It was the Green Ghost who touched the bell button and then stood with his weight against the door. It was Max Ganler himself who opened it, expecting the friend he had sent to strengthen his alibi.

"Wh-what—?" Ganler began.

HE CAUGHT sight of the incongruous headgear. But, before he could say more, before he could give a cry of warning, the muzzle of an automatic was jabbed into his belly. Suddenly white of face, Max Ganler put up his hands and stood back against the wall.

They were in the little entryway of the apartment, and could not be seen from the big living room unless somebody came to the doorway, which was shrouded with portieres. Through the slits in the hood he wore, the eyes of the Green Ghost gleamed malevolently.

"Wh—at—?" Max Ganler mouthed again.

"Quiet!" the Green Ghost hissed at him. "This is the night the cops get you, Max. They couldn't do it themselves, so I thought I'd help."

Ganler collected his nerve. He was trembling a bit, but managed to speak in whispers.

"What have you got against me?"

"Nothing any more than I have against all big crooks, Max."

"Why play the cops' game, Green Ghost? Maybe we can

make a deal."

"I've got almost all the Carstairs swag now, Max, so why should I?"

"That's only one job. I might let you in on—"

"I don't make deals with a thing like you! I work alone. There's a reason for it."

"You've got a nerve, coming right here to my apartment."

"Surprises you, does it? Here I stay, till I'm sure the cops are on their way for you."

"I don't know anything about that Carstairs job."

"You were there and bossed it," the Green Ghost said.

"You're crazy. I've been here since early in the evening. I've been giving a party to Lily Ratch, my girl. It's her birthday."

"Swell alibi, Max. The dumb cops probably will fall for it."

"It's the true goods," Max Ganler declared. "The superintendent of the building has been in and out half a dozen times. There have been twenty or thirty persons here since nine o'clock last night, coming and going. I've been seen almost every minute—"

"And yet I'm saying that you were at the Carstairs house, two miles away, between twelve and one this morning, and engineered a jewel robbery."

"You're crazy! I don't know anything about it. If some of the other boys—"

"Carns and Sorsten are in there now—they've told you their yarn, about how I knocked 'em out and took the jewels from them. They were bringing you the swag. You didn't have the guts to pack it yourself."

"The boys came here to ask my advice about a fence."

"SO THAT'S your story! You'd throw down your pals and make them take the rap. Not even a decent crook!"

"How could you know anything about it—if it was true?" Max Ganler asked.

"Listen, you! I'm the Green Ghost, out to get crooks. I had

you on my list. I've been watching you and your men for weeks. I know more about you than the whole police department could learn in five years!"

"What do you want here?"

Before the Green Ghost could reply to that, one of Ganler's male guests lurched through the portieres. He caught sight of the pair, and gave a squawk of terror when he saw the green hood. "He's here!" he howled, as he lurched back into the living room. "Snoopy! Sorsten! The Green Ghost—he's got Max out in the hall!"

NOW THE GREEN GHOST was in a position to jerk the door open and get out into the hall, dodge into the supply closet again, or make a run for it. But he did not. He jabbed Max Ganler with the muzzle of the automatic again, grabbed his arm with his left hand and whirled him around. He compelled Ganler to step through the portieres and face those in the room.

"Careful, everybody!" the Green Ghost called. "I've got a gun muzzle jammed against Max's spine. Make a bad move at me, and I'll let him have it!"

They recognized the situation instantly. Where they were sitting or standing, they seemed suddenly like statues. The Green Ghost saw Carns and Sorsten at one side of the room. There were half a dozen others, including three girls.

A glance sufficed to show the Green Ghost that there had, indeed, been an all-night party. Ample evidence of that in the ash trays filled with cigarette ends, the empty bottles and stained glasses. The appearance of those in the room showed it, too. Only Max Ganler looked fairly fresh. But it was common report that Max Ganler seldom drank to excess.

GANLER WAS still holding up his hands. Urged by the Green Ghost, he stepped along the wall a short distance. Those in the room seemed to be waiting for Ganler to indicate what he wished them to do.

Bill Sorsten lurched forward. He ran more to brutality than brains. Here was the man who had knocked him out and tied him up, and taken the stolen jewels he had been carrying.

"Why, you—!" Sorsten began.

One of the girls gave a scream of fear and sprang forward, threw wide her arms as she faced Sorsten.

"Back, you fool! He'll kill Max!" she cried.

That was Lily Ratch. She was violently in love with Max Ganler, said those who knew. She had courage enough to attempt anything to save him, and brains enough to know that this was not the time to make a move.

"Everybody sit down!" the Green Ghost ordered. "Be careful how you move! Don't give me an excuse for bumping off Max."

They obeyed him in silence. Every man there was looking at Ganler, wondering what to do. Ganler gave no sign. He was trying to think of a way out of the predicament. The Green Ghost commanded the situation at the instant. But here, in Ganler's apartment, and with half a dozen of Ganler's desperate friends in the room, he was at a disadvantage.

That did not seem to worry the Green Ghost. He compelled Ganler to sit down also, on a chair not far from the door.

"Looks like you've been having quite a party," he said.

"It's like I told you. I've been here all night," Max Ganler replied.

"I suppose everybody here would swear to it?"

Lily Ratch stepped forward. "You—whoever you are!" she cried. "I don't know what you're up to, but you've got Max wrong tonight. He's been right here since nine o'clock, when I came. He's giving me this party."

"Didn't lose sight of him a moment since nine?" the Green Ghost asked.

"Oh, he went back into one of the other rooms a few times, but he wasn't gone for more than five minutes. He hasn't been out of the apartment. You've got your dope mixed."

"You believe," the Green Ghost said, "that you're speaking the truth."

"I know it! Are you crazy?" the girl asked.

"You're due for a big surprise," the Green Ghost replied. "Tell me, Max, did I get all the Carstairs jewels off Snoopy and Sorsten?"

"I don't know anything about 'em, I tell you. It's none of my business what jewels Snoopy and Sorsten have. None of yours, either!"

"What the hell?" Snoopy Carns cried. "Are we goin' to let this guy walk in here and boss us around? He's the guy who tapped us for the sparklers, Max. We must be gettin' soft!"

"Let's get him!" Sorsten barked.

THE AUTOMATIC of the Green Ghost barked also at that instant. Sorsten's right hand had made a dive beneath his coat, in the direction of his armpit. But his gun was not there. The Green Ghost had removed it in the alley and tossed it away. And now the Green Ghost merely put a bullet past Sorsten's head for moral effect.

It thudded into the wall.

One of the female guests screamed.

"Quiet, you fool!" Max Ganler cried. "Want the cops to pay us a visit? That shot of yours might bring 'em, Green Ghost."

"What of it?"

"They might be interested in seeing you with that green hood off your head."

"You're afraid to have them drop in, aren't you?"

"Not particularly," Ganler said. "Just don't want to attract their attention. Might think I was giving a wild party, instead of a quiet, classy one for Lily."

"They might ask about the Carstairs business."

"Let 'em ask!" Ganler said. "I've been here all night. Got plenty of witnesses to that."

"MATTER OF fact, I was just going to call the cops," the Green Ghost declared. "May I use your phone, Max?" He bowed.

"There it is on the table."

"Walk over and stand beside me, Max. Just now, I crave your close companionship. And your friends better stay put. You're too young to die, Max."

He forced Ganler to go to the telephone with him. Watching carefully, automatic held ready, the Green Ghost dialed the operator.

"Police Headquarters—quick!" he said.

"You're sure crazy!" Ganler told him. "Let the cops come! I'm clean. How about yourself?"

"An alibi is something I never bother about," the Green Ghost declared.

A raucous voice growled at him over the wire.

"Tell the jewel squad to come to Max Ganler's apartment, quick, if they want the lowdown on that Carstairs job," the Green Ghost growled back.

"Who's talkin'?" the desk sergeant asked.

"The gentleman known as the Green Ghost. I sent a note a couple of days ago, and said I'd turn in Max Ganler. Tell them to hurry. I want to get home and to bed."

He slapped the receiver back into place and motioned for Ganler to resume his seat.

Ganler was smiling whimsically now, as though this situation amused him. He acted like a man not afraid of the consequences.

But Snoopy Carns and Bill Sorsten had no adequate alibis. They had no wish to remain there until the police walked in on them. The police might ask questions.

"Get 'im!" Sorsten barked.

SNOOPY CARNS had been standing at the end of a davenport table, upon which there was a small statuette. With a sweeping motion, he had the statuette off the table and had thrown it at the Green Ghost. At the same instant, Bill Sorsten sprang forward.

The automatic of the Green Ghost cracked twice. Sorsten, the nearest menace, dropped to the floor, his right leg sagging beneath his weight ominously. Snoopy Carns reeled back against the wall, clutching a wounded right shoulder.

"Max, get 'em out of here!" Lily Ratch cried. "You're all right, but these nuts may get us all in wrong. Give 'em the rush!"

But there was not time. Somebody pounded on the hall door. A stentorian voice commanded,

"Open up! It's the police!"

The Green Ghost knew that voice. It belonged to Sergeant Tim O'Ryan, in charge of the jewel squad—a police officer with whom no man trifled without being sorry for it.

CHAPTER V

CHAPTER V

DANNY'S TELEPHONE CALL HAD been superfluous. The Carstairs robbery having been reported a few minutes after it had occurred, the jewel squad had got busy immediately. It looked like a Max Ganler job, so Sergeant Tim O'Ryan took two men and hurried to Max Ganler's apartment.

Max Ganler had been flaunting himself in the faces of the police too long. Sure of his guilt in many nefarious enterprises, they had been unable to pin it on him. They could connect no suspects with Ganler's guiding hand. And Ganler himself always had a perfect alibi—not one of the ordinary crook variety, but an ironclad one. Ganler's alibis were always based on the axiom that a man can't be in two places at the same time.

"Open up!" Sergeant Tim O'Ryan pounded on the door again.

"We'll let 'em in," the Green Ghost said.

He prodded Ganler with the muzzle of the automatic and urged him into the entryway. He stood to one side as Ganler opened the door. Sergeant Tim O'Ryan and his men made the usual police entrance—striding into the room in determined fashion, slightly arrogant.

By doing this, they swept past the Green Ghost, and he slammed the door shut and stepped up behind them.

"Get your hands up!" he barked.

O'Ryan and his men turned, their hands groping for weapons. But they did not draw. The muzzle of the automatic menaced

17

them. The sight of the Green Ghost startled them. They put up their hands.

"What's all this?" O'Ryan demanded. "Why the trick costume?"

"I'm the Green Ghost."

"Oh, yeah? Cap'n got a letter of some sort. Thought it was a joke."

"I'm going to turn in Max Ganler, as I promised."

"Do that, and I'll shake hands with you," Sergeant Tim O'Ryan declared, "though I may be tearin' off that green hood afterward."

"I'm holding this gun on you because I don't want you to interfere with me," the Green Ghost said. "You might spoil the party."

O'Ryan motioned his two men to places against the wall. The Green Ghost stood at the end of the davenport, where all in the room were under his eyes.

"I SUPPOSE the Carstairs job brought you here, O'Ryan?" the Green Ghost asked.

"You're right. I thought Max might know something about it."

"Don't even know what you're talking about," Ganler said.

"O'Ryan, here's Snoopy Carns and Bill Sorsten. I had to stop 'em, but they're not hurt bad. Better send 'em in and have 'em patched up, though. A little judicious questioning—"

"I don't know nothin' about nothin'," Sorsten put in. "This guy comes in here and starts shootin' for no reason at all. Max has been givin' a party, 'cause it's his girl's birthday, and I dropped in with Snoopy to snatch a drink. What's wrong in that?"

"Yes, I've been giving a party," Max Ganler said. "If there's been a job pulled off, O'Ryan, I don't know anything about it. I've been right here since nine last night. Ask these folks. Ask the building superintendent, who's been in a dozen times to get a drink and see how we were gettin' along."

"Oh, he's got an alibi, O'Ryan!" the Green Ghost said.

O'Ryan snarled. "Yeah? We're goin' to bust this one wide open. This time, Max, you were seen!"

"How's that?" Ganler asked.

"You were seen not two blocks from the Carstairs house. That's a couple of miles from here. And you were seen between twelve and one o'clock. Laugh that off!"

"Between twelve and one tonight?" Max Ganler did laugh. "Wasn't I right here, Lily? Wasn't I, folks?" he appealed to the others.

A chorus assured him that he had been. "Of course, O'Ryan, these are my friends," Ganler went on. "You might not believe them on that account. But the building superintendent and his wife came up about midnight, and stuck around for an hour or more. A boy from the drug store at the corner brought up some cigarettes. I had sandwiches sent in at midnight from the café below—ask the man who brought them. They'll all say I was here. I couldn't have had time to get to the Carstairs place and back."

"SAME OLD alibi," O'Ryan said. "How about Carns and Bill Sorsten?"

"You'd better ask them," Max Ganler said. "They dropped in a few minutes ago. Old friends of mine—did some work for me once. It's Lily's birthday, and—"

"Here!" O'Ryan barked. He had seen Bill Sorsten make a move at the end of the davenport. Disregarding the Green Ghost for the moment, O'Ryan made a quick dive forward. Bill Sorsten was trying to ditch a couple of pieces of jewelry beneath the couch.

"Some of the swag!" O'Ryan barked. "This funny brooch, especially—the old Carstairs lady mentioned that. Got you, Sorsten!"

"I don't know nothin' about that; I saw it on the rug and kicked at it to turn it over."

"Trying to plant something on me?" Ganler snarled. "Why, you rat! Take 'em away, O'Ryan!"

"And you're tryin' to make us take the rap, huh?" Bill Sorsten snarled back. "Through with us, are you? Goin' to have us put away, so it'll be safer for you. You'll go along with us!"

"Talk, Sorsten!" O'Ryan said.

"'COURSE WE did that Carstairs job. Max planned the thing. And he was there with us tonight, bossin' the works. His alibi's a fake!"

Max Ganler's laughter filled the room.

"You see, O'Ryan?" he asked. "Sorsten and Carns may have pulled off something, but it'll do them no good to try to drag me in. Saying I planned the thing—you might have believed that. But Sorsten queers himself when he says I was with them. If he lied about that, he probably lied about everything. Any jury would say as much."

"You were with us, damn you! O'Ryan says somebody saw you in the neighborhood."

"Somebody was mistaken. I've been right here all night."

Max Ganler's tone was one of confidence.

Lily Ratch suddenly confronted O'Ryan. "Can't you see that somebody's trying to frame Max?" she demanded. "Use your brains! Look up his alibi. If these two cheap crooks—" She withered Snoopy Carns and Bill Sorsten with her flashing glances.

"He was there with us!" Sorsten cried.

"Yeah, he was!" Snoopy Carns added. "He opened the trick safe in the library wall. You know damned well, O'Ryan, that neither me or Bill is a box man."

"Let's stop this damned nonsense, and get on with the party!" Max Ganler said. "What are you going to do, O'Ryan? These two bums are trying to hang something on me. I've got twenty or more who'll swear I was right here all night. All that against the words of two bums."

Sergeant Tim O'Ryan dropped into the nearest chair. He extracted a cigar from his waistcoat pocket and ignited the smoke.

"I'm going to see what this Green Ghost chap does about it," O'Ryan said. "I don't know him or anything about him. But he says he can deliver the goods."

"With pleasure!" the Green Ghost said. "O'Ryan, I happen to know you cops have been after Max Ganler for a long time. A dozen times, you thought you had him. And you always ran up against a stonewall alibi."

"Right!" O'Ryan admitted.

"Max was always somewhere else when a crib was cracked and had reputable witnesses to prove it. He has tonight, O'Ryan. If you get to work, you'll find that a score or more are ready to swear Max was right here between nine and two tonight. And the joke of it is that they'll believe they're telling the truth. They are not just helping him out."

"What's the answer to that?" O'Ryan asked.

"THE ANSWER is that Max has a new sort of alibi. It's a pip. Not every crook can work it. You're due to be startled, O'Ryan. Tell me this—if you can prove that Max could have been out of this apartment an hour or so during the night, would you have him?"

"I would that, along with other evidence and the confessions of these two."

"Then, you've got him, O'Ryan! I started in after Max Ganler a couple of months ago. I've been studying him and his methods. I learned a lot about him. I camped around this building for hours at a time, always on the dodge. That ironclad alibi of his had me worried, too. I knew there was a trick, and I decided I'd get to the bottom of it."

"I'm still waitin' for the answer," O'Ryan complained.

"Promise you won't interfere for a few minutes and watch Max closely. He might get violent, when he understands that his game is up."

"It's a go!"

"MAX TOOK a long lease on this apartment and spent a lot of coin having it done over," the Green Ghost explained. "This closet in the corner has a trick panel door in the back. You can go into a small passage which leads to the cross hall, and you can get to the basement by the service stairs or out to a fire-escape."

"What of it? A lot of places have getaways in them," O'Ryan said.

"This is going to be interesting," the Green Ghost went on. "I was watching tonight. I saw Max leave the building and I saw him return. He left about midnight and he was back at a quarter after one."

"Give that testimony and I've got him!" O'Ryan cried. "That is, if you're a good witness. Take off that green hood and let's see."

"Wait," the Green Ghost begged. "When Max came back, I did what I'd planned—fixed the door at the end of the passage so it couldn't be opened from this side. Fixed it, O'Ryan, so nobody could leave this room through the closet and get out of the place."

"What damned nonsense!" Max Ganler cried. "O'Ryan, I'm sick of this. That big closet—why, it's where we hang coats and hats and I keep some liquor in there. I went into that closet several times during the night to get a bottle—"

"Take a look, O'Ryan," the Green Ghost said. "Better have your boys back you up and have your guns ready. Open the closet."

O'Ryan sprang up and motioned to his men. The closet door was opened. The police stood there, guns ready. They saw coats, women's wraps and two cases of liquor partially empty.

"Press along the wall in the right-hand corner," the Green Ghost instructed. "And be careful!"

O'Ryan and one of his men entered the big closet. O'Ryan fumbled at the wall. There was a click and a panel slid back.

"Come out of that!" O'Ryan barked. "Get your hands up!"

A man was crouching in the darkness behind that panel door. O'Ryan's companion reached in and grasped him by the shoulder and hauled him forth.

"Get into the room!" O'Ryan commanded.

He thrust the prisoner out into the bright light, where he reeled back against the wall.

THERE CAME a chorus of cries from those in the living room. Their astonishment was genuine, most of all that of Miss Lily Ratch.

Max Ganler, his face white and his eyes bulging as he saw a vision of the big stone house up the river, sat against the wall. But Max Ganler also stood there, his arms gripped by Sergeant Tim O'Ryan. The same in features, size, even to every detail of clothing.

"The ironclad alibi," the Green Ghost said. "A twin brother comes in handy some times, O'Ryan. There is your answer. Max slips into the closet and his brother comes out and goes right on with whatever Max was doing, and Max hurries away, does his job and comes back, signals, and the brothers change places again. Only, tonight, I fixed the door at the end of the passage, so this twin brother couldn't get out when the work was done."

"Got you, Ganler!" Sergeant Tim O'Ryan roared. "And now, Green Ghost suppose you tell me—"

But the Green Ghost had darted toward the entryway. As O'Ryan called to him to halt, as O'Ryan and his companions sought to stop him, the Green Ghost fired one shot over their heads as warning, jerked open the hall door and sprang out into the corridor.

Two bullets splintered the door a split second afterward. The Green Ghost darted along the hall and to the rear stairs. Down them he rushed, making little noise. Above, he heard the stentorian commands of Sergeant Tim O'Ryan.

To the basement the Green Ghost fled, and through the little door and out into the night. In the dark alley, he stripped off hood and gloves and stowed them away. He sped across a street and plunged into the darkness of the alley beyond.

A few minutes later, three blocks away, Danny Blaney engaged a cruising taxicab. He relaxed in the seat and yawned, like a man who had been keeping late hours. At a certain corner he dismissed the cab and entered a cigar store, where the night clerk was reading an early edition of a morning paper.

"Howdy, Boss! You're up late," the clerk said.

"Been paying a little visit uptown," Danny Blaney replied. "How's business?"

"Not so good, Boss. A few chauffeurs after cigs—that's all. Maybe it doesn't pay you to keep open all night."

"Oh, yes; it pays! It pays," Danny Blaney said.

THE DAY OF SETTLEMENT

CHAPTER 1

IT WAS EXACTLY NINE in the evening when Sato, personal Japanese servant of Lawrence Draite, entered the study of the latter's apartment.

Mr. Draite, a criminal lawyer of prominence, was doing some home work. He was searching through legal tomes in an effort to find some thread upon which to hang a trick which would result in the acquittal of a client. At such moments, Mr. Draite did not like to be disturbed.

"Well?" he snapped.

"Message, sar," Sato said.

Draite took the envelope the Japanese offered, and waved him aside. He ripped the envelope open. An instant later, having perused the message, he sprang out of his chair, scattering legal books and documents over the floor.

"Sato!"

"Yiss, sar?"

"Where did you get this?"

"Bellboy, sar."

"Go down to the office and find who left it, and all about it. Hurry!"

Sato faded from the study like a shadow. Lawrence Draite read the message again. There was not much of it:

The day of settlement is at hand. I am coming to collect, with interest.

The Green Ghost.

Lawrence Draite paced the floor a moment, making an evident fight to control himself, then with a quick motion grasped the telephone. The call he put through was to Police Headquarters.

He held speech with a certain sergeant of detectives who was named Tim O'Hara.

THEN HE took an automatic pistol from a drawer of his desk and thrust it into his coat pocket. He kept his right hand in the pocket, clutching the pistol.

It was about twenty minutes before the screeching of a siren down in the street announced the arrival of a police car in the vicinity. Mr. Draite had spent the entire twenty minutes in his study.

Sato had returned from downstairs with the information that the letter had been left by a uniformed messenger, and the clerk who had received it had given the messenger scant attention. He doubted he could identify him.

Detective Sergeant Tim O'Hara, who happened to be chief of the jewel squad, was a hard-boiled individual. Twenty years in the Department had wrecked his faith in human nature and soured him on the world. He read the note Lawrence Draite had received, and grunted as he dropped into a chair.

"Who's this Green Ghost?" O'Hara asked.

"I haven't the slightest idea," Draite replied.

"WHO'D BE comin' after you for somethin'?"

"I can't tell you that, either. I suppose I have some enemies, like any man in my position."

"Among crooks?"

"Possibly. I'm a criminal lawyer. I had a man threaten me once because I couldn't save him from prison."

"You're a lot of help," O'Hara said, sarcastically.

"Don't you know the identity of the Green Ghost?" Draite asked in turn.

"If I did, he'd be in jail. He's been gettin' busy around town."

"What is his line?"

"It seems to be robbin' crooks and turnin' them in, mostly. Always takes his percentage. I'll take a percentage out of his hide when I put hands on him. He's been makin' a fool of me."

"I demand protection," said Draite.

"You'll get it. I brought my squad along. I've got two men posted in the hall, watchin' the front and back doors of this apartment. There's a couple on the roof and one in the basement.

"Both stairways are guarded. There's a man at the elevator. And I'll be waitin' down in the lobby, with a couple more."

"THAT'S FINE, Sergeant! You may be sure that I'll not forget this."

"Anybody in the apartment except you and the Jap?"

"Nobody else, Sato has searched through it. But I'm expecting a couple of visitors—a lady and a gentleman.

"I don't want them to think there's anything wrong."

"I'll attend to that, Mr. Draite. Who are the folks that you happen to be expectin'?"

"A Mr. George Hadden and a Miss Marie Demaine. Do you know them?"

Tim O'Hara grinned. "Clients, huh? I know 'em for a couple of smooth swindlers."

"They've never done time, O'Hara."

"Which ain't sayin' that they shouldn't. I'll see that they ain't scared away, Mr. Draite. One thing's certain—this Green Ghost won't bother you tonight. He can't get in."

But the Green Ghost was in already.

CHAPTER II

DANNY BLANEY, FORMER MEMBER of the Police Department, detective branch, and now owner of a corner
cigar store, had left his place of business a few minutes
before eight. He remarked to his clerk that he was going to
take in a show.

Danny Blaney had a habit of buying a single ticket and going
to a show, alone. He was a man who lived by himself. His nature
had changed entirely in a year.

Danny Blaney, a conscientious officer, hoping to get up in
the department, had been framed by crooks. His aggressiveness
had enraged them. He was too zealous. Instead of catching
Danny in the proper spot and bumping him off, they did something which hurt him more—framed him so that he appeared
in league with certain underworld characters.

There had been suspension and trial. Danny was not con-
victed of anything, but even his comrades believed him guilty.
So he quit the force, his heart bitter against his comrades and
his hatred of crooks increased.

It was as the Green Ghost that he was making them pay. He
ran the cigar store as a blind. He continued detective work, but
did not send in reports. He robbed crooks, kept a percentage,
and turned those crooks in.

Lawrence Draite, Danny Blaney knew, had been one of those
instrumental in his ruin. Draite was a criminal lawyer. He had
taken stolen jewels as fees. Later, he had become nothing more

32

*Before he had a chance to use it, his gun was clipped out
of his hand by the other's quicker bullets.*

or less than a high-class fence.

So Lawrence Draite had gone down on Danny Blaney's list and had received the warning note. And now Danny Blaney was in the Draite apartment, watching and listening. Danny Blaney had let himself in through the service door.

The Green Ghost had gone into hiding in the closet in the corner of Draite's study—a closet where some old books and filing cases were stored, and which was entered seldom. It was probably the last place a searcher would look. Sato had not looked there.

THROUGH A keyhole in which there was no key, Danny Blaney could see the length of the room, see the desk and chairs around it, and the entrance to the hall which led to the living room.

He had witnessed Draite's receipt of the message, the delivery of which had been arranged for a certain hour. And he had listened to the conversation of Draite and Tim O'Hara.

O'Hara departed. Ten minutes passed while Danny Blaney sweltered in the closet. Then Sato announced the arrival of guests.

They were ushered into the study. George Hadden was an oily man of middle age. Marie Demaine was an ultra-fashionable woman of perhaps thirty. Danny Blaney knew them for what they were—smooth crooks who worked among the wealthy and fashionable.

"Sato, take the evening off," Draite ordered.

"Yiss, sar."

"But be back here by midnight."

Sato grinned and hurried away. Presently, the service door slammed to announce his exit.

Draite had put out drinks and cigarettes for his guests. Now, he got up and closed the study door, and turned the key in the lock. Back at the desk again, he sat before it and looked at the pair.

"Well?" he asked.

"We've got some fancy rocks," Hadden announced.

"How did you get them?"

"A lady got too much interested in me," Hadden revealed, smiling slightly. "She gave me some rocks to make me forget her."

"How about you?" Draite asked Marie Demaine.

"Oh, a gentleman who shouldn't have gotten so much interested in me," she replied. "I agreed to forget him if he'd get me a certain diamond necklace."

"Let's see 'em," Draite said.

Glittering jewels soon scintillated on the desk. Draite bent forward and examined them, taking jewelers' instruments from a drawer of his desk.

"This is the missing Harkland necklace," he said, after a time. "The newspapers have been full of that case."

"Passed on to me by the person who happened to get it," Marie Demaine said.

"And this other thing—stolen stuff, all of it! It's dynamite."

"That's why we've brought the stuff to you," George Hadden said. "You know how to handle it. You'll dismount those rocks and market 'em well."

"Dynamite! The price of dynamite is away down," Draite hinted.

"Oh, we expect to be robbed," the woman said.

"YES, IT'S been done before," Hadden added.

"If you're not satisfied with the deals you make with me, take your stuff somewhere else," Draite growled. "I should have something for the risk I run."

"Risk!" Hadden sneered. "How about those emeralds they traced to you? Told the cops that they'd been given you as a fee by some poor devil who'd told you they were family heirlooms. He got twenty years, and you got off. You'd do the same again, in a pinch."

"We are more clever now," Draite said, smiling slightly. "What do you want for these baubles?"

"You're setting the price," Hadden said. "Try to remember that you've got a conscience."

LAWRENCE DRAITE inspected the gems again, and named a price. It resulted in an angry argument, but Draite prevailed. "Get us the jack," Hadden said. "You sure drive a hard bargain, Draite."

Draite went to the wall of the study and pulled open what appeared to be double doors to a compartment for documents. The front of a safe was revealed.

Kneeling before the safe, the lawyer worked the combination and pulled the door open. He opened a strongbox, also, and put it on the floor of the safe, tossing into it the jewels the two had brought him. Other jewels were in that strongbox, gems which Draite had not been able to market.

Then Draite unlocked and opened another compartment of the safe and took out a bundle of currency. He started counting off bills.

"Need any help?" George Hadden asked, sauntering toward him.

Draite shook his head and went on counting. "I think we'll give you some, however!" Hadden snapped at the kneeling man. "We're sick of being robbed by you, Draite. This looks like a good time to collect."

"Get back to the desk!" Draite barked. "What do you think you're doing?"

"Only collecting some back pay," Hadden replied. "Stand up, Draite, and get away from that safe!"

To give emphasis to his words, Hadden bent forward and shoved the muzzle of an automatic against the lawyer's ribs.

CHAPTER III

DRAITE GOT UP AND staggered back against the wall. His face showed the fear he felt. With the muzzle of that gun before him, his courage oozed. "You can't get away with this—it's robbery!" he said.

"Coming from you, Draite, that's funny," Hadden told him.

"I've got plenty on you two. I'll see you sent up the river."

"Maybe you'll go along with us, if you try that."

"Are you the Green Ghost?" Draite asked, with sudden suspicion.

Hadden laughed. "I am not. Why?"

"I got a note from him, saying he'd come to collect. And you just remarked—"

"So the Green Ghost is after you, too?" Hadden asked. "Well, you can't get away with it forever."

"You fools!" the lawyer growled. "Didn't you have your eyes open when you came in? Tim O'Hara is in the lobby. His men are scattered all around the place, watching for the Green Ghost. How far do you think you'll get, if you rob me?"

"I noticed some dicks scattered around, George," Marie Demaine put in.

"They're always scattered around," Hadden replied. "Don't lose your nerve, Marie. Here's where we collect the price of a nice little jaunt over to Europe, where we may find some nice pickings this season."

"You can't get away with it," Draite stormed. "With Tim O'Hara and his men here—"

"How'll you explain some of that stuff in your safe?" Hadden cut in.

"I'll have explanations ready. Perhaps I'll say you brought it here and asked me what to do with it."

"And you think we can't make a move, because the Green Ghost has threatened you and the cops are waiting for him? Whatever happens here, Draite, might be blamed on this Green Ghost."

HADDEN HAD relaxed vigilance somewhat, since Draite was on his feet and standing against the wall a short distance from the open safe. And Draite had in his coat pocket the automatic he had slipped there after reading the Green Ghost's note.

Now, the lawyer made a sudden move. His hand darted into his pocket and came out holding the gun.

"So you'd—"

That was all he had time to say. Hadden saw the menace. His own gun barked, and Lawrence Draite dropped the weapon he held, clutched at his breast, looked surprised, swayed, tottered, and collapsed to the floor. "George!" Marie Demaine cried.

"Quiet!" he barked at her.

"You've killed him. The dicks know we came in here. You've got us in a trap."

"Quiet, you fool! Get some of this cash. Stuff it in your stockings. Thank heaven, you women are wearing long skirts again! The jewels—we can't have them found on us. Leave them where they are."

"But what—?"

"Can't you see? We've done for the crook! He was expecting a visit from the Green Ghost. We'll make a howl that the Green Ghost popped in here, stuck us all up, shot Draite—"

"That gun you're holding, George!"

"Yes. Must get rid of that. And his—we'll say he tried to pull a gun, but the Green Ghost shot him before he could fire."

"But the Ghost—where did he go? Where could he go, if the apartment is being watched?"

"That's something to puzzle the cops," Hadden replied. "All we know is that he told us to stay quiet for five minutes, then ran into the other room."

"The door's locked."

"I'll unlock it. You run out into the hall and howl for help. I'll telephone downstairs from the desk."

He telephoned first, hurled into the transmitter a jumble of words about holdup and murder. Then he darted across the room and unlocked the door. Marie Demaine, screeching, ran through the little hall and across the living room to the front door. Hadden followed her into the living room. He put his gun beneath one of the deep cushions on a davenport. Then he ran on to the front door in the wake of the girl.

Watching from the closet in the corner of the study, Danny Blaney had seen and heard all this. And now he found himself in sudden peril. Lawrence Draite was dead on the floor of his study. His safe was open, and money had been stolen from it. The Green Ghost had threatened him with a visit. Hadden and Marie Demaine were ready to say that the Green Ghost had entered and done the shooting.

And here was Danny Blaney, the Green Ghost, in a closet in the corner of the room, with police detectives watching every means of egress from the apartment, and more rushing to the scene.

CHAPTER IV

THERE WAS A TUMULT out in the corridor. Officers came running. Marie Demaine continued her cries, and to them was added now the ringing voice of George Hadden as he acted his part. Danny Blaney took from beneath his coat a hood made of thin green silk, which he put over his head and pulled down to his shoulders. He was the Green Ghost in truth, now. He must escape. And he had come to collect, too.

He left the closet and rushed across the study to the door, which he closed and locked. Then he darted to the safe and selected a package of currency, which he put into his pocket. There was no escape from the study except by way of the one door. There was a single window, opening into a court with a paved floor—but it was eight stories from the ground.

The Green Ghost opened the window wide. He could hear a confused din of voices in the living room, and ringing above the others the voice of Sergeant Tim O'Hara. They would be at the study door in a moment.

The Green Ghost darted across to the door again, and stood waiting. Somebody tried it and found it locked. Somebody pounded on it with a fist.

"Open up in there!" That was O'Hara's voice.

THAT THE door was locked startled Marie Demaine and George Hadden more than anybody. They had believed themselves alone in the apartment. And they were further startled now to hear the voice of a man in the study.

"Is that you, O'Hara?"

"It is."

"Send everybody else back. I've got something to tell you, and don't want others to hear."

"And who are you?"

"This is the Green Ghost."

"Is it, now? Then in we come, if we have to smash in the door, and we get you, Green Ghost, if we have to shoot it out with you."

"Then you'll miss some interesting information. Send the others away. You won't want them to hear this."

He heard Tim O'Hara barking orders on the other side of the door. Then the detective spoke again:

"All right! I'm alone here now."

"Listen carefully," the Green Ghost said. "First, Draite is nothing but a fancy fence. When you get in here, you'll find plenty of stolen jewels in his safe, and some of them can be identified easily."

"We've been suspectin' that. What else?"

"I HAD it in for him. I came here tonight to make him shell out to me, and then turn him in. I wrote you a note telling you to stand by, didn't I?"

"But this shootin'—" O'Hara began.

"Listen carefully, O'Hara. I didn't shoot Draite. I was hiding in here, when Hadden and the Demaine woman called. They had a row with him, after trying to sell him some stolen jewels.

"Hadden shot him. He stuck the gun under a cushion in the davenports—I saw him. The woman has a lot of currency in her stockings, taken from Draite's safe. They never saw me, but Draite told them the place was being watched because I'd threatened to come up here."

"Thanks for the tip. We'll get busy out here," O'Hara said. "And we'll get busy in there, too."

"You'll never get me, O'Hara."

"Won't I, now? Why don't you make a deal with me, Ghost? If you're after crooks, that's my job."

"I don't love the cops, either. I'm playing my own game."

"You always lift something."

"Only for expenses," the Green Ghost replied.

"We've got you, Ghost. You can't get out of there."

"There's a window. You'll find it open, and me gone. You'd better clean up in there first, O'Hara."

He could hear Tim O'Hara station a man at the locked door. And, kneeling close to the door and listening, he heard O'Hara handling George Hadden, heard Marie Demaine's cries of rage as the money was found on her, and her wild denunciation of Hadden when O'Hara unearthed the gun.

"He did it!" the woman screeched. "He was quarreling with Draite. I didn't have anything to do with it. I only took some of the money."

They would be at the study door again in a moment, the Green Ghost knew. His peril had not been lessened much. He might be absolved of the murder of Lawrence Draite, but the fact remained that he was the Green Ghost.

He looked around the study again. The closet would be one of the first places searched, no doubt. There was a huge sofa not far from the door, and the Green Ghost dropped down behind that, holding on to his automatic.

HE COULD hear O'Hara talking to some of his men, and realized that he was coming through the little hall toward the study door. The Green Ghost stood a moment, bent forward, and unlocked the door, then dropped behind the sofa again.

O'Hara pounded on the door.

"Open up, Ghost!" he barked. "Make it snappy! If we have to come in there for you, we'll come in shootin'!"

The Green Ghost remained silent. O'Hara pounded on the door again, and again shouted his demands. Then he happened to twist the knob—and found that the door was unlocked.

He kicked the door open. There was a moment of silence, while those outside undoubtedly peered into the room, weapons held ready for instant use.

Then there came a rush, and Tim O'Hara led three of his men into the study.

"Nobody here, Tim," one of the detectives said. "And the window's open."

"And a long way to the ground," O'Hara said.

"He may have used a rope."

"Where's the rope, then?"

"MAYBE HE had it doubled and hooked around that radiator, and pulled it down after him."

"Don't be a damned fool! Look at the distance. How much rope would it take, doubled? It'd make a load for a strong man to pack."

"But he's gone."

"Maybe," Tim O'Hara said. "Shut that door. Let the medical examiner in when he comes."

The door was closed. Tim O'Hara remained inside the study with two of his men. As the Green Ghost had expected, they made an immediate investigation of the closet.

They glanced beneath the desk, and behind a bookcase that stood out a few feet from the wall in a corner. No hiding place remained except the space back of the big sofa.

Tim O'Hara started toward that, glancing aside to motion for one of his men to cover Draite's body with a rug. When he looked forward again, he recoiled with a cry of surprise. The Green Ghost was standing in front of the door, automatic held in a menacing position.

"Drop that gun, O'Hara! You other men drop yours, too! Make it quick!"

The voice was hard, cold, promising instant annihilation if orders were not obeyed. Three guns dropped to the rug.

"Get your hands up!" the Green Ghost ordered.

Hands went up.

"How long do you think you'll last?" O'Hara asked. The Green Ghost snapped:

"Long enough! Don't make any bad move, O'Hara! I'd hate to hurt you. I always liked you."

"Did you now? You talk like maybe we're old acquaintances."

"Perhaps we are."

"And what do you think you'll do now?" O'Hara asked. "You'd better hand over your gun and surrender, Ghost. You've helped me some, and maybe I can get you off light."

"No deal," the Green Ghost said, promptly. "You three men walk to the opposite wall and stand facing it, with your hands above your heads."

"You can handle us like this now, Ghost, but it won't get you anything," O'Hara assured him. "You can't get out of the place. I've got men scattered all around."

"Move!" the Ghost said.

Grumbling, the three faced the wall and kept their hands over their heads. The Green Ghost reached back and got the key from the door. And suddenly, he jerked the door open and stepped out into the little hall, and closed the door again. He had inserted the key and turned it instantly. O'Hara and his two men were prisoners in the study.

CHAPTER V

THERE WAS NOBODY IN the little hall, but a group in the living room beyond. Hadden and Marie Demaine, handcuffed together, were on the davenport. Two of O'Hara's squad were there guarding the prisoners. More undoubtedly were in the hall outside.

The Green Ghost advanced to the curtained doorway, waited for the proper moment, and spoke:

"Hands up, everybody!"

The two detectives were caught with holstered weapons. They whirled at sound of the voice, saw the Green Ghost and his menacing automatic, and put up their hands.

There was no noise in the study. The Green Ghost guessed that O'Hara was using the telephone, calling the clerk downstairs, relaying orders for all his men to gather on this floor in the halls.

"Take off those handcuffs!" the Green Ghost ordered.

The eyes of Hadden and the woman bulged with surprise. They could not understand this kindness on the part of a man upon whom they had tried to fasten murder, unless it was a case of a crook helping others of his ilk against the police.

"Make it quick, or I'll start shooting!" the Green Ghost barked. "And be careful how you move."

ONE OF the detectives fumbled in a waistcoat pocket and brought out a key. He unlocked the handcuffs and tossed them aside, then put up his hands again at the Green Ghost's gesture for him to do so.

The Ghost waved toward the door. "Get going," he said to the pair who had been prisoners.

"But there are dicks in the hall."

"Tell 'em O'Hara turned you loose. Make for the elevators. Quick!"

They started toward the door. The Green Ghost motioned for the two detectives to go into the little hall. He waved them on, into a bedchamber, jerked the door shut and locked it, and sprang aside just as bullets crashed through the panels.

He ran to the living room again, darted to the door which Hadden was just opening.

"Quick!" he said. "You haven't much time."

They braced themselves for the ordeal. Hadden stepped into the hall with Marie Demaine beside him. The Green Ghost tried to imitate O'Hara's voice. "Get goin', you two. I know where to find you, if I want you."

The two detectives in the bedchamber were howling and pounding on the door. O'Hara was yelling in the study now, wanting to know what was happening.

George Hadden and Marie Demaine walked briskly toward the elevator, as some of the detectives in the hall watched. The Green Ghost waited a moment, holding the door open a crack. And suddenly, in the voice of O'Hara, he began barking:

"Grab them two, men! They're escapin' by a trick! Everybody after 'em!"

The detectives in the hall heard what they supposed was O'Hara's command. Hadden and the woman heard, also. They darted around a corner and started running for the stairway. The officers gave chase.

THE GREEN GHOST, chuckling slightly, darted into the hall. One man remained there. The Green Ghost fired a single shot over his head, and as the officer scurried to cover to fight it out, the Green Ghost ran along the corridor in the opposite direction.

Behind him, a gun barked twice. Bullets flew past his head. Then he was around the corner. O'Hara, who had ruined a door, came charging into the hall, his two men at his heels. The pair got out of the bedchamber and followed. Through the halls rang wild shouts.

The two prisoners were caught quickly, and brought back. But Tim O'Hara howled for the Green Ghost to be taken. It irked O'Hara that the Ghost had drawn the men away by releasing the prisoners and then shouting for them to be pursued and recaptured.

Search was futile. On the ground floor, all exits were watched, but the Green Ghost tried to use none of them. Tenants wishing to leave the building found they had to be identified by the manager. And they had to vouch for any guests with them. "We're goin' through this place from basement to roof if it takes us a week," Tim O'Hara declared. "I'm telephonin' for men from the precinct station. I'm goin' to have a look at the face of that Green Ghost!"

CHAPTER VI

IN A SUPPLY CLOSET in the hall, the Green Ghost crouched among mops and brooms. For some fifteen minutes he remained there, until he knew that all the officers were below with the possible exception of a guard in the Draite apartment.

The Green Ghost guessed that a methodical search would be made, since O'Hara knew he had not had time to get out of the building. In the event of such a search, he might be found.

Presently, he slipped out into the empty hall and rushed along it almost silently. He darted across a cross hall without being seen. At the end was a window, which he opened, and got out on a fire-escape landing. He did not descend, but ascended, until he came to a landing where the window was dark. There he crouched in the cold wind. He heard the search below him, as the windows on the landing were opened. He got on the fire-escape ladder again when they closed the window directly below him.

Down he went, cautiously through the darkness, passing the searchers as they went upward to the next floor. He was beneath them now, but not free. There would be policemen watching below, guarding every exit.

But he continued his descent, careful as he passed each landing, until he came to the second floor. There, after watching and listening for a time, he let himself in. Hurrying along the hall to the rear stairs, he descended to the ground floor, went through a service door, and on to the basement.

Only dim lights burned in the basement halls. From a room near the alley entrance came voices. The Green Ghost slipped along the hall carefully to the half opened door through which the voices were coming. He peered into the room. It was the quarters of the engineer of the building. Two negro firemen on night duty were sitting in there and talking.

"Don' lak so many cops around," one was saying. "Don' lak talk of ghosts. Anyhow, ghosts ain't green—de's white."

The Green Ghost strode through the door. The men looked up at him.

Came a howl from one, a choking sound from the other. The green hood shimmering in the light, the eyes glittering through slits in it, the automatic held ready for business struck terror to their hearts.

"Into the alley!" the Green Ghost barked at them. "Run for it!"

He stepped aside as he spoke. Howling their fear, they charged past him. Down the hall they dashed, to wrench open the alley door and dart into the night.

"Here, you—!" the officer stationed there shouted at them.

But no shout could stop them now. Down the alley they raced. They gave no attention to the command to halt. The bullet which enforced the command only made them run faster.

The officer yelled for help and started the chase. In the basement hall, the Green Ghost smashed the electric bulb, so no streak of light shot out into the alley. Then, through the darkness, he ran swiftly out of the building, to crouch against the wall of the building opposite.

TWO POLICEMEN, answering the alarm of the one who had fired the shot, rushed past within a few feet of him. The Green Ghost turned and made for the other end of the alley, away from the scene of excitement. He stripped off his hood, and stowed it away. It was Danny Blaney who emerged from the alley and turned into the street to walk briskly along it, head bent against the wind, like a man eager to get home.

Three blocks away, he engaged a taxicab. He left it a short distance from his cigar store, and walked the remainder of the distance. His clerk yawned when he sauntered into the store.

"How's business?" Blaney asked.

"Lousy," the clerk replied. "See a good show?"

"Oh, the show wasn't so bad," Danny Blaney admitted. "I'll get home now, and hit the hay. Try to make expenses, will you?"

III

SWIFT REVENGE

CHAPTER I

OVER THE EDGE OF the parapet came a ghostly figure that dropped noiselessly to the roof. Like a shadow, it merged with other and deeper shadows. Then it drifted toward the dark wall of the penthouse.

There were streaks of moonlight, and streaks of light which came through doors and open French windows. The nocturnal visitor avoided these. Close against the wall he crouched, watching, listening.

A musical voice drifted out at him—-a woman's voice in kind tones. That same voice, the watcher knew, could rasp like a file. Its beautiful owner had eyes which could be limpid pools of promise or blazing volcanoes of wrath.

A door slammed. There came the sound of footsteps. An elevator door clanged. Then there was silence save for the soft rustling of the wind through the tiny trees on the veranda of the penthouse.

The man beside the wall lifted himself, stretched, crept forward until he came to the edge of the first streak of light. He was a peculiar figure of a man. Dark clothing shrouded him. Over his head and pulled down to his shoulders was a hood of green silk. He wore green silk gloves.

IN FRONT of him was an open French door. Through this he went silently and crept into the big living-room of the penthouse. Unseen, his presence unsuspected, he surveyed the scene.

Only one person was in that lavishly furnished room—Coralie Farlowe. She was dressed in ravishing negligee. On a divan, she stretched with the grace of a panther, reached for a book, began reading.

This was Coralie Farlowe, at present a queen without a royal consort, legal or otherwise. She had come from Paris three months before. Crookdom did her homage. More than one Big Shot sought her favor, personally and professionally. An alliance with Coralie Farlowe meant something.

The intruder darted forward until he was within ten feet of the head of the divan.

"Beg pardon," he said.

She gave a little cry of surprise, dropped the book, half sat up, and turned her head. Her eyes dilated an instant, her breast rose and fell with greater rapidity, then she compelled herself to composure, and merely stared. Coralie Farlowe was a woman not easily startled.

"I am the Green Ghost."

"I judged as much from the costume. I suppose I should feel honored at this visit?"

"Pardon me for not sending in my card." The Green Ghost chuckled. "Let me inform you at once that you have nothing to fear from me."

"You're not after my jewels, then?"

"I am not. I have nothing against you. I merely wish you to help me."

"In what way?" she asked.

"You have become well acquainted with 'Butcher' Corgan, gang chief. If his life was in danger, would you save it if you could?"

"Certainly." She betrayed increased interest and sat up straight on the divan. "But Corgan's life is always in danger, more or less, is it not?"

"Never so much as tonight," the Green Ghost assured her. "Your telephone is there at the head of the divan. Telephone

A flash of flame and lead cracked the night.

Corgan and tell him to come to you at once."

"COME HERE!" she cried. "Are you mad? Mike Delane lives in this building. He and Corgan—"

"Don't waste time telling me how Corgan and Delane are mortal enemies. If you want to save Corgan, get him here at once. Don't frighten him. Make him think you want him alone, for a rendezvous. He'll come, if you call."

"I tell you that Mike Delane—"

"The safest place for Corgan is right here. Telephone!"

Coralie Farlowe reached out and got the receiver. She began dialing a number. The Green Ghost stepped closer.

"Be careful—don't make him suspicious. If he suggests meeting you elsewhere, hint that he's too much of a coward to come here. And he must come alone. If he brings any of his mob with him, even one rod-man for a bodyguard, Mike Delane's men will take it as a challenge."

Coralie Farlowe looked straight at the eyes which gleamed through holes in the green hood. "Why should I trust you?"

"Why not?"

"You may be having me decoy Corgan here so you—"

"I've nothing against him, just now."

SHE TURNED suddenly to the telephone as an answer to her ring came over the wire. It was Corgan speaking. She chatted a moment, then asked him to come to her at once. He hesitated, asked for a meeting at a night club. She pouted, teased, hinted at cowardice. Presently, she put the receiver up.

"He'll be right over," she said.

"Thank you. Thank you also for trusting me."

"Don't know why I did," she confessed.

"You are helping dispose of one of Corgan's enemies."

"Won't you explain?"

"It is too involved," he protested.

He stepped forward again. Now, an automatic appeared in his hand.

"Kindly stretch out on that couch," he ordered. "I regret it, but I must bind and gag you."

"What?" she cried. "So it is a trick! If you've made me decoy Corgan here for you—"

"Corgan will be all right. You also. But you must do as I say."

"If I scream a few times, you'll find yourself in a corner, Green Ghost."

"Your servants are gone—it's their evening out. Nobody will hear if you scream. Don't make me be rough with you."

She sprang from the couch and started toward a little hall which ran to a bedchamber. To get a weapon, the Green Ghost thought.

He jumped before her, grasped her wrist, twisted her arm a

little. She cried because of the pain. The Green Ghost whirled her around forcibly, so that she sprawled on the couch again.

"It's your own fault if I get rough," he said. "You're a beautiful woman, and look dainty and soft. But I know you for a swindler, thief, accessory to murder. I remember that when I handle you."

Her eyes flamed. "Some day I'll—"

"Get me for this? Wait and see."

From a pocket, he had taken lengths of fine, strong cord. A loop went around one of her wrists. Her struggle was short before the other wrist was caught and lashed to the first. The Green Ghost fastened her ankles together, then tied her elbows to her sides, so she could not bend and untie her ankles with her fingers.

She made herself as comfortable as possible on the couch.

"DON'T GAG me," she begged. "As you said, nobody would hear me if I screamed."

"I don't want you interfering when Corgan comes."

"Then you do mean harm to him?"

"No," the Green Ghost declared again.

He had a soft gag already prepared, and now he affixed it despite her savage attempt to bite him. He chuckled a bit as he finished; sitting at the side of the couch, he pulled the little telephone cabinet to him, and dialed a number.

"Hello!... That you, Mike Delane?... Listen carefully. And don't ask who I am. Butcher Corgan is making a monkey out of you. He's got a date with Coralie Farlowe. Going to her penthouse, right in the building where you live. Rubbing it in, huh? The town'll be laughing at you tomorrow."

HE PUT the receiver back on the hook. Then he removed the gag.

"Time enough for that again when we know Corgan is coming," the Green Ghost explained.

"You rat!" she cried. "Why don't you do your own killing, whoever you are? And who are you, anyhow? Crook or cop?"

"Neither," the Green Ghost said. "I told you Corgan would be safe if he came here."

"With him alone, and Mike Delane's mugs waiting all around the place?"

"Corgan has something I want," the Green Ghost said.

"What?"

"An overcoat."

He ignited a cigarette and put it between the girl's lips, then lit one for himself. Back and forth across the rugs he strode, smoking, waiting.

Presently, he turned to the couch again, took the cigarette from her lips and once more affixed the gag. Then he hurried out, to the elevator.

The dial showed that the car was ascending. On to the penthouse it came. It did not open directly into the penthouse, but upon a tiny porch.

The door clanged open, and Butcher Corgan stepped out. The door clanged shut again, the car began its descent. Corgan started along the porch to the door.

A shadow moved. The sound of a blow was heard. Corgan groaned and dropped.

Working swiftly, the Green Ghost removed Corgan's overcoat. He bound Corgan's ankles and wrists, and gagged him. Then he carried him inside, and put him on the floor near the couch.

"Tapped him on the head," the Green Ghost explained to the woman who looked at the unconscious Corgan. "He'll be all right in a jiffy. I'll leave you like this. If I don't get a chance to come back and turn you loose, your maid will find you when she returns."

He picked up the overcoat. There was none other like it in the city. Probably no man except Butcher Corgan would have worn one. It was an affair of huge plaids of tan and mouse color.

The Green Ghost folded the coat and hooked it over his left arm.

CHAPTER 11

RAVING LIKE A MANIAC, Mike Delane strode back and forth in his apartment. His massive shoulders twitched. He brandished his thick arms. His swarthy face now was almost purple with wrath.

One of his trusted men stood before him.

"So Corgan came, did he?" Delane roared. "There wasn't any fake about that message."

"He came alone—came right into the building and went to the penthouse, Mike. You want us to go up there and blast him and the jane both?"

"You damned fool!" Delane cried. "Not in the building. Get him when he leaves. Blast him to hell!"

"Leave it to us, Mike."

"Have the boys watch every exit."

"They're doin' that now."

"Blast him! And watch out for the cops."

An instant later, Mike Delane paced the room alone. He mumbled as he walked. He brandished his fists.

BIG SHOT Mike Delane had weaknesses. One was fear of ridicule. The unknown who had telephoned knew of Butcher Corgan's visit to Coralie Farlowe. Possibly, then, others knew it also. If Corgan lived to return to his own rooms, the laugh would be on Mike Delane.

It surprised Delane that Corgan would have the nerve to do

such a thing. Possibly it was a trap. Yet that did not seem possible, if Corgan had come alone.

The injunction to blast Corgan outside the building had been based on another fear of Delane's. Mike Delane would—and had—face blazing guns. But he had a terror of the hot chair. Let his men take the chances. He would not appear openly in this. What the police believed, after it was over, must not be proved.

He wondered how long Corgan would remain in the penthouse. If he did not leave before daylight, the blasting could not be done. Corgan would have to be reached and wiped out later, and that might be difficult.

"Get 'em up, Delane!"

Mike Delane whirled, a cry of surprise rushing from his lips, when he heard the command. The hand which had started for the automatic he packed in a shoulder holster suddenly was inactive. Delane found himself covered effectually.

"The Green Ghost!" he muttered.

"Sit down." The order came in an ordinary voice. "Keep your hands up." The Green Ghost came close, alert, watchful, gun held ready. He put forth a left hand and got Mike Delane's automatic, and slipped it into his coat pocket.

"What's the idea?" Delane asked.

"Thought we might have a little visit."

"Who are you?"

"Your enemy, to an extent. Delane, you're either a fool or an idiot."

"What do you mean?"

"Your mugs are scattered all around the building, waiting to get Butcher Corgan. They'll get him. And the cops will get you."

"I don't know what happens in the street. It's none of my business. If Corgan gets rubbed out, I won't know who does it."

"You'll let your men take the rap?"

"I'll have 'em sprung."

"You can't spring a man charged with murder. Your high-priced mouthpiece won't even be able to spring you. You're in a trap, Delane."

"What trap?"

"I know all about it, I telephoned you about Corgan's visit to Coralie. The cops know about it, too. They know you'll have your men waiting to rub Corgan out. Soon as it's done, the cops'll gather all of them in—then come up here for you. It's a plant. Dog eat dog. Corgan gets wiped out, and Mike Delane and his men are jugged for murder. Two gang chiefs gone, without the cops risking their lives."

"Who are you—a cop?"

"I WAS once. Crooks couldn't buy me, so they framed me. I was innocent, but got kicked out of the Department. Other cops believed me crooked. I haven't much love for cops. Nor crooks."

"What do you want here?" Mike Delane asked.

"Some of the jewels your mob got when they stuck up that society wedding party three nights ago."

"Don't know anything about it."

"Get up," the Green Ghost ordered. "We'll go into your little back room."

Delane was compelled to obey. The Green Ghost closed the door after Delane had snapped on the lights.

"Make a bad move, and you'll get it," the Ghost warned. "I don't know which I hate the most, you or the cops. You helped frame me, Delane.

"And my pals on the force believed me guilty. It wrecked my whole life—"

"You're Danny Blaney!" Delane interrupted.

"Not sure of that—you're guessing. Better not guess again, Mike. If you guessed right, I might be afraid to let you live. Understand? Now, open your safe."

"I tell you—"

"And be quick about it or you'll be sorry!"

MIKE DELANE did not wish to invite death. He could get more jewels. If this Green Ghost took them now, perhaps he would not get away with them. Delane did not forget that the building was watched by his men, waiting for Butcher Corgan. He could flash them a signal.

He pulled aside a painting, exposed the front of his safe. Working the combination, he stepped back.

"Keep your hands up," the Green Ghost warned. "And stand there flat against the wall, your face to it."

In a compartment of that safe were scintillating jewels. The Green Ghost put a few into his coat pocket. It was his manner of paying expenses. He retained others in his hand.

"Back to the other room!" he ordered.

In the living-room again, the Green Ghost stowed some of the jewels in a vase. Then he forced Mike Delane to put his wrists behind his back.

"SIT DOWN and be comfortable," the Ghost said.

Watching his victim closely, he used the telephone. He did not dial a number this time, but asked the operator for Police Headquarters. And then he asked for Detective Sergeant Tim O'Hara.

There was a short wait, during which the Green Ghost watched Mike Delane and hummed a popular air. Presently:

"O'Hara? Green Ghost talking. Come at once to Mike Delane's apartment. You'll find stolen jewels in a vase in the living-room, and an open safe stuffed with swag. Better make it snappy!"

He chuckled as he replaced the receiver.

"I have a lot of fun with O'Hara," he said. "He's trying to catch me. Just to show him how futile his efforts are, tonight I swiped his new overcoat. There it is on that chair, where I dropped it when I came in."

"How'd you get in?" Delane asked.

"Through your service door."

"And how'll you get out?" Delane's eyes glittered. "My men are waitin'—and the cops."

"I'll manage."

"I thought you hated the cops. Going to turn me in to them, are you?"

"You'll burn," the Ghost said. "You'll fry, Delane. And for planning the death of Butcher Corgan. Is it worth it?"

"If I could get away now—"

"You can't. Your number's up, Delane. You've killed several men, ordered a lot more killed. Your men may blast Corgan, but that'll be a decent death.

"You'll sizzle."

"Cut it!"

"Don't like to hear about it, huh? Day after day, Delane, you'll sit in the cell, looking at the death watch, waiting. Nobody in the world can help you then."

"Help me out of this, Ghost," Delane begged. "You've got the jewels. Take more. Make your getaway."

"You had me framed—you and others. Wrecked my life. As soon as Corgan is bumped off, the cops will come for you. I'll slip out, and they'll find you here alone."

"That's playin' the cops' game."

"If I let you go, what can you do?"

"I'll get down there and call off my men," Delane said. "The Corgan thing can wait."

"The cops will grab you if you show your nose. Your men won't know it. They'll go ahead and blast Corgan—"

"That overcoat!" Delane cried. "You said that that overcoat belongs to O'Hara."

"What about it?"

"I'LL PUT it on. If the cops are watchin', they'll think I'm O'Hara. They won't bother me. I can slip along the side street, get to one of the men, have him call off the others. No blastin' of Corgan, no charge against me."

"Yes, you could do it," the Green Ghost admitted.

"Don't play the cops' game. Let me go, Ghost. Settle with me later, when the cops aren't mixed in—if you're man enough."

The Green Ghost tossed him the overcoat.

"Go ahead," he said.

CHAPTER III

mIKE DELANE'S MEN, SECRETED in dark spots, were watching every exit of the building. They knew that Butcher Corgan had entered. They had seen him, had made special note of that unusual overcoat he wore.

Between Delane and Corgan was enmity of years' standing, a continual fight for control of the district. The arrival of Coralie Farlowe had intensified that enmity. She had played them against each other.

Members of the two gangs followed the leadership of their chiefs. It had been open warfare for some time. And here the Delane men had the chance to rub out Butcher Corgan and score a decisive victory.

They waited, watched, careful not to be observed. As time passed, they grew nervous. It might be hours before Butcher Corgan left the penthouse and descended to the street. They were alert against the police, against the possibility of some of Corgan's men slipping up on them.

They understood the situation perfectly. Corgan had come alone, to the building where Mike Delane lived, to visit the woman in whom Delane also was interested. It was an open insult, a sort of metaphorical thumbing of the nose.

Suddenly, one of the Delane men straightened, tensed, hissed a warning to others near. Down the alley and toward the side street a man was coming beneath the faint light over a service door. There could be no mistaking that overcoat.

With head bent, he hurried on, and reached the street. He turned down it. For an instant he was against the solid brick wall of the apartment building.

A blast of flame and lead cracked the night. The man in the overcoat swayed drunkenly, then crashed to the ground. His arms spread out in grotesque fashion.

Shuffling feet left the scene. Dark figures darted through the alley. At the corner, two taxicab chauffeurs began shouting. The doorman turned to look. A police whistle shrilled.

Up in Delane's apartment, the Green Ghost heard that blast of firing. From the window of a darkened room, he looked down at the street. He could see the overcoat.

Leaving the apartment, he darted to the rear service stairs. It took him some time to reach the roof and get over the parapet again. Cautiously, he advanced to the porch of the penthouse.

Things were as he had left them, save that Butcher Corgan was conscious. The Green Ghost acted swiftly, removing the gags. His victim worked stiff jaws. Corgan struggled to sit up, and the Green Ghost propped him against the wall.

"Mike Delane has just been bumped off," he said.

"What?" Corgan cried.

"BY HIS own men. He was wearing your overcoat, Corgan. I gave it to him."

"A good job, whoever you are!" Corgan declared. "But I'd rather have done the job myself."

"Oh, you may get credit for it," the Green Ghost assured him. "You're in the building, you know. It'll look like your men had been posted outside, and got a chance at Delane."

"But Coralie can swear—"

The Green Ghost's laughter stopped him.

"Of course they'll believe Coralie, especially since you two men were rivals. They'll say Coralie decided between you, and the man who lost was rubbed out. It'll look all the more like a planned job, with Coralie testifying for you."

"Let me get out of here," Corgan begged. "Turn me loose, Green Ghost."

"You'll run into the arms of the cops. Did you have any of your men trail you here?"

"I had three waiting a block away."

"They'll get blamed for the job, and you for planning it. You can be sure that Mike Delane's men won't admit they shot their chief by mistake."

"Cut me lose," Corgan begged again. "I can't be caught here. I've got a hideout I can go to, till this thing gets straightened out."

THE GREEN GHOST walked over to Coralie Farlowe, and cut the rope which bound her wrists.

"Coralie can get you loose," he said to Corgan. "I'll be on my way."

He hurried through the front door and to the parapet. But he did not descend. Behind a ventilator, he crouched in the darkness, and watched.

He saw Corgan and the woman come out on the porch. At the same instant, the elevator door opened. Detective Sergeant Tim O'Hara and three of his men emerged.

There was no time for Corgan to dart back into the penthouse. He was too wise to try for a weapon. He put up his hands at O'Hara's orders, stood still while O'Hara's men snapped handcuffs on him.

"What's this for?" Corgan demanded.

"A matter of precaution," O'Hara told him. "We haven't ironed out the angles of this thing yet."

"What's happened? Can't I visit a friend—" Corgan began.

"Mike Delane's been washed up, Corgan—if you don't know it."

"A good job—but I didn't do it."

"We caught some of your men in the neighborhood."

Coralie decided to take the center of the stage. "The Green

Ghost has been here. He left only a few minutes ago."

"He can't get out of the building," O'Hara told her.

"Mr. Corgan's been here with me for some time."

"You can do your talking later," O'Hara said. "I'll take a look at your penthouse while I'm here."

The search took fifteen minutes. O'Hara and his men went down in the elevator again, taking Butcher Corgan with them. Coralie Farlowe remained in her living-room, pacing back and forth, uncomfortable for once at being alone.

"Beg pardon," said a voice behind her.

THERE WAS the Green Ghost again. He had come through the open French window and advanced toward her, bowing slightly. She stood back against the wall.

"What do you want now?" she asked.

"This is the safest place for me just now. They've already searched here," the Ghost pointed out.

"You're quite a man," she admitted. "Got Delane rubbed out and Corgan nabbed for it. Make your enemies fight one another, do you?"

"Nothing new in that," the Green Ghost declared. "It's an old, old trick. But it's one that is always effective."

"Who are you?" she asked. "You know, we might make a good team of partners. This town could be handled right."

"I don't team," he told her. "I hate crooks and cops, so I work alone."

Watching her, he went to the telephone and called the office below. He asked for Sergeant O'Hara. There was a moment's wait, then he heard O'Hara's voice.

"This is the Green Ghost," he said. "I'm in the penthouse. You missed a bet, O'Hara. This Farlowe jane is one of the big fish. Ought to be jugged or deported. Better search the penthouse again. You'll find some jewels the Delane gang got three nights ago. Didn't know Coralie's trying to work with both Corgan and Delane, did you?"

"Where are the jewels?" O'Hara asked.

"Look in the piano, O'Hara."

He slapped the receiver in place and darted to the grand piano, the top of which was up. Some of the jewels he had taken from Mike Delane's safe came from his pocket, and were tossed down inside the instrument. Then he whirled toward Coralie Farlowe again. He held one of the cords with which she had been bound before.

"No you don't—" she began.

"Listen, crook! To me, you're not a pretty woman to be handled with gloves. You're Coralie Farlowe, over here because it got too hot for you in France. Turn your back and put your wrists behind."

She hesitated. The Green Ghost held her against the wall, bent her arms back, lashed her wrists.

"**NOW, LET'S** see you get those jewels out of the piano before O'Hara gets here. It can't be done. And tell him any yarn you please—tell him the truth. He won't believe you. Nobody will."

"Why are you—" she began.

"Because you're a crook."

He darted out of the room, across the porch, and to the door of the elevator. In a dark spot beside it, he stood waiting, merging into the darkness.

The elevator ascended. The door clanged open, and O'Hara and two of his men rushed out and charged across the porch and into the penthouse.

The Green Ghost stepped out of the darkness and into the elevator.

"Down—quick!" he snapped at the operator. He emphasized the command by jabbing the muzzle of his automatic into the boy's ribs.

The door was closed, and the elevator started down.

"Stop at the fourth floor," the Green Ghost ordered.

He got out there, and made the boy take the elevator on

down. Racing along a corridor, the Green Ghost got to the rear service stairs. Down these he went swiftly, and with little noise. As he ran, he stripped off his gloves and hood and stowed them away beneath his coat, and put on a cap he took from a pocket.

He reached the basement, went slowly and carefully along a semi-dark corridor there, approached the alley door. That police were stationed in the alley, he did not doubt. He listened a moment, heard nothing. He opened the door halfway.

"Help! Help!" he cried.

Then he darted to one side in the darkness and waited. Pounding feet in the alley. Heavy breathing. Two officers in uniform charged through the door and down into the basement hall.

The Green Ghost charged out, slamming the door behind him. The alley was dark for the greater part. He fled through the darkness to the side street. Behind him, a gun cracked, a hoarse voice bellowed to him to stop.

But he did not stop. He left the street, ran between two buildings, paralleled the alley and finally reached the next street. There, he sauntered along like any honest citizen homeward bound, sauntered for two blocks, and engaged a taxicab.

Twenty minutes later, Danny Blaney entered the cigar store he owned far downtown.

"How's business?" he asked the night clerk.

"Middlin'. Danny, I bet it's tough for you, not bein' a cop any more."

"How's that?"

"Well, you were used to excitement, and now you never get any."

Danny Blaney grinned. "Oh, I get all I want," he said.

IV

THE GREEN GHOST STALKS

CHAPTER I

THE VOICE CONTINUED, SPEAKING in sibilant whispers, just the mere suggestion of a voice that seemed to come from a far distance:

"Snap out of it, Lanwell! Easy!—don't make a sound! Blast you if you as much as whisper—"

Gus Lanwell stirred in his sleep. The noted criminal lawyer had been dreaming, and now the dream seemed broken by another.

"Come out of it, Lanwell—"

Suddenly, Lanwell was awake. He was stretched on the bed with his face turned toward the wall. There was no light in the room. He grunted, and started to turn over.

"Take it easy—"

The whisper seemed to come from across the room. It must be a dream, Lanwell was thinking. No enemy could invade his apartment and get into his bedchamber without being stopped. Lanwell was guarded carefully against that.

He continued turning over. He was getting to be himself now. He blinked, opened his eyes wide, and looked across the room toward the door.

"What—!"

The word strangled in his throat. Fear and surprise mingled to choke him. He sat up straight in the bed, trembling, the perspiration popping out on his face. His tongue sought to moisten lips suddenly parched.

That thing across the room, by the wall! A sort of greenish light that moved toward the bed. It looked like the outline of a skull. There was a slit for the mouth, and circles for eyes. Coming toward him through the darkness, it was a terrifying sight.

There came a chuckle, too—a sort of fiendish chuckle that seemed to promise dire things. Lanwell heard it plainly. He was shocked to inaction. His mind was telling him he should make an immediate move, but his body was as if paralyzed.

"Careful, Lanwell! I'm watching every move you make. I can see in the dark."

"Who are you?" Lanwell managed the words in a hoarse whisper.

"I'm the Green Ghost."

"What?" Lanwell gasped.

"Keep your voice down, or I'll blast you!"

Gus Lanwell was silent. The Green Ghost! For some time, that elusive personality had been menacing crooks and playing tag with the police. He seemed to possess uncanny knowledge of what was going on in the underworld. He preyed upon those who preyed upon others.

"Green Ghost," Lanwell mouthed, finally. "But, why come to me like this? Are you in trouble? You want me to act for you professionally?"

Again that eerie chuckle came through the darkness, and the green skull seemed to dance.

Lanwell watched the cavorting green death's-head. He knew that the Ghost was wearing a hood over his head, and that luminous paint outlined the skull on the hood. But that knowledge did not make the sight any the less terrifying.

"When I want legal advice," the Green Ghost said, "I'll go to a lawyer."

"And what am I?" Lanwell asked.

"A legal racketeer—a crook!"

Then the business-like automatic of the
Green Ghost barked quickly, twice.

"See here, whoever you are—"

"Oh, don't use that tone of injured dignity to me, Lanwell! I know everything. Lanwell, the lawyer! Lanwell—the One Spot!"

"What?" There was genuine terror in that word.

"Oh, I know, Lanwell! Lead a double life, don't you? Gus Lanwell, the famous criminal lawyer, is also the One Spot, the disguised head of a mob of crooks—"

"Who *are* you?"

"Merely the Green Ghost. I've come here to tell you something, Lanwell. My motives are none of your business. Listen! You think you're wise, but you're a sap. You're being double-crossed, as you've double-crossed so many others. Max Martin is putting it over on you.

"The International Import jewels, Lanwell!"

"I don't know what you're talking about."

"Oh, don't be afraid of me—I'm no cop. Three days ago, the showrooms of the International Import Company were raided, and a fortune in jewels was taken. Max Martin's mob pulled off the job, but you furnished the brains. Bail is ready, if any of them is pinched on suspicion, and you'd be their mouthpiece.

"And Max Martin is going to walk out on you this time, and take all the swag. And he's taking more than that, Lanwell—he's taking Corrine Frane with him."

"What's that?"

THE LAST remark seemingly had been like a smash in the face. Gus Lanwell started to get out of bed, but changed his mind quickly when the Green Ghost growled a low warning.

"You don't believe it, do you?" the Green Ghost asked. "Let me give you a tip, Lanwell. It's one o'clock in the morning. In half an hour or a little longer, Corrine Frane will go to Max Martin's apartment. Lou Hatch will be there, too—Max's pet gunman. Possibly a couple of the others. They'll handle the swag between them, and away they'll go—"

"Who are you? How do you know all this stuff? Why are you warning me?"

"My motive is my business. I've warned you, Lanwell. The rest is up to you."

THERE WAS a soft click, and the bedchamber was bathed in light. Lanwell's man-servant stood in the doorway in pajamas, bending forward, blinking, holding a revolver in a hand that shook.

The Green Ghost was revealed as a medium-sized man dressed completely in black, with a black hood over his head and black gloves on his hands. He had been invisible in the darkness, save for the greenish glow on the hood. His identity was effectually hidden—he might have been any one of ten thousand men in town.

"Drop that gun!" There was unmistakable menace in the Green Ghost's voice.

The man-servant had some vague idea of helping his employer. He started to lift the weapon. The automatic the Green Ghost held promptly cracked. The servant recoiled with a cry, dropping his gun, lurching back against the wall with blood dripping from a wounded forearm.

"Steady!" the Green Ghost warned. "Hop out of bed, Lanwell, and do exactly as I say."

The servant was whimpering with pain and cringing in fear. The Green Ghost forced Lanwell to walk past him and go into the living room of the apartment, compelled the servant to go along and sit in an easy chair.

"Telephone for a doctor," the Green Ghost instructed the lawyer. "When he comes, say that I broke in here and shot your man."

Lanwell telephoned.

"Now, walk with me to the door. We'll turn off the lights, and I'll get out. Then you can telephone for the cops."

"That—what you told me—" Lanwell stammered.

"It was the truth. It's up to you, Lanwell. Let yourself be double-crossed if you like. The swag and your girl! Let Max Martin get 'em both—if you haven't got red blood enough to take care of your own interests."

"Whoever you are, thanks for the tip."

"You needn't bother to thank me for anything."

"If there's anything I can do for you at any time—"

"I may be seeing you again," the Green Ghost said.

The lights were snapped off. The Green Ghost listened at the hall door a moment, then opened it slowly and cautiously and peered out.

"Sorry I had to shoot your man," he whispered to Lanwell. "He's probably the only decent one around here. It's not a dangerous wound, though. Good-by, Lanwell, for the present."

"Wait! How'd you get in here?" Lanwell asked.

"Your safety measures don't commence until you're ready to retire," the Green Ghost replied. "I got in hours before that. Been hiding in a closet."

THE GREEN GHOST opened the door wider, glanced up and down the hall, suddenly darted out and pulled the door shut behind him. Nor did Gus Lanwell have the courage to jerk that door open again and see where the intruder went. He hurried back to the wounded servant, his brain busy with a story to be told the police.

IT **WAS THE GREEN GHOST** who left Gus Lanwell's apartment, but it was Danny Blaney who slipped through the dark alley a moment later, his green hood and gloves tucked away beneath his dark clothing.

Flattening himself against a wall, Danny Blaney made sure that he was not being observed. He did not want to be noticed in that section of the city. He wanted nothing to happen that might endanger the success of plans he had made.

He was out to get Gus Lanwell, Max Martin and any of the others who might be caught in the net. The profit he might acquire while so doing was of secondary consideration.

There had been a time when Danny Blaney had been a member of the Police Department, Detective Branch, a zealous and ambitious officer who respected the oath he had taken. His zeal had won for him the enmity of the underworld.

Assassination was denied him. Those he fought had decided it would serve their purpose better to ruin him, and give the Police Department a black eye.

So Danny Blaney had been framed neatly, been made to look like a crook himself. His trial had not resulted in conviction, but he had been dismissed from the Department. And many of his comrades believed in his guilt.

So Danny Blaney had become bitter. His career had been ruined. But he continued his detective work. He made a study of the underworld, its leaders, its methods. He learned more than he possibly could have learned as a detective. He masked his activities by running a corner cigar store.

He had learned that Gus Lanwell, noted criminal lawyer, was also the One Spot, a crook leader known only to a couple of his confederates, who always appeared before the others wearing a robe and hood which disguised him effectually. And Danny Blaney knew that Gus Lanwell had been one of those instrumental in his downfall.

To expose Gus Lanwell and his pals was Danny Blaney's task now. The robbery of the International Importing Company gave him the chance. The eternal suspicion crooks have toward one another furnished him with a means.

DARTING THROUGH the alley and across a side street, Danny Blaney came to an avenue and strolled along it after the manner of an honest citizen. At an all-night drug store, he entered a telephone booth and called Police Headquarters. He asked for Detective Sergeant Tim O'Hara.

The connection was made immediately. O'Hara's gruff voice demanded the name of his caller.

"Green Ghost speaking," came the reply. "I phoned you in the afternoon to stand by. Just want to let you know that you can get set for a trip with your jewel squad."

"Where are you?" O'Hara demanded.

"In a pay booth. Won't do you any good to trace the call. I'll be gone before anybody can get to me. Listen! I'm going to call you in a short time. Be ready for a quick ride."

"What's the game?" O'Hara asked.

"Going to put you next to the International Import jewels, and also give you a chance to catch the One Spot."

"Wait, Green Ghost! Why can't we get together and work? You've put me wise to a lot of stuff—"

"Get me right!" the Green Ghost interrupted. "If you knew me, my value to you would end. I hate crooks and cops both. I don't give you tips to help the cops. I do it because I want you coppers to land the crooks.

"Don't forget to stand by. May call you in half an hour or so."

Danny Blaney walked out of the store when the night clerk was busy attending to a customer. He went through another side street, keeping to the shadowy spots as much as possible. Once more, about five blocks away, he entered a dark alley.

Along this alley he slipped, keeping close to the walls of the buildings, wary for the approach of a night watchman. He stopped, finally, in the rear of a huge apartment building, where there was a little door.

Danny Blaney knew all about that door. It was not the service entrance it seemed to be. It was the private rear entrance to the apartment of Max Martin, notorious gang leader.

A member of the Martin mob was always just inside that door, ready to open it only when a certain knock was given. The person admitted ascended a short flight of stairs to a hallway, and suddenly found himself in the Martin apartment. It was not unlike the secret entrance to some gambling den.

IT HAD taken time for Danny Blaney to learn all this, as it had for him to learn other things. But now he crouched against the dark wall not far from the door, and watched the mouth of the alley. He drew in his breath sharply when he saw a woman dart into the alley from the street.

Danny Blaney had only a swift glimpse at her, but he knew she was Corrine Frane—beautiful, exotic, poisonous. She had come from Europe to dodge the results of a swindling escapade, and had gone to Gus Lanwell for legal advice. Lanwell had become infatuated with the siren from across the Atlantic. Their alliance had resulted in her being admitted to the Max Martin mob—and its profits.

Shortly before midnight, having made sure of Max Martin's whereabouts, Danny Blaney had telephoned Corrine Frane, pretending to be Lou Hatch, Martin's right-hand man. He had succeeded in the deception.

"Max says for you to come to headquarters about two o'clock tonight," Danny Blaney had told her. "Somethin' important. No, he ain't here. He's downtown seein' the mouthpiece. Be sure to show up."

Now it was the appointed time, and here came Corrine Frane through the alley.

Danny Blaney crouched against the wall. He heard the rustle of her skirts as she slipped through the black night and up to the door. He heard the knock, the slight creak of a hinge as the door was opened. Then all was silent again.

Danny Blaney continued to watch the mouth of the alley. He saw a man stroll by it, swinging a stick, the picture of a gentleman taking a late stroll before turning in. Danny Blaney recognized him—Gus Lanwell.

AN INSTANT later, Lanwell retraced his steps and darted into the darkness of the alley.

Danny Blaney crouched against the wall once more.

Again there came that knock on the door, and again the hinge creaked. Gus Lanwell disappeared into the building. Danny Blaney knew he had put a hood over his head before entering, so the doorman would not see his face. Before ascending to the Martin apartment, he would wrap his body in a long, thin robe.

Danny Blaney remained against the wall for a moment, then went cautiously to the door himself. He took out his own hood, and put it on. He drew on the gloves, got out his automatic, and took from beneath his waistcoat a length of rope and a prepared gag.

At the door, Danny gave the signal. The hinge creaked again. With his left hand, Danny felt the door being opened. He slipped quickly inside.

"Who—" the door guard began to question.

Danny Blaney smote him once with the automatic, tripped the half-stunned man, hurled him to the floor. Working swiftly, he bound and gagged him. He took away a gun the other had in a shoulder holster. Then he started silently up the stairs.

CHAPTER III

MAX MARTIN HAD, IN truth, been downtown that night. But it had been a trip for pleasure, not business. He had shown himself at a couple of night clubs, with his bodyguard along, trying to give the impression that he and his mob were inactive at present—in case the police were wondering about his being implicated in the recent jewel robbery.

Now, Max Martin sat in his living room, dressed in silk lounging pajamas and flowered dressing gown. He was tall, thin, with an inscrutable face which always expressed cruelty. With him was Lou Hatch.

Lou Hatch was of the thug type, a dependable ruffian Martin liked to have near him. Hatch was a killer, and toward Max Martin expressed the loyalty of a dog for his master.

"We'll split the swag when the One Spot says to do it," Martin was saying. "This thing is big, and the cops are on their ears about it; won't hurt to take it easy for a time."

"I'll say it's big!" Lou Hatch agreed. "And this One Spot gets a big cut—"

"Stow that! He's entitled to it," Martin interrupted. "He got the lay and planned the job."

"I'd like to know who he is. He sure has a way of findin' out the right dope."

"You can stow that, too," Martin warned. "None of your business who he is. You tend to your line of work and forget the rest."

Lou Hatch gulped a drink to cover his embarrassment at this rebuke. A soft buzzer sounded.

"Somebody comin'," Hatch said.

"It's almost two," Max Martin added. "Wonder who it can be? I haven't told any of the boys to show up."

Lou Hatch promptly got his automatic out of its holster and held it ready. Max Martin lit a fresh cigarette and strolled to a niche in the wall, where he turned on a tiny light. There was a knock, and a panel slipped back.

"Corrine!" Martin gasped.

"Yep, it's little Corrine!"

SHE SWEPT into the room and tossed aside the long cloak she was wearing, which had covered a rather elaborate costume. Corrine Frane was the type of woman who never went anywhere without being gowned to create a splendid impression.

Max Martin closed the panel and followed her into the room. She nodded in friendly manner to Lou Hatch, sat on a couch, and motioned toward a cocktail shaker on a table near-by.

Max Martin poured her a drink, gave her a cigarette, held the lighter, then sat beside her. He looked at her appreciatively. He always had regretted that Gus Lanwell had seen Corrine Frane first.

"Sure glad to see you," Martin said. "It's a pleasure to have you drop in, Corrine. But to what do I owe the honor of this unexpected visit?"

"You should know," she replied. "What do you mean by 'unexpected'? I'm here because Lou phoned me that you wanted me to come about this time."

"What?" Martin cried.

"I didn't do any phonin'," Lou Hatch declared.

"YOU CERTAINLY did—just a bit before midnight. You gave the code word. And I recognized your voice. You said that Max wanted me to come here around two, and that it was important."

"Mistake somewhere," Martin declared, looking slightly worried. "Lou couldn't have telephoned you at that time. He was with me downtown. Didn't leave my side a second."

"If Lou didn't phone me, who did? It certainly sounded like Lou's voice," she insisted. "He seemed to be in a hurry."

"I sure didn't call," Lou Hatch reiterated. "Maybe it was one of the other boys."

"It's got me puzzled," Max Martin admitted. "I'll look into it. Anyhow, Corrine, you're here." He slipped his arm about her shoulders. "Have another cocktail and I'll take you home later. You can blow now, Lou."

"Sure!" Lou Hatch slipped his automatic back into its holster and reached for his highball, to finish it and get going.

"Lou needn't leave," Corrine said.

"Afraid to be with me alone?" Martin bantered.

"Don't be silly, Max!"

On impulse, she turned her head and kissed him lightly on the cheek. Martin's arm tightened about her. And, at that instant, the panel in the niche slid back.

"A very pretty picture!" a deep voice, evidently disguised intoned.

"The One Spot!" Lou Hatch gasped.

"Thought I'd drop in," the hooded and gowned figure said.

The panel closed noiselessly, and the One Spot strode into the room.

"Seems to be a night for the unexpected," Martin offered.

"No doubt my visit is unexpected," the One Spot replied. "A friend gave me a little tip." Through slits in the hood, his eyes blazed at Corrine Frane.

"A tip about what?" Martin asked. "There seems to be something funny going on."

"So I've been led to believe," the One Spot said. "Max, I understand that you've planned to double-cross me."

"What's that?"

"This last haul. You intend to decamp with all the swag. Also, you intend to take Corrine along with you. You can have her, Max. I don't want any double-crossing wren. She'll probably do the same to you some day. But you don't get away with all the swag!"

"Are you crazy?" Martin cried, springing to his feet.

THE ONE SPOT suddenly exhibited an automatic.

"Careful what moves you make!" he warned. "And you keep out of this, Hatch! Maybe you were to be one of the suckers, too."

"Anybody who says Max would double-cross—" Hatch began.

"Shut up, and sit down!" the One Spot ordered. "It's all up, Max. I was tipped off. I was told Corrine would be here at two o'clock, also."

"Wait!" Martin barked. "Somebody phoned Corrine and told her to come here tonight. She thought it was Lou, but it wasn't. We were just wondering who—"

"You think I'll fall for a thin yarn like that?" the One Spot demanded. "I walk in and find you sitting side by side, you with your arm around her, and her kissing you."

"Why, that was—was just—" Corrine began.

"Just double-crossing," the One Spot said. "You and Max are the only ones who know the identity of the One Spot, except the man who warned me tonight."

"Who warned you?" Martin cried. "Man, don't you realize that if somebody else knows—"

"THE GREEN GHOST warned me. I don't know who he is, any more than you do. He got into my bedroom, woke me up and warned me, then shot my servant, and got away."

"The Green Ghost! How could he know?" Martin cried.

"He seemed to know everything. He certainly knew about you and Corrine, and how you're planning to walk out on me.

Well, Max, we'll have a showdown right now. Get the swag, and we'll split, and I'll take mine away. Then you can go to blazes, all of you!"

"Going to get rid of us just like that, huh?" Martin asked, sneering.

"Just like that! And there's no comeback. If you or Corrine disclose my true identity, nobody will believe you. My tracks are covered. There isn't as much as a fingerprint left behind. Get the swag!"

Max Martin sprang to his feet. "All right! Have it your own way. We'll split right now."

"Please—" Corrine Frane extended her hands toward the One Spot.

"Stay right where you are," he barked at her. "And, after this, you and Max better really blow the country. I've got ways of taking care of double-crossers."

Lou Hatch made a movement, but Martin motioned for him to remain quiet. Hatch was about to go to the defense of his idol, regardless of the weapon the One Spot held.

"Maybe it's best," Martin said. "We'll split the stuff now, and have it over with."

Max Martin walked to another couch, worked there for a time, and finally exposed an aperture in a false bottom, so cleverly contrived that only by taking the couch to pieces could it have been located by one not in on the secret.

FROM THIS aperture he drew forth several packages, which he carried to the table in the middle of the room. He opened the packages, and upon the table cascaded a flood of scintillating gems.

Corrine Frane, despite the situation, gave a cry of delight. Lou Hatch's eyes glittered.

"We'll split," the One Spot said. "I'll take half this time, instead of the usual third. You pay extra for trying to double-cross me. Be glad I don't take all."

"Where do you get the idea you'll take half?" Max Martin cried.

"I'm holding a gun," the One Spot explained. "Stand back from that table, and get your hands up. Corrine, you stand beside him."

"Playing a high hand," Martin observed, as he and the girl obeyed. "If there's a muss here, and you're exposed—"

"There wouldn't be anybody left to expose me," the One Spot said significantly. "Hatch, you stand beside the others. I suppose you're packing a rod?"

"Sure!" Hatch replied.

"Get your hands up. Might be dangerous to order you to take out the gun and drop it. Stand back, now!"

They stood in a line against the wall. Lou Hatch was frankly furious. Max Martin's face was mask-like, save that his eyes were glittering. The girl was deathly white.

The One Spot advanced to the table and sat down beside it. He continued to watch them and hold his weapon ready as he made a swift inspection of the haul. Glancing repeatedly from the jewels to the three against the wall, he began shoving some of the loot to one side of the table.

"I'll play square with you double-crossers," the One Spot said. "I'll have to guess at values, but I'll try to split this stuff fairly. More than you deserve."

"You're only wastin' time, One Spot!" said a voice from the other side of the room.

"Drop that gun!"

A chorus of gasps came from the three against the wall. The One Spot seemed to flinch. His body was motionless except for the head, which he turned slowly. The Green Ghost was there, and the panel was sliding shut behind him.

"You!" the One Spot cried. "You certainly knew what you were talking about when—"

"Drop that gun!"

"But if you're my friend—"

"You saw me shoot in your apartment. Quick!"

THE ONE Spot dropped the gun to the rug and got slowly out of the chair.

"Back up beside the others," the Green Ghost ordered. "A wrong move, and I start some target practice. Four of a kind— all crooks!"

"Don't class me with double-crossers," the One Spot cried.

"Far as I know, they're not double-crossin' you," the Green Ghost replied. "That was just a yarn to get you here. I was the one who phoned Corrine Frane, too. Wanted to have you all here together.

"Thought you might get the International Company's jewels out of their hiding-place. Wanted them, too."

"Who are you?" the One Spot cried.

"Not sayin'."

"Why not come in with us, Green Ghost?" Max Martin asked. "Why work alone?"

"I'm not a crook. I've been invited to join better mobs than yours, anyhow, and refused. And you can't take care of yourselves. Look where I've got you now."

LOU HATCH decided that this was a time to do something about the situation. His hand made a quick dive for his holster as he threw his body aside. But the automatic of the Green Ghost barked quickly, twice. The first bullet missed and tore into the wall. The second cut down Lou Hatch as he was about to press the trigger.

The gun fell from his hand. He reeled back against the wall, and slowly sat down against it.

"Steady!" the Green Ghost warned the others. "Only a shot in the shoulder. He'll not die. He'll live to do plenty time."

For a moment he held them so, then looked at the glittering jewels. Working swiftly, he selected a few, and stowed them away.

"I collect only for expenses," he remarked. "As I said, I'm not a crook. I fight crooks. And what a sensation the newspapers will carry tomorrow!"

"Let me make a deal with you?" the One Spot asked.

The eyes of the Green Ghost glittered. "You're the last man in the world who could buy me off! This whole thing was planned to get you! Steady, now, or there'll be more shootin'. All I need is an excuse."

Watching them closely, he stepped to the telephone and dialed for the operator.

"Police Headquarters!" he said.

"So! You're some sort of trick cop!" Max Martin accused.

"Wrong again! I hate cops almost as much as I hate crooks, and with mighty good reason for it! Hello! Police Headquarters? Get me Tim O'Hara. This is the Green Ghost!"

There was a short wait, while the Green Ghost menaced the three with the weapon he held.

"Don't be a damned fool, man!" the One Spot barked at him. "Take all the swag—there's a fortune—and go!"

"Got all I need," the Green Ghost replied. "Hello! O'Hara? Bring your squad to Max Martin's apartment. Be quick about it. And you'd better break right in."

He clicked the receiver on the hook and walked back to the table in the middle of the room.

"Martin, you'll probably get a few years," the Green Ghost said. "So will Lou Hatch. Maybe some of the others. But that's all a part of the game you play. The fair Corrine will either go up or be deported. She may get off a trip to the big house if she makes eyes at the jurors.

"But the One Spot—ah!"

"Make some kind of deal with me," the One Spot begged.

"No chance! These jewels—jewels of vengeance! It's you I'm after, One Spot, and probably you'll never know why."

"I'll say I was framed—"

THE GREEN GHOST laughed. "You're a criminal lawyer, aren't you? You know you're doomed. You can't give any explanation for being here in that make-up."

"I can say I came here to hold a conference with my clients."

"And, of course, Max and the others will stand aside and back that up, and take the rap for you. Especially since you've been holding out on them—and planning to have them framed and put out of the way."

"Prove that and I'll confess everything and have him sent up for a twenty stretch!" Max Martin cried.

"He'll go up anyhow," the Green Ghost replied.

So they waited, afraid to move, except that the Green Ghost allowed Corrine Frane to lower her hands and sit on a couch.

AFTER A time, there was a racket in the corridor, and feet pounded to the door. A fist crashed against it.

"Open up!" That was the stern voice of Detective Sergeant Tim O'Hara, of the jewel squad.

"Smash in, O'Hara! This is the Green Ghost!"

He backed toward the niche which held the panel. Something crashed against the door. Again! It rocked on the hinges, splintered around the lock and bolt, caved in, and detectives sprawled into the room.

"Hands up!" the Green Ghost barked. "No shootin', O'Hara. Just grab those people. That's Lou Hatch on the floor—shot through the shoulder!"

One glance at the thug and the invading officers snapped handcuffs.

"There are the International jewels on the table," the Green Ghost said, "all but a few I've taken for expenses. The Max Martin mob did the job. They'll probably talk. And there's the mysterious One Spot. Take a look at him."

O'Hara stepped forward swiftly and tore the hood away.

"Gus Lanwell!" he cried.

"A criminal lawyer turned criminal. Got tarred from handling the stick," the Green Ghost said.

"I protest that—" Gus Lanwell began.

"Don't worry, O'Hara. I'll tip you off tomorrow where you can get conclusive evidence against him. And Max Martin will probably talk."

"And how about you?" O'Hara demanded. "Take off that thing you've got on your head."

"One moment, gentlemen!"

The right hand of the Green Ghost, still holding his gun, went toward his hood as though to take it off. His left hand, behind his back, felt for the button which released the sliding panel.

"Watch him!" Lanwell cried.

But he cried it too late. The panel opened, and the Green Ghost sprang backward into darkness. The officers in the room started forward. As the panel closed, bullets splintered it. But it clicked into place.

Tim O'Hara shouted orders. It took a moment to find the button and open the panel again. It stuck half-way open because of the splinters. They wrenched it open, finally, but precious time had been lost.

Down the stairs the Green Ghost had darted. He tripped over the bound and gagged door guard. He opened the little service door and darted silently into the dark alley. As he went swiftly toward its mouth, he stripped off hood and gloves and stowed them away.

Behind him was a chorus of shouts. From the darkness ahead, a voice answered. A policeman came pounding along the alley. He charged past the man crouching against a wall in the black night. And Danny Blaney knew that no other guardian of the law was between him and freedom.

HALF AN hour later, Danny drifted into his cigar store, to be regarded in amazement by a sleepy clerk. "Boss! What are you doin' up at this hour? It's almost half-past three," the clerk said.

"Couldn't sleep," Danny explained. "How's business?"

"Rotten!"

"Well, maybe we've made expenses, anyhow," said Danny Blaney.

V

THE MURDER NOTE

CHAPTER I

PALLOR OF DEATH

STYGIAN BLACKNESS SHROUDED THE end of the blind alley in the rear of the big apartment house; yet, only a short distance away, was the brilliantly-lighted street with its midnight traffic, its alert police officers, its somewhat questionable citizenry.

Crouching against a brick wall, Danny Blaney watched the alley's mouth. In this section of the city, midnight was not an hour of dull wits after a busy day. This was a district of denizens of the night, nocturnal birds of prey who arose in the early hours of afternoon and sought beds at dawn. He who clashed with them at this hour matched quick brains, tense nerves, swift violence—else went down to ignoble defeat.

A slight creaking sound reached Danny Blaney's ears. He crouched lower against the wall.

Two men passed him like shadows, whispering softly as they passed.

"Everything's set."

"And everything's settled."

They went toward the alley's mouth. There was no other manner of egress. Danny Blaney knew they had come through a small door which was supposed to be a service entrance. Soon, they were against the light, and Danny Blaney could see them.

But he was unable to make sure identification. They kept close to the building, awaited an opportunity, and darted out to the street. Danny Blaney could see nothing except that they

A trap was all set for Blaney—and he walked right into it.

were dressed in inconspicuous dark clothing. That was natural.

That made all of the gang—except Rod Rordan himself. Rod Rordan had sent forth his men, and had remained at home. Danny Blaney would have a chance he wished—to meet Rod Rordan alone. But not as Danny Blaney!

Like a shadow, he drifted along the wall. The squeaking sound came again as Danny Blaney got through the door and closed it behind him carefully. He went up a flight of steps to the basement level.

Swiftly, unseen, he ascended to the third floor of the building, using the rear stairs. He darted into a supply closet there, for a moment of rest.

He wanted quiet nerves, for he had work to do. He was going to face Rod Rordan alone in his den—Rod Rordan, the gang chief, the jewel thief supreme, the cold killer.

From beneath his coat, Danny Blaney took a garment of thin green silk. It was a hood, which, when slipped over his head, concealed his identity completely. He put on thin green silk gloves. He extracted from one pocket a bunch of keys, and from a shoulder holster an automatic pistol.

A moment longer he waited, listening for sounds in the

corridor. And during that moment his nature changed. Cold hate surged through him—not the hot flush of hate that causes a man to do violent things, but cold hate, that makes a man plan and scheme to his enemy's undoing.

Rod Rordan! One of the group of crooks that had framed Danny Blaney, then a respected and hard-working member of the city detective force! Framed him, so that even his own comrades believed him guilty, though investigation had resulted in an acquittal! Wrecked his career, caused him to resign from the Force, because he could not endure the thrusts of his fellow officers!

Danny Blaney hated crooks. He knew underworld secrets. Lone-handed, he fought the criminals of the upper order, pinning crimes upon them when the police could not, turning them in for justice.

Nobody guessed that Danny Blaney, discredited member of the police department of a year before, was the Green Ghost, a being crooks learned to fear.

IT WAS the Green Ghost who darted from the closet and went swiftly into a cross hall, to stop at the service door of Rod Rordan's apartment. He let himself in with a skeleton key. Not a sound reached his ears.

Like the ghost he impersonated, he went swiftly and silently along the hall, until he came to an archway through which he could peer into the living room.

Lavishly furnished, this apartment. Rod Rordan spent plenty of money, though not in the best of taste. The rugs were thick and expensive, for which the Green Ghost was glad. They muffled the slightest footfall.

Not a sound. He peered cautiously through the curtained archway. Then he saw the back of Rod Rordan's head. The gangster was sitting asprawl in an easy chair, his arms hanging loosely over the sides of it, sitting before a fireplace in which there was a crackling log fire.

Either dozing, or planning some new crime, the Green Ghost thought. Rod Rordan was due for a shock. None knew better than the Green Ghost who had engineered the Barlow jewel robbery three nights before. Even the police thought Rod Rordan had, but they had been unable to connect the gang with the crime.

The Green Ghost had come to snatch the swag—and turn it and Rod Rordan over to the police.

Now he went forward slowly, automatic held ready, alert eyes shifting about the room, ears strained for any sound which might presage danger.

Rod Rordan did not move. The man in the easy chair seemed oblivious of the nearness of a foe.

Suddenly, the Green Ghost spoke. His voice was a low, tense monotone charged with menace:

"Don't move, Rordan, except to lift your hands straight up! Make a break, and I'll let you have it!" Rod Rordan did not move his head, did not even lift his hands as commanded.

"You can't think your way out of this, so don't stall for time," the tense voice continued. "Up with 'em, or I'll blast you!"

The man in the chair remained motionless. The Green Ghost did not underestimate Rod Rordan's cleverness. He was not foolish enough to go up to that chair and get within grasping distance. Walking slowly, watching alertly, he circled, the automatic held ready.

"I'm not a fool, Rordan. This it the Green Ghost! Might as well put up your hands. We've got some talkin' to do."

THE GREEN GHOST made a quick movement—got around in front of the man in the chair, automatic menacing the crook he had come to face.

A cry of surprise escaped him.

The eyes of Rod Rordan were open, fixed. His countenance bore the pallor of death. From his breast protruded the hilt of a knife which had been plunged through his expensive dressing gown and into his heart.

CHAPTER II

BETWEEN TWO FIRES

THE GREEN GHOST DID some swift thinking. He had seen men leave by the little alley door, and had supposed them to be members of Rordan's mob. Had Rod Rordan been executed by his own men? Or had Sam Dorrich done it?

The Green Ghost, informed well as to movements in the underworld, knew that the city was not big enough for both the Rordan and Dorrich gangs…. Even the police knew that, and had been expecting a clash. But they had expected a battle royal, with gunfire ripping through the night. And this was simple murder.

It flashed upon the Green Ghost that here he was alone with the body of a murdered man. If caught there, he would be unable to prove his innocence of the murder. No doubt the hilt of that knife was clean of fingerprints—and the Green Ghost wore gloves!

He would get out immediately, he decided, without searching for the stolen Barlow jewels. One of his objects—handing Rod Rordan over to the police with evidence to convict him of crime—was impossible now of attainment.

He stepped nearer, looked at the dead man more closely. He had been stabbed, the Green Ghost decided, while sitting in the chair. That meant he had been killed by somebody he did not fear, somebody able to get near enough to deliver the thrust unexpectedly. Possibly one of Rordan's own gang—one of the last two men the Green Ghost had seen leave the building.

He whirled to retrace his steps through the hall, and came to an abrupt stop. On the end of the long table, directly before his eyes, was a large square envelope, propped against a book rack. Across it, in large and sprawling handwriting, was: "For the Green Ghost."

An exclamation of surprise escaped the Green Ghost. He picked up the envelope and ripped it open. From it, he took a folded sheet of paper, and unfolded it to find a note in handwriting plainly disguised:

It you are reading this, Green Ghost, it means the end of you. You poor sap! We planted tips for you to pick up—that Rordan did the Barlow jewel job. A good chance to be rid of you and Rordan both. Now we'll learn who the Green Ghost is, when you're jugged for murder.

We're watching. When we know you're in the apartment, we'll tip the cops. They'll find you there, for you'll not be able to get out. Maybe you think this letter will clear you of the murder charge. Watch it a few minutes, Green Ghost.

A tumult of thoughts raced through the Green Ghost's brain. Here was a trap! He had got a dozen tips that the Rordan gang had pulled off the Barlow job. Too many, and too easy, now that he came to think of it.

Somebody had scattered that misinformation, thinking the Green Ghost would pick it up and act on it. They had even spread the report that tonight at a late hour the swag was to be split in Rordan's apartment.

It was plain enough now. They expected the Green Ghost to act on the tip. Rod Rordan had been executed. If the police caught the Ghost there—

BUT, HOW could they be watching? How could they prevent his leaving, now that he saw the trap? He could fight his way out, if necessary. And why couldn't the letter be used to clear him?

He glanced at the letter again—and understood. The writing

was fading already. Trick ink, which would disappear in a few minutes after being exposed to the open air; a schoolboy trick— but it menaced the Green Ghost.

He stuffed the letter and envelope into his pocket, and glanced swiftly around the room. Perhaps they expected to face him as he sought to leave, drive him back and hold him there until the police came. Perhaps some watcher had telephoned for the police already.

Automatic held ready, the Green Ghost started slowly back across the room toward the hallway. He intended to leave as he had entered, if he had to shoot his way through.

He heard no sound, saw nothing to alarm him. It was hot in the room, he thought. Perspiration was streaming from him, and his heart was pumping wildly. He berated himself mentally for letting this situation get him so excited. This was time to keep cool, to think logically and act without hesitation.

He seemed to be choking, and his eyes were smarting, his vision becoming blurred. It was as though some gas—

Gas!

From a large vase on a table in a corner, he saw a wisp of smoke curling up. It had a sweetish, sickening odor. So that was it! They had left chemicals burning, to poison the air in the room, to send the Green Ghost into the realm of unconsciousness, so the police would find him there.

A FEELING of terror came to him. He lurched across the room toward a window. He was growing weaker rapidly, tried to keep from breathing. He fumbled at the window, and found it locked. The catch had been fastened in some manner so he could not turn it.

His heart was pounding, his breath coming in little gasps, his senses were reeling. He opened his smarting eyes an instant, saw another vase on a table, grasped it and smashed wildly at the window pane.

Glass crashed. Cool, fresh air rushed in. He drank it greedily. Far below, glass tinkled as it struck the walk. A whiff of that sickening gas brushed past him, trailed into the night. His vision cleared.

Now, if he could narrow his eyes to slits, and hold his breath until he could get through the rear hall and to the kitchen, and let himself through the service door—

An imperative knock on the front door of the apartment! A stern voice:

"Open up! Anybody in there?"

The Green Ghost knew that voice. It belonged to Detective Sergeant Tim O'Hara, an officer who could not be taken lightly.

CHAPTER III

BOLDNESS DOES
THE TRICK

CHOKING, GASPING, EYES SMARTING, the Green Ghost hurried on across the big living room. He could hear O'Hara giving orders, so the sergeant must have some of his squad with him. The Green Ghost knew that some officer was hurrying to the service entrance, so escape that way would be cut off. And they were at the front door also.

There was no fire escape outside any of the windows of this apartment, no standpipe or ledge to offer a precarious means of exit. And O'Hara was pounding on the front door again. The Green Ghost heard him speak to another man, evidently the manager of the apartment house.

"Get busy with that master key. If the door's bolted on the inside, we'll smash it in."

Trapped! Caught in this apartment, disguised, with the dead body of Rod Rordan there in the chair before the fireplace. If captured, the Green Ghost would be revealed as Danny Blaney. The police knew that the Rordan gang had helped frame Blaney. It would be assumed that Danny Blaney had come there to settle outstanding accounts, and had settled them.

He fled into the rear hall as he heard them fumbling at the front door. He did not doubt that the officers sent to the service door had instructions to enter there and come on into the apartment.

THE GREEN GHOST got as far as the pantry. There was a high, small closet, for brooms and cleaning apparatus, and the Green Ghost wedged himself into it quickly, leaving the door open a fraction of an inch, so he could get air, and could peer out. Sounds told him entrance had been made to the living room. He heard O'Hara's ejaculation as he found the body of Rordan, his swift orders, heard another officer talking monotonously over the telephone, notifying Headquarters of the find. Other sounds told the Green Ghost that policemen had come in through the service entrance.

Through the crack in the door he saw an officer, weapon held ready, pass through the pantry and into the hall. More orders were barked by O'Hara:

"Search the joint from one end to the other."

They had noticed the gas, and some of them were coughing. But the draft created between the open corridor and the window the Green Ghost had smashed was clearing out the gas rapidly. It was safe for them in there now.

The Green Ghost was not so safe. They were starting to search the apartment. He knew O'Hara—an officer who was thorough in everything. His squad members would not overlook even this small closet.

The Green Ghost opened the door wider, slipped into the pantry and to the kitchen door. The kitchen was dark. Into it the Green Ghost hurried, and on to the outside service door, which was standing open a few inches.

Peering into the side hall, the Green Ghost saw a policeman standing a few feet away. He was looking down the corridor toward the front door of the apartment. The Green Ghost went through the door silently, crept forward. The policeman turned.

There was a startled cry, a quick rush, the explosion of a gun, and a blow that thudded home against the side of the policeman's head. The shot the officer had fired cracked into the ceiling. The Green Ghost was past him and racing along the corridor.

Behind him was a chorus of yells. Guns cracked, and bullets

whistled down the corridor. Doors were being jerked open by tenants curious to learn what was happening. They put out their heads, saw the police and heard the bullets zipping, and jerked their heads quickly back again.

THE GREEN GHOST made the rear stairs and started racing down them. Behind him was the pursuit. On the ground floor of the apartment, he darted into a closet and swiftly removed hood and gloves, to hide them away beneath his coat. He did not try escape by the blind alley. He stepped from the closet and walked boldly forward, through the little foyer of the building. The Green Ghost was gone, and Danny Blaney was himself for the moment.

He was a little excited in manner as he passed close to the desk and spoke to the night clerk from the corner of his mouth:

"Raidin' a poker game upstairs."

"Hell!" the clerk said. "Noticed the dicks go up. Can't let the boys have their little game, huh?"

Danny Blaney went on to the street and along it rapidly. The raid story had satisfied the clerk for an instant. Things like that always were happening in that section of the city. Poker game raids were but subterfuges of the police to haul in suspects, excuses to see whether known criminals from other cities were visiting here. The personnel of a poker party often gave detectives inklings of partnerships in the underworld.

Danny Blaney went to a drug store on the corner and got into a telephone booth. He called the apartment building he had just left, and asked to be connected with Rod Rordan's apartment. He wanted to speak to Detective Sergeant O'Hara, he said.

There was a short wait, for O'Hara had to be summoned from the corridor. He barked his identity into the phone and demanded to know what was wanted.

"Listen carefully, O'Hara. This is the Green Ghost. If you standby, I'll call again shortly, and let you know who killed Rod

Rordan and where you can grab the Barlow jewels and the men who stole 'em."

"Say, you—" O'Hara began.

"Just stand by," Blaney interrupted. "No more talk now, O'Hara. I'm not being stalled here till you can trace this call. And say, O'Hara—your men are rotten shots."

THE RECEIVER was snapped back upon its hook, and Danny Blaney walked out to the street. He turned a corner and walked a couple of blocks before he beckoned the chauffeur of a cruising taxicab. He did not want to take a cab from a stand. That phone call might be traced, and the cab chauffeurs in the neighborhood questioned.

Danny Blaney left the cab twelve blocks from where he had engaged it. There was a dance hall half a block down the street, and he started toward it, as though that had been his destination. But he passed the dance hall and went on.

SAM DORRICH, rival and ancient foe of Rod Rordan, had a large apartment, but did not run to lavish furnishings. Dorrich was more of the type known as "roughneck." He disliked anything that hinted at beauty or the effeminate. He had called Rordan a "perfume-stinkin' dude."

Rordan had been clever, and Sam Dorrich depended on violence almost entirely. Danny Blaney knew well the sort of man with whom he had to deal. Nor did he expect to find Sam Dorrich alone.

Preliminary investigation had acquainted Danny Blaney with the place. Dorrich's rooms were on the second floor, rear, with a fire-escape landing at one of the windows. Other means of swift egress were the rear stairs, by which a person could hurry to the basement.

There were two entrances to the basement from outside—an alley door and a service door opening into the side street.

Danny Blaney opened the latter calmly and entered. He found himself in a basement hall dimly lighted, and nobody in sight. He hurried to the stairs, stood back against the wall, donned green hood and gloves again, and got his pistol ready.

There was risk ascending to the second floor dressed like that, for his unusual garb would attract the instant attention of any who saw him, even from a distance. And, this district being full of crooks, the Green Ghost was not unknown.

But boldness would do the trick this time, he thought. So he skipped up the stairs without being seen, reached the landing on the second floor, and stopped there an instant in a niche in the wall to collect himself and get his breath back.

Like a shadow, he drifted along the hall until he came to the front door of Sam Dorrich's apartment. There, he listened. A hum of voices came to him—he could make out three distinct ones. He had three with whom to deal, then—and possibly more.

The Green Ghost touched the bell button, jabbed at it so the distant bell made three short, jerky rings. Then, holding his automatic ready, he waited, standing to one side of the door. He guessed there was a chain on that door. He stood so he could not be seen unless the chain was removed and the door opened wider.

The door was opened promptly, and there was a chain, as the Green Ghost had supposed. He heard somebody grunt in surprise to find nobody there.

"Some comedian, huh?" the man at the door growled.

The Green Ghost heard him undo the chain, and slid closer along the wall. A head protruded. The Green Ghost struck with the weapon he held. The blow did nothing more than disconcert the victim a moment, but that was all the Green Ghost wished. As the other gave a cry of pain and surprise, the Green Ghost hurled himself forward and through the door, tossed the man aside, and slammed the door behind him.

"WHAT THE devil—" he heard somebody say in the living room. "Hey, Stubby—what's wrong?"

Quick feet shuffled over the floor. The Green Ghost sent his victim reeling, sprawling into the room from the entry with another blow. He straddled the body and held his pistol ready. Sam Dorrich and two other men were hurrying toward him....

"Up with 'em!" the Green Ghost barked. "Quick!"

CHAPTER IV

THE BARLOW HAUL

SAM DORRICH AND HIS two companions recoiled before this unexpected apparition. The man at the feet of the Green Ghost groaned and started crawling toward the others.

"Don't do anything foolish," the Green Ghost warned. "Better wait till you know why I'm here. Back up, gents, and sit down, but keep your hands above your heads."

They backed slowly before him, did as he ordered. Dorrich's face was working with rage. The others waited for him to deal with the situation. So far, this mysterious Green Ghost never had stepped on the toes of any of the Sam Dorrich crowd. Possibly he was an ally instead of an enemy.

"Pardon this melodramatic entrance, gents," the Green Ghost said. "But you understand I had to be in the position of the boss for a moment, till we understand each other."

"Who are you, and what the devil do you want?" Dorrich demanded. "Bustin' in here, and crackin' Stubby on the head—"

"Stubby should be careful how he opens a door," the Green Ghost replied. "I came to thank you, Dorrich, for bumpin' off Rod Rordan."

"What's that? Rordan blasted?"

"You can't act worth a damn," the Green Ghost told him. "He's not blasted, and you know it. He was stabbed. The last two men with him tonight were one of his gang, that man right there beside you, and one of yours who was pretending to turn against you for Rordan's benefit. A real traitor and a fake one."

"You seem to know a lot."

"Your little effort to pin the thing on me failed. Oh, I got your charming note! And I escaped the gas; and Tim O'Hara broke in—after you'd notified him some way. But I managed to dodge O'Hara, too. And now I'm here!"

The Green Ghost walked toward them a couple of steps. His eyes were glittering through the slits in his mask. His automatic was held menacingly.

"You got the Barlow jewels, too, didn't you, Dorrich? The dumb cops were sure Rod Rordan got 'em. I'm not in love with the cops, understand. Nor with anybody who tries to frame me. So I think we'll square the books."

"Yeah?" Sam Dorrich snarled. "Just how are you goin' to do that?"

"Plug the lot of you, and stage it here so it'll look like you'd got into a row about dividin' the swag and gunned one another. Then take some of the loot and get away—and telephone the cops to come and pick up what's left."

"What'd we ever do to you?" Dorrich demanded.

"Why did you try to frame me tonight?"

"We wanted Rordan bumped, and we wanted to hang it on somebody else, naturally. You've been handlin' guns pretty rough, so we thought—"

"Thought you'd kill two birds with one stab, huh?" the Green Ghost asked. "Well, you slipped, Dorrich. It doesn't pay to slip, you know."

Dorrich was sitting beside a long table, upon which a scarf had been tossed carelessly over a heap of something. One of the men sat opposite him, and one directly behind. The man the Green Ghost had struck at the door was sitting on the floor at the end of the table, and all had their hands up.

"'Splittin' the Barlow jewels, were you?" the Green Ghost asked. "Got 'em all handy for me, I see."

"You'll never touch 'em," Dorrich said. "You'll never get out of here alive, Ghost. You're goin' to be found sometime in the mornin', down by the river, with about fifty slugs in your body."

"Do tell!"

"Before you can make a move against us—blast him, Jim!"

As Dorrich shouted that last, he sprang to his feet and to one side. The others were on their feet instantly, too. Dorrich had looked past the Green Ghost, toward the door of a bed-chamber. But the Green Ghost did not indulge in the folly of turning his head to see "Jim."

Instead, he dropped prone to the floor, and with such speed that the shot one of Dorrich's men fired flew over him and thudded into the wall. Because nobody fired from behind, the Green Ghost knew that "Jim" had been mythical.

The Green Ghost's automatic barked, and the man who had fired dropped his gun and reeled backward, to sit down against the wall. The second man was getting out a gun also. The Green Ghost let him have it through the shoulder. He staggered aside. Sam Dorrich, his face livid, thrust his arms high in the air.

"So! Caught you without a rod on you, huh?" the Green Ghost said. "Sit down there, Dorrich. One more bad move, and I'll put a slug right between your eyes. Quick!"

Dorrich dropped into the chair. His momentary fear, which had been mirrored in his face, had left him. Rage was there again.

"Your men aren't dead," the Green Ghost said. "One has a shoulder wound. That traitor of the Rordan gang may be more seriously hurt—I shot a bit low. And this Stubby of yours, with a cracked head—sit up in that chair, Stubby!"

Dorrich glanced at Stubby, and the man obeyed the order. The Green Ghost, watching the two at the table carefully, walked around and collected the weapons dropped by the wounded men. Then he confronted Dorrich again.

At one o'clock in the afternoon, the shooting probably would have attracted attention. At one in the morning, in that district, few heard it. Radios were going full blast in most of the apartments. Wild parties were in progress. Windows were closed because of the nip in the air. Charging trucks in the street were backfiring constantly....

The Green Ghost stepped back to the doorway, always alert and on guard, ripped down the portieres and got the heavy cords off them. He hurried back to the table.

"I'll feel safer with you gents tied to chairs," he said, as he ran a noose in one of the heavy cords.

"Ghost, I'm willin' to overlook what you've done, if we can make some kind of deal," Sam Dorrich told him.

"Afraid you can't offer anything good enough. I'm not forgettin' how you tried to frame me for the hot seat tonight."

"The Barlow jewels—"

"I've got them without makin' a deal."

"If you carry on, I'll get you if it takes me years!"

"You'll get a cell, then sit on the wires for killin' Rordan."

"I didn't kill him."

"You engineered it—admitted as much," the Green Ghost said.

He tossed the noose around Dorrich's body and the chair, and jerked tight. Working swiftly, and not relaxing vigilance for a moment, he bound Dorrich to the chair. Then he formed a noose in the other cord, and tied Stubby in the same manner.

"That'll hold you," the Green Ghost said. He glanced at the wounded men. The traitor of the Rordan gang was moaning, and seemed half unconscious. The other was clutching his wounded shoulder, from which blood oozed, and his face was white.

"You can give it, but can't take it," the Green Ghost commented. "Now we'll take a look at the loot."

He swept aside the scarf on the table. Jewels scintillated in the light.

"Some haul!" the Green Ghost said. "Your last one, Dorrich. It's a pity you can't profit by it. Might need all a fence would give you to pay off your mouthpiece. But it'd be a waste of money this time. The chair's waitin' for you, Dorrich."

Sam Dorrich volleyed curses. Behind his hood, the Green Ghost chuckled. He began making a close inspection of the jewels.

"I COULD use some of these baubles for expense money," the Ghost muttered, "but they're needed here for evidence. Even if you dodged the Rordan murder charge, Dorrich, how'd you explain the presence of these stolen jewels here in your apartment?"

Dorrich only cursed again. The Green Ghost picked up the telephone on the end of the table. He called the other apartment house.

"O'Hara?" he asked, presently. "This is the Green Ghost. Listen carefully, O'Hara, and I'll tell you some things you wish to know. The Dorrich gang pulled that Barlow job. The jewels are on the table in Dorrich's living room at his apartment. Know where it is? Good! You'll find Dorrich and one of his men tied up, and a couple more wounded. Dorrich engineered Rordan's murder, too, and the actual killer is right here. Come and get 'em!"

He slapped back the receiver and looked swiftly around the room again. Seizing the scarf which had covered the jewels, he tore it into strips. He muffled Sam Dorrich's curses with a gag, gagged Stubby, and turned toward the wounded men.

The one by the wall was unconscious now. But the wound of the other was not serious. The first shock of it over, this man might be able to prove a menace.

The Green Ghost got another portiere cord and bound this man's arms and legs, and gagged him also. His work here was done, he decided. Time to go. It was up to Tim O'Hara to get evidence regarding the Rordan murder, and O'Hara was the man who could do it. O'Hara knew how to use violent methods on men such as these, who used violent methods themselves. As for the Barlow robbery—there were the jewels for evidence… and Dorrich was a two-time loser already.

The Green Ghost swept a glance over his victims again, looked at the jewels glittering under the light, and hurried toward the door. He stopped there to listen. Somebody stopped outside. The door bell sounded.

CHAPTER V

DESPERATE TAG

FROM THE PECULIAR MANNER in which the bell rang, the Green Ghost guessed it was a signal, that one of Dorrich's mob had come to report. He glanced back, and caught a gleam in Dorrich's eyes. He slipped close to the door, and whispered hoarsely:

"Who is it?"

"Bert Baines."

"Who's with you!"

"Shorty."

"Lam! The bulls are on their way here."

The Ghost heard hurrying steps in the hall. He decided he would wait.

But there was a sudden tumult in the hall. Somebody bellowed a command to halt in stentorian tones. Scurrying feet—and the sound of a shot! A wild cry, muttering voices.

There had not been time for O'Hara and his squad to get there from the other apartment house. But somebody had been sent there anyhow, the Green Ghost judged, possibly to look in on Sam Dorrich and do some questioning. Any member of the police force was a potential danger for the Green Ghost.

Heavy feet in the hall—another ring at the doorbell. No signal this time, but a long ring that bespoke a determination to gain entrance.

The Green Ghost rushed through the living room to a window and looked out. He saw the fire-escape landing at the next window, and hurried to that. Swiftly, he raised the window, put out his head. He was just in time to see the beam of a flashlight on the pavement of the alley below.

Somebody was on guard there. No doubt, the police had come to drop in on Dorrich, and were taking precautions against the escape of him or any of his gang. They might have thought instantly that Dorrich had something to do with the killing of Rod Rordan.

They were pounding at the front door, and the bell was ringing continuously. Loud voices sounded in the hall. The Green Ghost was trapped in an apartment for the second time that night.

Dorrich's eyes were gleaming. Stubby betrayed excitement. The other conscious man seemed stunned by the turn of events.

The Green Ghost quickly turned the chairs in which the two bound men were sitting, so their faces were toward the wall; now they could not see where he went, and tell later. Then he dashed to the entry again.

Somebody was still pounding on the door and demanding that those inside open. Somebody crashed against it. The Green Ghost darted behind the thick curtains which masked a little coat room, and stood flat against the wall.

"Get that night clerk up here—tell him to bring his master key!" somebody outside was ordering.

More steps sounded in the hall, then O'Hara's voice:

"What is it, Murphy?"

"They won't open up. I've sent for the clerk."

"Don't wait! Smash the door in."

Another crash! The door flew open. Officers sprawled into the entry, service revolvers held ready, rushed on into the living room.

There was a chorus of exclamations, then came O'Hara's voice again:

"Eyes open, now! Take those gags off and untie 'em! Ring for an ambulance—"

In the corridor, some policeman was demanding that the curious keep back. The corridor was filled with tenants and their guests of the evening. From open doors down the hall came blasts of radio music.

"Well, Dorrich?" O'Hara was asking.

"The Green Ghost—here a moment ago—planted those jewels and tied us up—shot those two—"

"Planted, hell!" O'Hara exploded. "You're not talkin' to a baby, Dorrich. Got the goods on you and your man this time. These jewels—and Rordan's murder—"

"What's that? Rordan killed?" Dorrich cried.

"And you know it! Your men made some mistakes—left a trail a blind man could follow."

"I—I don't know anything about it," Dorrich cried. "You can't frame me—"

"Oh, shut up!" O'Hara barked at him. "We nabbed a couple of your boys. One was a weak brother, and talked."

Pure bluff, the Green Ghost guessed. But Sam Dorrich did not know for sure.

"I'm tellin' you this is a frame. I think Rordan planned it. The Green Ghost—he's around here. He was here when your men came to the door."

"We'll tend to him," O'Hara said. "But we're handlin' you now. One of this crowd has a chance—if he'll talk. No danger for him afterward, 'cause you and your gang won't be in a position to harm him any."

"I'll talk, O'Hara!" cried the man with the shoulder wound. He had been moaning and gulping since gag and bonds had been removed. Now he lurched to his feet. "Sam planned it. He had Dinky Lewis and—"

"Shut up, confound you!" Dorrich cried.

O'Hara grinned, motioned, and an officer yanked the wounded man toward the corridor.

But all this did not aid the Green Ghost. He remained in

the coat room behind the thick curtains. O'Hara would search that apartment, without doubt. There was but one chance—a wild dash.

The Green Ghost made it. He darted from behind the curtains and rushed into the corridor. His automatic spoke once, the bullet crashing into the ceiling. His sudden appearance and the crack of the shot stampeded those in the wide hall.

They lurched and jostled to get out of the way. They bothered the officer stationed there, so that the Green Ghost got through the crowd before the policeman could recover himself and get into action. Behind him, as he fled, the crowd surged to the center of the hall again to look after him, thus coming between him and O'Hara and the others who came running. Things were working out as the Green Ghost expected.

He dashed around a corner and into a cross hall. Before him was the open door of an apartment. He ran into it, to find it empty. Those who had been enjoying themselves there were in the corridor.

Slamming the door behind him, locking it, the Green Ghost fled to a window. Another fire-escape landing was there. Quickly, he extinguished the lights, then raised the window and crawled through.

Down in the alley, men were shouting at one another. In the hall behind, there was bedlam. The Green Ghost went swiftly down the fire-escape, but not to the bottom. He came to the window of a bathroom, lifted it, and crawled through.

He went forward, into the apartment. Nobody was at home, though the lights were burning. They too, had gone to see what the tumult was about, the Green Ghost supposed.

He hurried to the telephone.

"Hello! Connect me with the Dorrich apartment. This is an officer. I want to talk to my sergeant—quick."

The connection was made

"O'Hara—quick!" the Green Ghost said to the man who answered.

Then he waited until O'Hara could be called in from the corridor. He listened intently, and knew that the line was not open, that the switchboard operator was not listening in.

"Well?" O'Hara's voice boomed.

"Listen, O'Hara. This is the Green Ghost. I'm out and away, old boy. Don't waste time lookin' for me. Take care of Dorrich and his gang. Did you get the jewels?"

"Got 'em, Ghost! Thanks. Murder evidence is weak, but maybe we can get enough out of one of 'em to send Dorrich away to the hot seat. I want to tell you—"

But the Green Ghost cut the connection. He heard somebody outside the front door, and fled. In the bathroom, he got behind the curtains of the shower, and listened.

For an hour he stood. In the living room, six persons resumed their party. They drank, danced to radio music, played cards. It grew quiet in the building. The police had taken their prisoners away.

Finally, the Green Ghost left the shower, locked the door of the bathroom, and crawled through the window again. He watched and listened, but nothing alarmed him. Down the fire-escape he went slowly.

He reached the bottom. The dark alley was a few feet below. Only a short distance away, it emptied into the street.

A slight sound attracted his attention. Below him, a match flared. The Green Ghost saw a uniformed policeman lighting a cigarette.

So, somebody had been left in the alley on guard. But not a detective, only a harness bull. He was between the Green Ghost and liberty.

The Ghost guessed direction, and dropped. He crashed against the man below. The surprise was complete, but that was not enough. Though he disliked to do it, the Green Ghost struck with his gun. The blow was true. The policeman groaned, muttered something, struggled weakly.

The Green Ghost sprang to his feet and ran, tearing off his

hood and tossing it away, taking his cap from a coat pocket and putting it on, tossing away the green silk gloves last of all. He heard a weak shout behind him, as the policeman tried to call for help. But the Green Ghost gained the street, turned up it, and walked along in a natural manner, touching flaming match to a cigarette—

Half an hour later, Danny Blaney suddenly appeared in the corner cigar store he owned, and greeted the sleepy night clerk.

"Gosh, boss, you're up at all hours!" the clerk said.

"Don't worry, boy. I'm not checkin' up on you. Just couldn't sleep."

"Pretty tame for you, after bein' on the Force once, huh?" the clerk suggested.

"Yeah!" Danny Blaney said. "Pretty tame!"

VI

DEADLY PERIL

CHAPTER I

SMOOTH MACHINERY

HARRY DARSON FLINCHED WHEN he heard the sound, jerked to one side quickly and brought up against the wall, trembling. But his condition at that moment was such that he would have flinched at any slight sound.

He needed the "stuff," and Matt Lobinger had issued orders against his having it. For some queer reason, Lobinger disliked dope, though he availed himself of the services of men who were its slaves.

There was the sound again! Harry Darson knew what it was—something tapping against the window of the bedchamber. Somebody probably was trying to attract the attention of those inside.

Matt Lobinger and "Grouchy" Bill Weaver were in the living room. Darson was in the bedchamber only because Lobinger had sent him to get a bottle of whiskey out of the closet.

Darson fought himself to control his jumping nerves. His thin nostrils were quivering, his white and sunken cheeks were tinged with pink, his eyes were glittering and his body trembling from head to foot. He inhaled deeply and straightened his shoulders. Somebody tapping at the window—that was all.

His first thought was to rush through the hall to the living room and tell Lobinger. But it might be something so important that there would be danger in delay. Perhaps one of the boys had come up the fire-escape, for reasons of his own, in a hurry to see Lobinger.

The tapping sound at the window was repeated. Darson decided that he would attend to this himself. But he would have sense enough to snap off the lights in the bedchamber first. He went swiftly across the room to the switch and pressed the button, and the lights went out. Then Darson sped to the window and rolled up the shade.

HIS SCREECH rang through the apartment. He whirled to crash against a chair, to hurdle it as it toppled, to spring out into the hall and rush along it wildly, meeting Lobinger and Weaver as he came to the living room door.

"What—" Lobinger began.

"Green Ghost—window—"

"What?" Lobinger cried.

An automatic appeared in his hand, seemingly materializing from nowhere. His short, thick body tensed. Behind him, Grouchy Bill Weaver thrust the frightened Darson roughly aside and brought out his own gun. Lobinger rushed along the hall and into the bedchamber, with Grouchy close behind him.

"WINDOW—FIRE-ESCAPE—" DARSON was muttering.

Inside the bedchamber, Lobinger came to a quick stop. Behind him, Weaver made a peculiar sound deep down in his throat.

"Wait, Grouchy!"

The whispered command from Matt Lobinger came just in time. Grouchy was bringing up his gun, to send a fusillade through the window and at what was beyond.

Outside, on the landing of the fire-escape, was the thing which had startled nervous Harry Darson. Faint light came from somewhere to illuminate it—a faint green light that made the thing eerie and spine-tingling. Gleaming eyes, the outline of a skull in luminous paint, what seemed to be a green silk hood pulled over a human head!

"The Green Ghost!" Lobinger muttered.

As Darson settled back, he felt something cold and hard pressing just behind his ear.

"Boss, do you suppose he knows—" Weaver began.

"Shut up, you fool!"

"Let me blast him."

"Hold it! Slip to your side of the window, and I'll get to this side. I'll turn the catch, and we'll grab the window, and when I give the word snap it up. I'd like to have a look at the face of this Green Ghost, and so would the cops, from what I've heard. We've nothing to lose."

"That's what I'm thinkin', so why not blast him and have it over with?" Weaver asked.

"Rather have him alive," Lobinger whispered. "This Green Ghost, whoever he is, knows too much. He's put the skids under a bunch of real guys—got the goods on 'em and turned 'em over to the cops along with plenty evidence. But the cops don't know who he is or why he's doin' it."

"Maybe they don't," Weaver replied, skeptically. "I'm for blast-in'—"

"Slip to the window!"

The night was pitch dark, and with a fine drizzle falling. The thing outside the window moved slowly from side to side, as though the wearer of the green hood was trying to peer into the dark chamber. Then it began descending.

"He's startin' down the fire-escape," Weaver whispered.

"Quick! The window!" Lobinger ordered.

THEY DARTED forward. Lobinger undid the catch and they threw the window open. Heedless of possible danger, Lobinger thrust out his head. He could see nothing. The fire escape dripped with the drizzle. Three floors below was the paved alley, blind at one end. Above was only darkness. Light was not streaming through any of the windows on the fire escape.

"Darson, get below!" Lobinger ordered. "Use the stairs— quicker than waiting for the elevator. Guy Marsh is standing lookout in front. Tell him to get around to the mouth of the alley. We'll follow this bird down the fire-escape—"

"Follow him?" Weaver interrupted.

"That's what I said, Grouchy. Come on!"

Darson rushed back through the apartment, wrenched open the front door, and fled toward the stairway. Lobinger crawled through the window to the slippery fire-escape landing, and Weaver squeezed after him.

With Lobinger going first, they started down the ladder slowly, silently, automatics ready to spray a sheet of fire. No sounds came to them from below. It was so dark they could see nothing.

Somewhere down there, they supposed, the mysterious, elusive Green Ghost was either waiting to receive them violently, or else was trying to get away. Possibly, if he was slow enough, Guy Marsh would catch him at the mouth of the alley.

BUT IT happened that the Green Ghost was above them.

From the fire-escape landing one floor above the window of Matt Lobinger's bedchamber, he had lowered a toy balloon on a weighted cord. Over the balloon had been draped a green hood with eyes painted on it and the skull outlined in luminous paint. A pocket flashlight with a green lens had been used to illuminate the thing faintly.

With a key tied to another cord, the Green Ghost had managed that tapping at the window by swinging the key in and out for a short distance and letting it strike against the pane. When he was sure that those below were in the bedchamber and had seen what was outside, he lowered the balloon past the landing, making it appear that the Green Ghost was descending. The flashlight was turned off, the cord cut—and the balloon dropped to the floor of the alley.

He heard two men below start the descent of the fire escape. Then he went down to the open window and crawled through. He darted across the dark bedchamber and into the hall. After listening a moment, he continued to the living room. Not until he peered through the doorway was he sure he was alone in the apartment.

He had known three men were there. He knew that Lobinger and Weaver had gone down the fire escape in pursuit, and now guessed that Harry Darson had been sent out the other way.

They might return at any moment. The Green Ghost hurried to the hall door and snapped the lock. He glanced around the living room swiftly. On a table at the end of a couch were glasses, an empty bottle, ash trays filled with ends of cigarettes.

The three had been in conference for some time, he judged.

Somebody rattled the front door and called because it was locked. At the same instant, the Green Ghost heard Lobinger and Weaver getting back into the bedchamber through the window. They would be in the lighted hall before the Green Ghost could reach it.

But he had anticipated something like this when he had gained entrance to the apartment by his schoolboy trick. He did not wish to escape, but remain and overhear. He darted behind the big couch, which was back almost against the wall, got down and wormed beneath it. A ruffle of upholstery which touched the floor prevented anybody seeing him from in front.

LOBINGER AND Weaver came into the living room. The knocking on the front door continued. Lobinger opened it, and Harry Darson came in.

"I told Gus—"

"The Ghost got out of the alley before Gus got there," Lobinger interrupted. "Like to know why he was prowling around here."

"Do you suppose he knows about the armored car job?" Weaver asked.

"If he does, he'd better not come around here looking for a split," Lobinger growled. "Gus will be watching the alley, if he comes back again."

"I left the door unlocked when I went to tell Gus, and it was locked when I came back," Darson put in.

"You probably didn't set the spring lock," Lobinger told him. "You're jumpy."

"If I could have—"

"You can't—not while you're here," Lobinger said. "Let's get down to business. It's time to split the swag. We've waited a month. Everybody's fingers are itching, but I knew it was best to wait. The cops have been watching every mob in town."

"PRETTY SMOOTH," Weaver offered.

"Yeah, pretty smooth, catching that armored car at the airport and raiding it of that hurry-up currency shipment. Caught some good bonds, too. Rushed the stuff to the liquor store where I trade, and they put it in the bottoms of some cases of booze and sent it up here in a wagon."

"Over a hundred grand!" Weaver said, softly.

"And one less to split it with, since Eddie Richmond isn't with us any more," Lobinger hinted.

"Too bad about Eddie," Weaver said. "Had to stop a slug of lead."

"Which makes it murder, so the less said the better," Lobinger growled at him.

"Anyhow, the cops are off the track," Weaver added.

"I've kept the stuff here, and kept you mugs from hanging around," Lobinger said. "Now, we can make the split without doing too much worrying. You two boys will carry yours away. And you'll take the others' shares to them. I've planned a way for you to get it out of here safely."

Beneath the couch, the Green Ghost heard all this. Only his mind was not that of the Green Ghost now, but of Danny Blaney, who had reason to hate all crooks, and especially Matt Lobinger and his friends.

Once, Danny Blaney had been a respected member of the detective force of the city. He had been too aggressive to suit certain criminals, and they had framed him. He had been acquitted, but even some of his comrades on the force had believed him guilty. So Danny Blaney had resigned from the job he loved, and had opened a corner cigar store.

But the cigar store was only a blind. Danny Blaney's real work was running down crooks and handing them over to the police. As the Green Ghost, he struck terror to the hearts of those in crookdom.

Danny Blaney had an advantage. The police waited until a crime was committed, then endeavored to find and arrest the guilty parties. Danny Blaney watched crooks, saw crimes being planned, and knew exactly where to look when the deed was done.

"YOU RAN a big chance, didn't you, Matt, keepin' the swag in your apartment?" Weaver was asking.

"Maybe not, unless the cops had come here and taken the place to pieces. I've had feelers out. The cops never suspected us of the job. They've been hunting wild. They still think an out-of-town mob pulled it."

"And all small bills that can be passed," Weaver exulted.

"But they'll be passed carefully," Lobinger warned. "I don't want any of you mugs flashing a roll. They might wonder where it came from, and check back to me. And you go easy on the hop, Harry."

"I'm keyed up better when I've got it," Darson replied. "Got my wits about me then. It's only when I haven't got it that I go to pieces and get careless."

"Better not get careless this trip," Lobinger growled. "It's not only robbery, remember. Eddie Richmond was bumped off. And the fool cops think he was an honest hero who died defending the money he was guarding."

Weaver laughed.

"Eddie wasn't to be trusted," he said. "Might have weakened and spilled everything. Matt, isn't that why you ordered me to—"

"**SHUT UP,** you blasted fool!" Lobinger snarled. "Forget it, will you? Keep it out of your mind."

"Let's split the swag and get out of here," Darson begged. "We don't want to leave too late, and maybe get picked up."

"Can't wait to get to your hop peddler, can you?" Lobinger sneered at him.

"Will it take you long to get the swag?" Weaver asked.

"It's within a few feet of us," Lobinger replied. "You'll notice that the hardwood floor of this room is parqueted. One of the squares is loose and has a hole beneath it. The swag is in the hole."

"And where's that?" Weaver asked.

"Beneath the couch. We pull the couch out three or four feet, lift the corner of the rug, loosen and lift out the square of wood—and there we are."

"Smooth," Weaver praised. "Let's have it over with."

"Get hold of the other end of the couch," Lobinger said.

Stretched beneath the couch, squeezed in between it and the floor, the Green Ghost gripped his automatic and prepared for swift and violent action. When they pulled that couch forward and exposed him, he would have to come up shooting. At first sight of him, realizing that he had heard their conversation, their confession of robbery and murder, these men would go for their guns.

The Green Ghost had not expected that murder angle as these men had revealed it. He had thought, with almost everybody else, that Eddie Richmond, the guard with the armored car, had died in the line of duty. Now it appeared that he had been one of the gang, and had been murdered by his pals.

The Green Ghost tensed himself as he felt the couch move a trifle when they grasped it. Shooting these men was not his object. He wanted to turn them over to the police, with evidence to convict. It meant the electric chair for them now, on account of Eddie Richmond. But he would have to shoot in self defense.

He was spared the necessity of doing it just then. The doorbell sounded.

CHAPTER II

CHANGED PLANS

"**W**HO'S THAT?" WEAVER GROWLED.

"None of the boys. I told them to keep away," Lobinger replied. "Flop, you muggs. Fix drinks, quick, Grouchy. Light up a cig, Darson. Try to look natural, like we were having a little chat."

The Green Ghost could hear their swift movements. The bell rang again. Matt Lobinger stepped swiftly across the room to the door and pulled it open.

"Oh! Come in, Miss Gray," he said, cordially, and with a note of relief in his voice. "A couple of the boys are here, having a little drink. You know them both."

"Yes." The answer came in a rich contralto.

The Green Ghost could not see her, but he knew who she was. Madge Gray, the sweetheart of Eddie Richmond. Her picture had been in the papers at the time of the robbery and killing. The sob sisters had written a lot about the pretty fiancée of the hero.

"This is rather a surprise," Lobinger was saying.

"I know it's late—after midnight," she replied. "I had to see you, and had sense enough to be careful. That's why I didn't telephone. I managed to get invited to a party in the building, and slipped out and came down here. Nobody knows I came, and nobody saw me in the hall."

"Good girl," Lobinger said. "You have got sense. But I always knew that. As sensible as you're pretty. Sit down, Madge."

She sat on the couch, and Lobinger sat beside her. The Green Ghost knew that Weaver was in a chair not far away, and Harry Darson in another against the wall.

"Have a drink," Lobinger invited. "Cigarette? What's on your mind, Madge? I hope you just dropped in for a visit with me personally. If so, I'll have the boys scram."

"I came for the split," she said.

"The split?" Lobinger questioned her.

"You know what I mean, Matt. I get Eddie's share, don't I? Not going to hold out on me, are you?"

"SO YOU think you should have Eddie's share?"

"Why not? You roped him into your mob. He tipped off when there was easy swag in the wagon. If it hadn't been for Eddie, you couldn't have made the haul. He told me all about it."

"He went wild and stopped a slug," Weaver growled.

She laughed a little.

"That didn't fool me a bit. You bumped him, didn't you, Grouchy?"

"I'm not sayin'," Weaver replied.

"You don't have to say. And you didn't do it because he went wild. Why should he? He was in with you."

"Got cold feet at the last minute and made a wrong move. Was goin' to turn honest," Weaver said, a sneer in his voice.

"Oh, no, he didn't!" Madge Gray said. "He didn't even have his gun out of the holster. He was standing there with his hands held above his head, and you let him have it. I understand, Grouchy. Orders, wasn't it?"

"ENOUGH OF this!" Lobinger barked.

"Why, Matt? I'm wise. It wasn't because you didn't want to split with Eddie. For you'll give me Eddie's share. Wasn't it because you wanted Eddie out of the way, Matt—so you could have a little more of my attention?"

"There might be something in that," Lobinger admitted.

"Then everything's understood."

"Dames are always gettin' things tangled up," Weaver said.

"Dames figure things out sometimes," she replied. "Just like I've figured this out about Eddie. You bumped him off, Grouchy, because Matt told you to do it—"

"Let's forget about Eddie," Lobinger put in. "And don't worry about the split. I'll take care of you, Madge."

The Green Ghost noticed that she got up off the couch. He heard her put on the table the glass Lobinger had handed her.

"What's the idea?" Lobinger asked. "Madge, you're looking so funny—"

"Watch out, Matt! Grab her, Darson!"

Grouchy Weaver snapped out the words, even as the Green Ghost heard him spring out of his chair and rush forward, and as Harry Darson jumped to his assistance.

There was a short scuffle. Matt Lobinger gave a cry of surprise, then voiced a smothered oath. Madge Gray began a scream which was promptly choked back into her throat. She was tossed upon the couch, held there.

"She was goin' to shoot you, Matt, and I suppose me, too," Weaver said. "Pick up that rod, Darson, and stow it away."

"What's the idea, Madge?" Lobinger demanded.

"I just wanted you to confess," she said. "You had Eddie killed—had Grouchy kill him. Thinking I'd turn to you. I came here tonight to kill you both. You see, I loved Eddie."

Panic seized the nervous Harry Darson.

"She knows everything, Matt, and she'll spill it to the cops."

"She won't spill anything," Matt Lobinger replied. "Gag her, Grouchy. Tie her wrists behind her back, and tie her ankles together. Get the cords off those portieres, Darson. They'll do. No, you won't spill anything, Miss Gray! So you slipped here without anybody knowing where you were coming, and were careful that nobody saw you in the hall, huh? That's fine!"

SHE TRIED to scream again, and again the scream was choked back into her throat. There was a short struggle on the couch.

"Good enough!" Matt Lobinger said presently. "Prop her up in that chair over by the wall. Gag her before she tries to howl again!"

"How are we goin' to handle this, Matt?" Weaver asked.

"We'll send word to Gus Marsh to get the sedan and drive it into the alley. We'll take her down the fire escape. Then the river, with plenty of weights on her. Sorry, but it's got to be done."

"Want me to go tell Gus?" Harry Darson asked.

"Stay where you are!" Lobinger ordered. "You're too shaky to do anything, can't be trusted. We'll make the split tomorrow night. Plant the dame in that easy chair. You hustle down and explain to Gus, Grouchy."

THE GREEN GHOST remained beneath the couch. It was stifling, and he was bathed in perspiration. He heard Weaver leave the apartment, knew that Lobinger was pacing back and forth. Harry Darson sat silently in the chair against the wall.

Weaver returned.

"Gus will have the sedan in the alley in ten minutes," he reported. "He'll use the swiped plates. Car looks like ten thousand others."

"We'll take her down the fire-escape," Lobinger directed. "Darson, you'll stay here. Hit some of that booze, and maybe it'll quicken you up, even if you haven't any hop. None of the boys will show up. If anybody else barges in, say you've come to spend the night with me, and that I've gone out to take a walk before going to bed."

"Which way we drivin', Matt?" Weaver asked.

"The Long Pier," Lobinger replied. "Don't forget, the watchman is a pal of ours. He'll keep his mouth shut. We'll drop her off the end of the dock. Water's deep there, plenty deep enough so she can't be seen from the dock—and the current's swift."

"Goin to bump her off before we take her there?"

"Might be better to drown her," Lobinger replied. "No marks of violence, then. People will think she committed suicide grieving over Eddie."

"But if they ever find the body, and she's bound and gagged," Weaver hinted.

"You can hold her under till it's over, then we'll take off the ropes and gag. The current will carry the body away from the dock."

The Green Ghost felt sympathy for the girl sitting a short distance away and listening to these men plot her fate. He imagined what she must be feeling.

"Better tell Darson to keep away from the swag," Weaver then suggested.

"Oh, he won't touch it," Lobinger said coldly. "He won't even think about it, because he knows what'll happen to him if he does."

The Green Ghost listened carefully.

As clear as though he could see it, he knew when Lobinger and Weaver carried the bound and gagged girl out of the living room and through the hall to the bedchamber, Darson aiding them. Darson soon returned, and sat on the end of the couch. The Green Ghost heard glass tinkle as he poured a drink.

IT WAS a time for swift action, the Green Ghost knew. He began worming out from beneath the couch, moving carefully, cautious about making the slightest noise. Harry Darson unconsciously aided him by turning on the radio. The strains of an orchestra blared. Darson began humming the tune the musicians were playing.

That covered any slight sound the Green Ghost made as he backed out from under the couch. He knelt behind it, then began lifting himself slowly, automatic held ready. He heard the tinkle of glass again, and knew that Harry Darson was bending forward to pour himself another drink.

As Darson settled back against the cushions, he felt something round and cold and hard pressing just behind his right ear.

"Put that glass down! Put your hands above your head! Then stand up!" a voice whispered hoarsely into his ear.

READY FOR MURDER

HARRY DARSON DROPPED THE glass to the rug and gave a cry of fright. His nerves already at the breaking point, this was the needed added touch to wreck him completely. He sprang to his feet, holding his hands high above his head, and whirled.

He gulped and gasped again when he saw the Green Ghost within a few feet of him, eyes glittering through slits in the green hood, automatic held ready for a blast of fire.

"Sit in that chair!"

The Green Ghost indicated the chair in which Madge Gray had been kept prisoner. Harry Darson collapsed in it. The Green Ghost walked slowly toward him. Darson seemed incapable of speech.

Ripping off the other cord from the portieres, the Green Ghost formed a loop, then made Darson stand and put his wrists behind his back so the loop could be jerked tightly around them. Working swiftly, without any resistance from the prisoner, the Green Ghost lashed his victim's legs, hurled him back into the chair again, and tied him there securely. Then he prepared a gag by tearing a strip off a table runner.

"I'm going to leave you here, Darson," the Green Ghost said. "For the cops. You'll give yourself a break if you talk frankly to them. It's the hot seat for Lobinger and Weaver. Want to go along with them?"

"No—no." Darson's speech was a mere whisper.

"Then you'd better open up to the cops and the D.A. Don't worry about reprisal. You'll be safe in prison for a lot of years, but there's always a chance when a man's alive. No chance at all after he's been in the hot chair. It's squeal or frizzle, Darson. Remember that."

Then the Green Ghost affixed the gag.

He hurried to the telephone and called Police Headquarters, and asked for Detective Sergeant Tim O'Hara.

"Green Ghost speaking, O'Hara," he said. "That armored car robbery—got news for you. Send a squad to Matt Lobinger's apartment. Tear up the floor under the couch, and you'll find the swag. You'll also find Harry Darson bound and gagged and he's ready to talk."

"Be right there, Ghost!" Tim O'Hara barked.

"Wait! Lobinger, Weaver and Gus Marsh are taking Madge Gray for a ride. You know—Eddie Richmond's girl. Eddie was in with the mob, and Weaver bumped him off because Lobinger was making a play for the girl. Understand? They're taking her to the Long Pier. Hustle!"

The Green Ghost replaced the receiver and darted over to Darson again.

"I'd like to take a little of that swag for expenses," he said, "but it'll be better not to touch it. Remember what I said, Darson—you'd better cave."

THROUGH THE hallway and bedroom he hurried, and went down the fire-escape in the fine drizzle. At the bottom, he dropped to the floor of the alley. As he hurried to the street, he stripped off the green hood and gloves and stowed them away. The Green Ghost had disappeared.

It was Danny Blaney, former cop, who slipped into the street and hurried along for a block to a dark spot where he had parked his own car.

Only a cheap flivver, that car, as far as appearances went. But there was a powerful engine under the hood.

Danny Blaney drove furiously through cross streets, and made for the river. Lobinger, he guessed, would proceed carefully and by a circuitous route to the Long Pier, having no special reason for haste which might attract attention.

Danny Blaney knew police work. Headquarters, acting on his tip, might send a squad roaring in a siren-screeching car to Long Pier. It might arrive in time, and it might not. And the life of a girl depended on what happened.

Danny Blaney rather admired the girl for the stand she had taken. Undoubtedly, she would have shot down Matt Lobinger and Grouchy Weaver, had she not been prevented. Danny Blaney wanted her to live—she would be an important witness. If she knew as much as she had seemed to in the apartment, the late Eddie Richmond certainly had told her more of the mob and its plans. Her testimony might be very valuable.

AS HE neared the docks, he slackened speed and began watching the streets closely. Only a few night owl pedestrians were abroad. He ran the car into a recess between two buildings and turned off the lights. An instant later, he was darting from shadow to shadow and making way toward the Long Pier.

Keeping close beside the warehouse, he slipped forward carefully toward the water end of the dock. The Long Pier extended far into the river, and, as Lobinger had said, the water was deep and swift out at the end of it. That was where they would consign the girl to the river, so the current could carry the body away.

A form loomed up before him out of the darkness. Danny Blaney flattened himself against the wall, and the prowling watchman passed within a few feet of him. Out came green hood and gloves again. An instant later, Danny Blaney had become the Green Ghost.

THE WATCHMAN turned back, and a collision could not be avoided.

"Who's there?"

The watchman's shrill voice called the question. His flashlight gleamed. Before its bright beam could strike the Green Ghost and reveal his identity, he sprang forward and struck with the automatic.

The flashlight was knocked out of the watchman's hand. He made an effort to get out a gun, as the Green Ghost struck again. The watchman went down unconscious. The Green Ghost went on toward the end of the pier.

He heard soft voices, and footfalls, and dodged back against the warehouse again. In the black night, he could see nothing. But he heard Weaver calling cautiously for the watchman.

"Funny he's not here," Lobinger's voice said.

"What's this?"

Weaver had stumbled against the body of the watchman. A light gleamed. In its glow, the Green Ghost had a momentary sight of Weaver and Lobinger carrying the girl, and of the unconscious watchman stretched on the dock.

"Somebody's slugged him," Lobinger said. "Put out that light, you fool! Something's wrong."

"Might be some gang robbin' the warehouse."

"Let's hurry with this job and get out of here. Gus will be cruising back with the car in a few minutes."

In the distance, a screeching siren.

The Green Ghost growled his rage. Why did the police advertise their approach so well? There was little danger of traffic down there at that hour—no need for making that warning siren shriek into the night.

Nearer it came; then the sounds of a car rushing over the rough pavement could be heard.

"Cops!" Weaver cried. Fear was in the one word.

"Hell, they can't be after us," Lobinger said.

"That watchman slugged—maybe there's been a job pulled off—if they catch us here—"

"Toss the girl over as she is," Lobinger ordered. "She'll drown, and maybe the current will carry her away. Quick!"

Then it was that the automatic of the Green Ghost cracked, and its amber flame split the black night. Two bullets thudded into the planking within a few feet of the pair and their victim.

AS HE fired, the Ghost darted swiftly to one side. There was an answering blast of flame, as he had expected. But his shots had startled them, and possibly had been heard by the police tumbling out of their squad car and commencing to play their flashlights around.

"Quick!" he heard Lobinger's voice shout.

The Green Ghost started forward. But he heard the swift movements of feet, then a splash. They had tossed the girl into the river at the side of the pier.

They turned, started to run around the end of the warehouse, possibly with some wild intention of getting down among the pilings. The Green Ghost darted to the edge of the dock, and dropped down into the water, thrusting his automatic back into its holster before he leaped.

He explored swiftly, furiously. The girl would be helpless even if she were a good swimmer, with arms and legs bound and her mouth stuffed with a gag. He made a deep dive, came up groping, happened to bump against her.

An instant later, he broke surface and held her while he tore off the gag.

"KEEP QUIET! I'm a friend!" he said, loudly enough to be heard above the lapping of the water against the piles.

He did not know whether she heard, whether she was conscious. Perhaps she had drowned already, he thought, or else was in such condition that she needed treatment. He swam with her to a place where stringers had been fastened between the piles, got upon one and pulled her up beside him.

He could use two hands now. He worked swiftly, taking off the cords which bound her, began whispering to her again. He dared not use his flashlight. On the dock above him, the police were charging around, calling to one another, flashing their lights. Some of the light came down through a crack, and the Green Ghost caught sight of her face. Her eyes were fluttering, and she gulped and moaned.

"Careful!" he whispered. "I'm a friend. Don't make any noise now."

She was alive. But there were reasons why the Green Ghost did not call for help and hand her up to the police above. His identity must be preserved from the police, else his work was at an end, and prosecution might follow. As the Green Ghost, he had stepped outside the law a few times in order to get results.

"You're all right now. Just be quiet," he muttered to her.

But she had been on the verge of death by drowning. She regained consciousness to find herself in the darkness, being held by some man she did not know. Without realizing what she did, she gave a wild scream that cut through the night and reached the ears of the police.

Too late, the Green Ghost clapped a hand over her mouth. Up above, the police were shouting to one another. Heavy feet pounded the planks.

"LISTEN! I'M a friend. I got you out of the water. I don't want to talk to the cops. Understand? Keep quiet," the Green Ghost begged.

"Oh, I—I'm sorry." She seemed to be herself now. "Who are you?"

"I'm the Green Ghost. I was in Lobinger's apartment and heard everything, and got here to save you. Lobinger and Weaver are somewhere around, so be careful. The cops'll get Darson at the apartment, and get the swag.

"You want to square things for Eddie, don't you? There's an easy way—tell the cops all you know. Let Lobinger and Weaver fry in the chair. That's better than shooting them yourself, and standing trial."

"I'll tell everything," she whispered.

"Good! Can you swim?"

"Yes."

"Swim along the dock and get to shore, and yell for the cops. Wait a minute."

Directly above them, some of the police had stopped and were flashing their lights. On the opposite side of the dock, more lights were being flashed. Came a yell, a shot.

"Come out of that!"

Lobinger and Weaver had been found, under the dock, clinging to the pilings.

Guns blazed down in the darkness and up on the wharf. The Green Ghost whispered to the girl to go, to swim carefully, and pushed her into the water. He submerged himself, all except his head, and clung there, waiting, watching.

Lobinger and Weaver were swimming for shore, keeping under the edge of the dock as much as possible. The Green Ghost swam in that direction also, but on the opposite side of the dock. He heard the girl call out again, and knew she had reached land. He heard some of the police answer her, and then ply her with questions.

Somewhere in the darkness below the dock, possibly close to land, Lobinger and Weaver were hiding. If they escaped now, perhaps they would hide out until Lobinger's friends could get money to him, and then make a getaway.

The Green Ghost clung to a piling and submerged again, all except his head. He waited till there was a lull on the dock above, then shouted:

"Lobinger! Weaver! The girl's got ashore! The cops will learn you tried to drown her, and why!"

CHAPTER IV

NIGHT'S PROFIT

THEN HE HEARD A curse, saw flame split the night as they fired at the sound of his voice. The police above had heard, too. They knew Lobinger and Weaver were somewhere below the dock.

The Green Ghost swam quietly a short distance from where he had spoken. He heard another swimmer near, as the police overhead prepared to descend and get their men, even in the face of fire. The Green Ghost got out his automatic. It was more happy accident than perfect timing and judging of distance which caused him to crash the gun down on the head of the swimmer in just the right spot.

He caught the other and pulled him along. The blow had stunned the man partially, paralyzed him enough so that the Green Ghost could handle him easily in the water. He swam toward the shore, not knowing which of the fugitives he held.

At the shore end of the dock, a flight of steps ran up to the street level. The Green Ghost crawled from the water, pulled his quarry after him. A streak of light came from the distant street and revealed the victim as Lobinger.

That streak of light also disclosed the Green Ghost to a watchful policeman. He shouted, started running, flashing his light. The Green Ghost made a quick dive back into the water, and swam beneath the surface.

He came up a distance downstream. Lights were flashing. The searchlight on the police car had been turned on the end of the wharf. The Green Ghost saw Madge Gray standing there with water streaming from her clothing, a policeman supporting her. Matt Lobinger was sitting on the dock, handcuffs on his wrists. Lobinger's car was there, Gus Marsh standing handcuffed beside it.

"Who helped you if you were bound and gagged?"

The Green Ghost heard those words drifting to him on the wind.

"He said he was the Green Ghost. I couldn't see him in the dark."

"The Green Ghost!" somebody bellowed. "I want him as badly as the others."

THE GREEN GHOST smiled behind his hood as he floated on the surface. Then it flashed through his mind that the voice was that of Detective Sergeant Tim O'Hara. He had come here instead of going to the apartment.

"O'Hara!" The Green Ghost shouted with all the strength of his voice.

"Yeah?" O'Hara answered the call out of the darkness.

"Get to Lobinger's apartment, quick! Darson there—witness. Swag where I said—remember? Hurry, or something may happen to make you miss it."

"Hey! Where are you? Who are you?"

"This is the Green Ghost. Did you get Weaver?"

At that instant, the Green Ghost knew they had not caught Weaver. For Weaver came through the water at him, only a few feet away.

"Now, blast you!" Weaver roared.

A gun exploded within a few feet of the Green Ghost, and a bullet whistled past within inches of his head.

The Green Ghost dived. He had no time to get out his own automatic. In the dark water, he kicked forward, and bumped against his man. He seized him, pulled him down.

He knew that the other was trying to strike with the gun,

but the water robbed the blows of strength. Twisting suddenly, the Green Ghost jerked Weaver aside, got hold of the gun and let it sink.

THEN BEGAN a furious fight to reach surface and the life-sustaining air. Weaver was a rough-and-tumble fighter, only a dressed-up thug. He was an expert swimmer also. The Green Ghost submerged again, pulled the other down, fought to get free of his grasp.

He broke away, panting for breath as he got to the surface once more. Weaver was at the surface also, and making for him. Up on the dock, a gun cracked, and bullets sang around them. Far away, the *put-put* of a launch could be heard.

The Green Ghost made a quick dive and came up behind his man. He had lost his own gun, too, but he got out the heavy flashlight. With that, he struck a glancing blow. The force of it tore the light from his grasp, and it sank. It was hand-to-hand now.

The Green Ghost's fist slammed home in a wet face. He felt a return blow graze his shoulder. Then they were grappling each other again, and Weaver plainly was trying to get the other below the surface, hold him there until his struggles ceased.

The launch was coming nearer. On the shore, the chauffeur of the police squad car backed it until he could swing the search-light across the tumbling water of the river. The bright beam cut over the surface and revealed the struggling men.

The Green Ghost gathered his strength for a last effort. He tore free of Weaver, submerging again, came up behind. His fists struck as he was sinking, and one blow had effect.

He pulled Weaver under again, swam with him despite the man's weak struggles.

He got out of the path of the searchlight, and made for the darkness beneath the dock, where the light could not reach. The launch was coming on swiftly now, and the Green Ghost could hear O'Hara bellowing orders.

HE WAS in peril now. If he were captured, the world would learn that the Green Ghost was Danny Blaney. Even if he escaped the consequences of the Green Ghost's acts, his work of fighting crooks would be at an end. The police would prevent it. And the criminal element would make short work of him, by way of revenge.

Weaver was giving him no more trouble now. The Green Ghost swam along beneath the dock and toward the shore on the other side, toward the spot where he had landed with Lobinger. It was the last place they would expect him to appear.

He grew doubly cautious as he neared the shore. When he came to the steps, he waited a moment, lifting Weaver half out of the water. The thug was unconscious.

The launch was cutting toward shore on the opposite side of the dock. The searchlight of the police car was being played back and forth on that side also. The Green Ghost crawled from the water and up the slimy steps, dragging Weaver after him.

THE LAUNCH stopped. Orders were shouted. The craft began cruising rapidly around the dock. The Green Ghost pulled Weaver to the top of the steps. He had taken considerable water, yet it was possible that he might recover and crawl away through the darkness if left there alone.

"O'Hara!"

The Green Ghost bawled the word into the night. Detective Sergeant Tim O'Hara heard.

"Yeah?" he called. He had not been certain from which direction the shout had come.

"Here's Weaver for you!"

Then the Green Ghost doubled and sped through the darkness toward the street, passing swiftly through a streak of light.

"Halt, there!" O'Hara shouted after him. "Get him, men!"

The Green Ghost sped on. He reached the street and ran along it swiftly, keeping to the dark spots as much as possible. Behind him, guns cracked, but no bullets came near. He darted across the street in a dark streak, stumbled over cobblestones and almost sprawled headlong; righted himself and rushed on.

Now he was in the dark recess between the two buildings where he had left his car. He sprang into it, tore off green hood and gloves and thrust them into his pockets. He kicked the starter; the motor roared.

It was Danny Blaney who turned the car into the street and swung it away from the dock. He snapped on the headlights, and went into high gear. The powerful engine beneath the hood roared into life.

Behind him a siren wailed, and he knew he had been spotted and that there would be instant pursuit. He went around a corner with a sickening lurch, dashed away through a cross street, thankful that there was little traffic at this hour.

Around two more corners, and he knew he had lost the chase. He slackened speed and went ahead in an ordinary fashion. In the far distance, he heard the screech of the siren warning traffic to clear the way.

Danny Blaney parked his car half a block from his cigar store, behind a small shop. He was soaked to the skin. He pulled a water-drenched cap from his pocket and put it on, and slipped along the deserted street.

The sleepy night clerk in the cigar store glanced up as Danny Blaney, minus his wet cap, entered. Standing behind the counter, the clerk did not notice his employer's wet apparel. He had his mind on a book he was reading between customers.

"BEEN PROWLIN'" around at night again, boss?" he asked.

"Some," Danny Blaney admitted, as he hurried along the counter toward the room in the rear, where he lived. "How's business?"

"Rotten tonight!"

"Not much doin'," Danny agreed. "Guess I'll hit the hay. Good night!"

He went through into his private room, locked the door and

turned on the lights.

"Not much financial gain in this night's work," he muttered, as he began peeling off his wet clothes. "Yet there's profit. There's always profit, when crooks are put away."

VII

BLOODSTAINED BONDS

CROUCHING IN THE DARKNESS beside the clump of shrubs, with the high wind slashing around him and scudding clouds obscuring the light of the moon at intervals, Danny Blaney waited.

He could not hear the man he sought, but knew he was near. Like a shadow, he was moving close at hand, an obstacle in Danny Blaney's path. But this was a night when Danny Blaney would allow no obstacle to stand in his way.

Danny Blaney was grasping a blackjack, a reminder of the days when he had been an honored member of the force. He had been honest, hard-working, ambitious—had aspired to great things in the department. Being promoted to the detective branch, he had made himself so obnoxious to leading criminals that they had turned upon him.

Danny Blaney had been framed neatly by them; he had been accused of accepting a bribe. His trial had resulted in acquittal, but he had been discredited, and even many of his own comrades had believed him guilty. So Danny Blaney, under pressure, resigned from his beloved force, his life plans ruined, and opened a corner cigar store.

But he did not stop his police work. In the dark, he worked, gathering evidence, watching, striking when he could. Nobody thought that Danny Blaney, quiet and timid around his place of business, was the Green Ghost, the terror of crooks and the wonder of the police.

*The Green Ghost tossed the
man through the window.*

Tonight, Danny Blaney was the Green Ghost again. And he was after Phil Cardon, a man of prominence in the underworld, one of the group that had caused Danny Blaney's disgrace. He had been after Phil Cardon for some time.

Now he was crouching in the grounds of a big roadhouse beside a tumbling river, a half-secluded district which was still within the city limits and under the jurisdiction of city police.

It was about ten o'clock. In the roadhouse, the orchestra was playing dance music. The parking place in front was packed with cars. Song and laughter rang through the windows and could be heard above the noise of the rushing wind. An open public place, seemingly.

But Danny Blaney knew that the front was being watched by Phil Cardon's spotters.

Back here well toward the rear, where there were no bright electric lights, others lurked in the darkness, alert and watchful. Phil Cardon was being well guarded tonight. And Danny Blaney dared not be seen, either as himself or as the Green Ghost, or his plans would be ruined.

When the evening newspapers had told, under black headlines, of the robbery of a fortune in negotiable bonds from a messenger, Danny Blaney had not been surprised. He had expected the robbery. But he had not expected that Phil Cardon's men, usually so careful, would kill the messenger.

Generally, the Cardon gang killed only by way of revenge. They prided themselves upon their cleverness. This time, somebody had erred. And their erring had thrown the police off the track; because of the killing, they did not seriously suspect Phil Cardon.

But Danny Blaney knew—so the Green Ghost prowled again, intending to trap Phil Cardon. It might mean more than prison for Cardon now—it might mean the chair.

With the blackjack held ready, Danny Blaney listened and watched. This one guard removed, he could get to the rear of the big, sprawling building. He saw a shadow drifting among the trees—the shadow of a man.

Crouching, tensed, scarcely breathing, Danny Blaney held himself ready. The drifting shadow came nearer. The guard would pass where Danny Blaney was in hiding.

At the proper instant, Danny Blaney sprang and struck. He knew how to use a blackjack, and he used it properly now.

His man groaned and fell. Working swiftly in the darkness, Danny Blaney turned his pockets inside out and took what they contained—and tossed the loot far into the shrubs. He wanted this man to think that he had merely been blackjacked and robbed.

Then Danny Blaney glided through the shadows himself and got to the rear of the building. At a corner was a waterpipe half obscured by a tangle of tough vines. Danny Blaney ascended by means of this, until he came to the roof of a one-story addition to the building. Up this sloping roof he crawled cautiously. Stretching upon it, he could peer through a window without being seen. He was looking into a hallway on the upper floor of the roadhouse.

Waiters passed along the hall. Guests went along it to private rooms. A door opened—and Danny Blaney caught sight of Phil Cardon glancing up and down nervously. Blaney knew what that meant. Cardon was waiting for Harry Leloy, who would have the bonds.

Leloy undoubtedly had been detained. He would not approach Phil Cardon until it was safe. Nor would Danny Blaney approach until Leloy had been there. He wanted to turn Phil Cardon over to the police with evidence to convict.

BLANEY PULLED back his head as another man came along the hallway. It was Harry Leloy—tall, lean, nervous—a man with ever-shifting eyes. He knocked peculiarly on the door, and it was opened instantly. Harry Leloy darted inside. Danny Blaney noticed that he was carrying a bulging briefcase.

The hall was deserted now. Raising the window slowly and cautiously, Danny Blaney thrust his head inside. An instant later, he had crawled through. He darted to a little recess just across from the door, waited a moment, then glided to the door and listened.

"—didn't have to give him the heat!" Phil Cardon was declaring angrily.

"Couldn't be helped, Phil."

"Been gettin' careless lately, Leloy. My orders don't seem to mean anything to you any more."

"Aw, now, Phil—"

"You know my rules. This is a mess."

"The cops ain't even thinkin' about us, because we gave that guy the heat. They know that ain't Cardon's way. Here's the stuff, Phil—more'n a hundred grand. None of it too hot, either. It can be handled easy."

"Give it here, and let me get it put away. Then you can get the devil out, and don't come back for half an hour or so."

"All right, Phil."

"Stella Kenwell's comin' here to see me about a little deal. You watch downstairs, and when she comes tell her to get right up here."

There was a moment of silence, during which Danny Blaney got back into the recess and in hiding again, holding his black-jack ready. Then the door across the hall opened and Harry Leloy came out and hurried along the hall toward the stairs. So, Phil Cardon had the bonds in that room, hidden cunningly. And Stella Kenwell was about to visit him. He would not be disturbed while she was there.

Danny Blaney had reason to hate this Stella Kenwell. She had given false testimony at his trial. She was a beautiful woman of about thirty, absolutely unscrupulous and heartless, one of the most dangerous female crooks in the city.

He might do considerable tonight in his work of revenge, and also put out of circulation some outstanding public enemies. But he did not underestimate the peril. Phil Cardon would have the right to shoot down the Green Ghost, since the latter had no legal standing.

A waiter passed swiftly along the hall and disappeared. Danny Blaney's hands went beneath his vest. He took out his hood of thin green silk and put it on, drawing it over his head and down to his shoulders. He put the blackjack away, and brought out an automatic. Then he glided across to the door, and knocked in that unusual fashion he had heard Harry Leloy employ.

He could hear somebody grumbling inside the room, heard steps, and the door was pulled open. The Green Ghost stepped inside swiftly, menacing with the automatic, kicked the door shut behind him as he whispered for Cardon to put up his hands.

"Wh-what—" Phil Cardon was startled. He had expected that this was Harry Leloy returning, or that Stella Kenwell had arrived.

"Sit down!" the Green Ghost snapped. "Make a bad move, Cardon, and you'll be blasted!"

"You're the Green Ghost, huh?"

"I sent you a note some time ago, sayin' I'd pay you a visit."

"All right, Ghost. You're here. Sit down and take it easy."

PHIL CARDON was taking it easy, now that the first shock of surprise was over. He had some ideas of his own about this mysterious Green Ghost.

"What can I do for you?" Cardon asked.

"I've come for the bonds."

"What bonds?"

"Those Harry Leloy left with you a few minutes ago. Dig 'em up, Cardon. I was listenin' at the door and heard you say you'd hide them."

"I don't know what you're talkin' about, Ghost."

"Don't stall for time. I'm workin' fast tonight. I can blast you, Cardon, find the bonds myself, and get out. Won't be hard to do. You've left orders not to be disturbed. And if your friend, Stella, comes, I'll take care of her."

"You seem to know a lot," Cardon said, his eyes glittering.

"I do."

"Ghost, I'm glad you're here. I think we can do business. I've been thinkin' a lot about you, and to me you aren't any mystery at all. You're simply a crook hijacking other crooks. You're wise; you wait till somebody pulls off a job, then step in and collect."

"Got it all figured out, have you?"

"You've turned in a few gents to the cops, but I figure that was by way of revenge. We might make a deal."

"What kind of a deal?" the Green Ghost asked.

"Why not throw in together? I've got a few weak links in my chain just now. Might get rid of one of them and make a place for you. Better yet—you get rid of him and make your own place."

"I work alone, Cardon."

"Keep right on wearin' that trick hood and hidin' your face, if you want it that way. I don't care who you are, long as we work together."

"Who's in the way, Cardon? Whose place do you want me to take?"

"Now, you're talkin' sensible. I don't fancy Harry Leloy any more. He forgets orders too easy, or else he's got the idea that he's a bigger man than he really is."

"GETTIN' UNDER your skin, is he?" the Ghost asked.

"I'll fix it for you, so it'll be easy, Ghost. Get rid of him for me, and step into his shoes."

"Why don't you do your own killin'?"

"It's a messy job, and I run to brains."

The eyes of the Green Ghost glittered through the slender holes in his hood.

"I'll keep right on workin' alone," he said. "Far as hookin' up with you is concerned—you'd be the last man I'd hook up with. I'm out to get you, Cardon!"

"What'd I ever do to you? Who are you?"

"I'm not tellin'. Put your hands behind your back!"

"If I don't—"

"I'll give you the heat! My finger is itchin' to pull the trigger, you rat!"

"You'll never get away with this, Ghost."

"That's to be seen."

He walked around behind Cardon's chair. From a coat pocket, he took a noose of fine, tough cord. He slipped it over Cardon's wrists, jerked it tight, looped it securely, then fastened the wrists to the back of the chair.

"Where are the bonds?" the Green Ghost demanded, standing in front of his victim again.

"You know so much, suppose you tell yourself that, too."

The Green Ghost glanced swiftly around the little room. His eyes darted back to Cardon—and caught him glancing toward a corner. The Ghost hurried there, tapped on the wall and baseboard, got a hollow sound from the latter.

He looked back at Cardon again, to find his face a picture of rage. Stooping, the Green Ghost removed a section of the baseboard, and got out the briefcase.

"Bloodstained bonds," he said, as he carried the case to the table. "This will make it tough for you, Cardon."

"It was against my orders—givin' that messenger the heat."

"It'll be strictly accordin' to orders when they give you the heat in the chair, Cardon."

"Listen, Ghost! Take the bonds and go. More'n a hundred grand. That'll set you up in business for a while."

"I don't want the bonds," the Green Ghost said. "They aren't mine, see. I'm goin' to use them to pin this thing on you, Cardon. You've got me wrong—I'm not a crook. I've made it my business to go out to get certain crooks and you're one of them."

The Green Ghost opened the briefcase and dumped the packages of bonds on the table.

"Bloodstained bonds," he said again.

"Don't keep sayin' that!" Cardon begged. "I didn't have anything to do with it."

"Cardon, the first tip you got about that messenger, and how easy it'd be to get his bundle, came from me—indirectly," the Green Ghost said. "You walked into the trap, you rat. But I gambled on the idea that you never had your men kill. Knew you never would yourself—you haven't the nerve."

"Take 'em and go, Ghost."

"They're goin' to stay right here, and be evidence. And you talk too much, Cardon. I'm goin' to gag you."

He took a gag from his pocket and advanced, threatening Cardon with the automatic again.

This thing had happened so speedily, so easily, that Cardon had not had a chance to put up a fight. And he dared not try a hostile move now. His hands were lashed to the chair. He could do nothing but howl for help. And he sensed that he would get a chance to howl but once.

Then his head was jerked back, and he was gagged effectually. He could only glare at his captor—and hope that help would come unexpectedly.

And at that instant there came a knock on the door—that peculiar signal.

The Green Ghost glided across the room, automatic held ready. He turned the catch, the knob, pulled the door open. He expected to see Stella Kenwell, but it was Harry Leloy who darted silently into the room.

He had stepped past the Green Ghost, and the door was closed again before he caught sight of Phil Cardon helpless in the chair. At the same instant, he felt the muzzle of a gun jabbing against his spine. "Put 'em up, Leloy!" a cold voice commanded.

Harry Leloy put up his hands. From behind, the Green Ghost's left hand explored, and got a gun from a shoulder holster. Then he thrust Leloy away from him.

Leloy's eyes bulged as he turned swiftly and saw the Green Ghost in front of him.

"So—it's you," he said. "I heard somebody talkin', and thought it was one of the boys. I heard Cardon tellin' somebody to give me the heat—"

"Yes, Mr. Cardon doesn't like you any more," the Green Ghost said.

"Give me my gun," Leloy said, in a hoarse whisper. "Take the bonds and get out. Just leave me my gun—and leave me alone with Cardon."

"That might be an easy solution," the Green Ghost said. He glanced over at the helpless Cardon. "Might be justice, too. He's ordered others bumped off in his time."

"The double-crossin' rat!" Harry Leloy hissed. "Give me a chance at him, Ghost."

"You've killed your share today, haven't you? That messenger—"

"The devil with that! Had to do it, no matter what Cardon

says. He recognized me—I could see it in his face. They'd have traced it right to Cardon—but he doesn't stop to think of that. Doin' him a service, I was—fool that I am!"

"SIT DOWN!" the Green Ghost ordered. "In that other chair."

"What's the idea?"

"You're going to be tied up and gagged, like Cardon."

"What'd I ever do to you?"

"Nothin' in particular, Leloy. But whenever I get hold of a murderer, I'm turnin' him in."

"A man'd think you were a cop."

"Sit down!"

Leloy, drug addict and killer, did not possess any particular amount of courage. He was the kind to wilt when another held the advantage. He wilted now. He sank into the chair, muttering appeals for sympathy.

"Please, Ghost—take the bonds and go—leave me the gun, leave me alone with this rat. Toss the clip in a corner, if you're afraid I'll open up on you."

His wrists were lashed, but not before, in desperation, he had made a move. One blow from the automatic half-stunned him, and caused a trickle of blood down the side of his face. Then, the Green Ghost gagged him.

"Bloodstained bonds," he muttered, as though a sudden thought had come to him.

He darted to the table and got a couple of packages of the bonds. Back beside Harry Leloy again, he wiped the bonds across the bleeding face, smeared them with blood. His two victims were struggling ineffectually, glaring at him, gurgling in a vain attempt to speak.

"Bloodstained bonds," the Green Ghost said again.

He went behind Phil Cardon's chair, fumbled with his fingers. Cardon writhed and groaned. He knew what the Green Ghost was doing. He was pressing the tips of Cardon's fingers to the wet blood smears, causing damning fingerprints.

Then he went behind Leloy's chair and did the same with another package of bonds, then put the bonds on the table beneath the light, with the others.

"Plenty of evidence," the Green Ghost said. "I wish I could tell you why I'm doin' this, Cardon. It'd be a lot of satisfaction. But it might get out, and that'd put some others on guard. You're not the only crooks I'm after."

Cardon twisted his head and gurgled behind the gag, but the Green Ghost would not take the gag away.

"Now, I'll send in a call for the cops," he said, speaking in low tones. "That makes your eyes sparkle, huh, Cardon? The call will go through the switchboard downstairs. Any call to Police Headquarters might cause a little investigation up here, and bring you help, huh?" The Green Ghost laughed a little. "But we won't do it that way, Cardon. I contacted Jim Malloy, the Detective Sergeant in charge of the bond detail, before I came out here. Told him I'd turn in the bonds and thieves tonight. So we've got an undercover man planted."

The Green Ghost chuckled again, and went to the telephone on a stand in the corner. He called the number of the Hotel Magnificent. No doubt the switchboard operator downstairs knew that number.

"I want Mr. William Green, in Room 809, please," the Ghost said. "Hello! Green? Come out to the Riverside Roadhouse, and make it snappy. Big party on."

HE PLACED the receiver and turned toward his victims again.

"Understand, gents?" he asked. "Riverside Roadhouse—big party. That means come prepared to raid. And they'll come, Cardon—Jim Malloy and his men. They'll find you and Leloy here, with the stolen bonds, and your bloody fingerprints on 'em. Try to explain all that away."

He watched as they struggled again at the bindings which would not give, as they glared murderously at him. Then there came another knock on the door.

Again, the Green Ghost glided swiftly and noiselessly across the room. He opened the door halfway, standing behind it, and closed it swiftly as a woman in an evening gown swept in.

Stella Kenwell, a welcoming smile on her face, expected to find Phil Cardon alone, to negotiate a deal with him as she had often done before. Cardon, she supposed, had need of her services and would pay well for them.

As the door closed, she caught sight of the two men bound and gagged. With a little cry, she whirled swiftly, to see the Green Ghost standing before her, menacing her with a gun, his eyes glittering.

Stella Kenwell was a woman of poise, and she recovered herself swiftly.

She had been in many situations where swift thinking and tact had saved her.

"Rather startling," she drawled, flashing a smile at the Green Ghost. "Looks as though I'd walked in on something. If it's all the same to you, I'll walk out until this is finished—whatever it is."

"Sit down," the Green Ghost said. "I hate to contradict a lady—but you're not walking out just now."

"Like to have me around, do you?" she asked.

She smiled at him again, laughed a bit, glanced at Cardon and Leloy, and sat down on a sofa.

"I take it that you're the Green Ghost," she said. "I've been hearing about you. Perhaps I'd better explain. I dropped in here because Phil Cardon sent for me. Whatever this is—I have nothing to do with it. If I give you my word to say nothing about this, may I leave?"

"Your word is absolutely valueless, as I have reason to know," the Green Ghost told her, coldly.

She peered at him intently, swept her glance over him.

"You'll probably not be able to guess my identity, so don't waste time trying," the Ghost said.

"Well, what is this?" she snapped angrily. "What are we

waiting for?"

"For the cops."

"Cops? Don't get me mixed up in this. I don't know what it's all about."

"Tell the cops that," the Green Ghost said, coldly. "You see those bonds, don't you? Blood marks on them, too."

"Bonds? Blood marks?" She looked at them wildly. "I don't know anything about any bonds. You're getting me mixed up in something, Green Ghost."

"You've got plenty of people mixed up in your time. I can't be bothered with you when the cops come. Have my hands full with them. Pardon me, fair lady, but I'll have to tie you up and gag you."

"If you dare do that—"

"You're supposed to have sense, Stella Kenwell. If you have, you know you're not in a position to do any threatenin' just now."

He took a piece of cord from his pocket and strode across the room toward her.

"You can say that you walked in here, as you did, and found this, and that the Green Ghost tied you up. You'll have to make up the rest of the yarn yourself. Maybe Cardon and Leloy will help you out of this scrape—but they're goin' to be pretty busy gettin' out of it themselves."

He seized one of her wrists and looped it with the cord. She offered no resistance as he caught hold of the other and lashed it to the first. Then he took a gag out of his pocket.

"I imagine you'll not have to be gagged long," he said.

Then Stella Kenwell screamed.

IT WAS a piercing scream that must have sounded up and down the hall, down the stairway, and into the big room below, which was thronged with merrymakers. The Green Ghost gagged her swiftly, and not as mercifully as he had intended. Then he tied her wrists to the arm of the sofa, and darted across to the door.

Feet pounded in the hall. Somebody tapped on the door—not the usual Cardon signal. Some waiter, the Green Ghost judged.

"Well?" He tried to imitate Phil Cardon's snarl.

"Everything all right in there, sir? We heard a scream—"

"Not in here," the Ghost replied.

He heard the man outside go away slowly, as though suspicious, and prepared to receive him if he returned. But there was a sudden commotion downstairs. Men were shouting, and women shrieking.

"Raid! Raid!" the Green Ghost heard somebody cry.

Detective Sergeant Jim Malloy and his squad had arrived.

The Green Ghost opened the door a crack. Men and women were darting out of the private rooms and rushing toward the rear stairs. From below came sounds that told of furniture being overturned. Employees were shouting at one another. The stentorian bellow of Jim Malloy could be heard above the din.

The Green Ghost could not afford capture. He was a malefactor himself, in a way. And, if his identity became known, his work would end. No longer could he punish the crooks who had framed him and taken away his life's work.

The hallway cleared, just as some of the squad came pounding up the stairs. The Green Ghost sprang out and closed the door behind him.

"Malloy! Malloy!" he shouted.

"Comin'!" he heard Jim Malloy reply.

THE GREEN GHOST knew Malloy; had worked beside him in the old days. He did not desire to clash with Malloy in any way, for the latter was a conscientious officer who always "mopped up." He would be determined to see the face behind the Green Ghost's hood.

Malloy and two other squad members appeared at the head of the stairs.

"Malloy! This way!" the Green Ghost cried. "In this room,

Malloy."

Malloy saw him pointing.

"Comin'!" he roared. "Just a minute—you! I want to see you!"

The Green Ghost darted into the recess across the hall. A gun barked and a bullet whistled past as Jim Malloy fired a warning shot.

In the recess, the Ghost crashed against another man—one of the waiters, new to this sort of thing, and half terrified.

"Come out of there, Ghost!" Malloy was crying.

The Green Ghost had a sudden inspiration. He grasped the waiter, a smaller man, and got to the window. He tossed the man through it, so that he rolled screeching down the sloping roof to drop to the ground. And with his automatic the Green Ghost smashed the glass, then darted back behind the curtains again.

"He's gone through the window!" somebody shouted.

Malloy and one of his men rushed up, saw the smashed glass, heard the waiter cry out again as he struck the ground. To Malloy, it looked as though the Green Ghost had taken the shortest route to a getaway.

He began bellowing orders, and members of the squad rushed to carry them out. Then Cardon and Leloy were discovered in the room with Stella Kenwell, the bloodstained bonds on the table, and Jim Mallloy was called.

Police were at either end of the hallway. Others were searching down in the grounds. The frightened waiter had been found, and had told his story of being tossed through the window by a man with a hood over his head. So they would be back in the building, after the Green Ghost instantly.

The Ghost got through the window and crawled slowly down the sloping roof, keeping to the darker shadows. At the edge, he listened.

Men were crashing through the underbrush below. There was a crowd in front of the resort. Many of the guests had been gathered in the big dance hall, to be released after Jim Malloy had looked them over.

In the upper hallway, Malloy was issuing more orders. He had the bloodstained bonds and his prisoners. The Green Ghost knew what the result would be. It would mean the end of Phil Cardon and his band. Harry Leloy, facing the electric chair, was the sort to drag Cardon along with him, especially since he had heard Cardon plotting his death.

The Green Ghost looked over the edge of the roof again, trying to see into the shadows. Behind him somebody put his head through the window.

"Get out on the roof and take a look," Jim Malloy was ordering.

The Ghost let himself over the edge, held a moment, and dropped.

He had hoped to drop silently, but he crashed into some of the brush. His fall was heard.

"There he goes!"

The Green Ghost snapped a shot in the direction of the voice, firing high only to deter pursuit. Then, bending low, he ran.

A blast of fire came from behind him. Bullets whistled near him as he fled. He raced around the corner of the building, to crash into another of Malloy's men and send him sprawling. On he raced, darting from shadow to shadow. He swung around in front, and tore into the crowd, scattering men and women as he rushed on. The police did not dare to fire into the crowd.

Down the line of automobiles he dashed, to where a light police car was standing, its chauffeur having left it to join the hunt. The Green Ghost sprang into it, and kicked the starter. The engine roared to life.

An instant later he was swinging out into the driveway. There was more shooting behind him—and now they were trying for a hit. One of the windows cracked as a bullet struck it. And then the Ghost was out on the highway.

THEY WOULD be after him in squad cars, but he had the advantage of a flying start. He snapped on the bright headlight and roared down the highway, warning with the siren. He knew this car—it was the pet of Detective Sergeant Jim Malloy. The sergeant would consider the theft and use of it no less than a deadly insult.

A warning would be flashed ahead, the Green Ghost knew. So he swerved off the highway when he came to a dirt crossroad, and snapped off the lights, but kept on running slowly in the shifting moonlight.

Back on the highway, sirens were screeching in the distance. One of the cars might turn into the crossroad—the pursuing police might guess that the Green Ghost would make that move. So he swung the car off the road and into thick brush and sprang out.

Along a creek he raced, dodging the brush and keeping in the dark spots. A mile across country was a suburban car line. When he neared it, the Green Ghost stripped off his hood and stowed it away, and put on a cap. He stepped out and signaled when a car came along.

An hour later, Danny Blaney walked into the corner cigar store he owned, and was greeted by his night clerk.

"How's business?"

"So-so, Mr. Blaney."

"Guess I'll get to bed."

"Been prowlin' around town again?" the clerk asked, grinning. "Never saw a man who likes to prowl around at night like you do."

"Comes from havin' been a cop once, maybe," Blaney said. "And then—the city's so quiet at night. Nothin' much doin'.'"

THE ROLLICKING ROGUE

CHAPTER I

A MOCKING LAUGH

SOMEWHERE IN THE HOUSE a door slammed, and Hiram Doles flinched. His nervous pacing of the library floor came to an abrupt stop. His face paled, and then the color surged back into it until it was almost purple.

Though he was trying desperately to fight it off, abject fear revealed itself in his countenance. He was not a man to show fear where ordinary things, ordinary situations were concerned. But here was something so unusual, so different! It was the uncertainty, the quality of the unknown that frightened him.

At the end of the library, through an open archway, could be seen a small anteroom which was used as an office. Peters was there now, James Peters, the confidential secretary of Hiram Doles. He was working on some books, the household accounts for the month.

Peters was middle-aged, stoop-shouldered, wore thick spectacles, and gave the general impression of being a timid soul. He was humble in manner, especially in the presence of his employer. Not the sort of man to call on for physical assistance in case of an emergency, not Peters!

"Peters!" Hiram Doles called, his voice a trifle shaky, that voice which could roar in stentorian tones down in his magnificent suite of offices and make men and women quail.

"Sir?"

"You—er—you're sure that the safe is locked?"

"I locked it after I took out these account books, sir."

"That window in the study—it is fastened?"

"Securely, sir."

"Very well, Peters."

Hiram Doles resumed his pacing of the library floor, from the hall door to the bookcases and back. It was eleven o'clock on a splendid summer morning. Save for this one room, there was an atmosphere of peace and beauty about the country estate of Hiram Doles. But every window in the library was closed and locked, despite the balmy air. The hall door was locked, also.

"Peters!"

"Sir?"

"You have a gun?"

"I believe there is one in the lower drawer of the desk, Mr. Doles."

"Good heavens, man! In the drawer of the desk! In case of

The Rollicking Rogue's weapon spat flame and lead at his pursuers.

an emergency, Peters, what good would the gun do you in the lower drawer of the desk. Get it immediately and slip it into your pocket! At once!"

"Really, sir," said Peters, "I'd rather not. I do not fancy handling the thing, sir. Violence is repugnant to me."

"And I can danged well believe you!" Hiram Doles exploded. "In case of a physical clash, you'll not be much of a help for me, Peters. I'll be glad when Martin Shane gets here. Just what did you tell him?"

"When I telephoned him in the city, sir, I merely said that you had been disturbed greatly by a threat, and that he should come to you at once."

"And what did he say?"

"He said to leave it to him."

"There's a man, Peters! Detective Martin Shane! We didn't make any mistake, the small group of us, when we took him from the police department and got him to handle our special work. Self-reliant—that's Shane!"

"I have understood that he is very good in his line, sir," Peters said.

"Did he say when he would get here?"

"Not exactly, sir. He said just to leave it to him and he'd bring home the bacon. I did not understand what the last remark meant."

"You wouldn't!" Hiram Doles said.

"I thought it might be in private code, sir, and you would know."

"Never mind, Peters. I understand. Confound this business! It has upset me terribly. Understand, Peters, I am not exactly afraid—"

"Certainly not, sir!"

"But a man in my position has to take care of himself. There are so many disgruntled cranks in the world. Irresponsible persons, Peters."

"Quite so, sir."

"There may be nothing to this, but I thought it best to have Shane come out and offer me his advice and protection. He couldn't have caught the early train. Possibly he'll motor out."

Doles had stopped at the door of the anteroom, and was watching Peters work on the books as he talked. With a hand that trembled, he ignited a cigar. He puffed a few times, then hurled the cigar from him and at the nearest ash receptacle. Fear had made his taste bitter.

"Peters, there are certain qualities lacking in your make-up, but you do have a modicum of brains."

"Thank you, sir!"

"Tell me again—what do you think of it?"

"I scarcely know what to think, sir. As you said half an hour ago, it may be only a hoax, a practical joke, or it may be something very serious."

"The Rollicking Rogue! What a name for a man to call himself! No sense to it!"

"One never knows, Mr. Doles. I'd be inclined, in your place, if you'll pardon me for saying so, to be very cautious. I'd not get too close to that window, sir."

"How's that?"

"Suppose it is serious, and the confounded fellow was lurking at the edge of the woods, say with a high-powered rifle, waiting to try a shot at you?"

Hiram Doles got away from the vicinity of the window swiftly. "Confound it, Peters, you can be extremely disagreeable at times," he said.

"I regret it, sir."

"The fellow did not intimate that he was going to kill me."

"Did you gather that impression, sir?" Peters asked. "I was of the opinion that he was very threatening. May I look at it again, sir?"

"There's the thing on the table. Don't touch it. There may be fingerprints on it, and Shane will want to—er—examine them."

"I quite understand, sir," Peters said.

He left the anteroom and entered the library, marching across it to the long table in the middle of the room. He adjusted his spectacles and bent forward to look.

On the table was a card about the size of an ordinary postal card, which had been received in the morning mail brought out from the neighboring village. It had been in an ordinary envelope. The message on the card, and the name and address on the envelope, had been printed with a pen.

Peters read swiftly:

THE ROLLICKING ROGUE
"He Laughs While He Loots!"
It is our pleasure to call upon you
Thursday of the present week.

Peters picked up a letter-opener and used it to flip over the card. There was another message on the back:

Your sins have been found out, and you must pay!
I am coming to collect!

"You see, Peters?" Hiram Doles asked. "He says that he is coming to collect. That means he will try to rob me, try to get into the safe and steal something."

"But, sir, if he really means you must pay with your life—" Peters began.

"Confound it, Peters, are you trying to frighten me? You are always looking on the darkest side of things."

"I'm very sorry, sir."

"You should be! Great heavens, what is that?"

Hiram Doles stopped his nervous pacing again. To his ears and those of Peters' had come a roaring sound. Peters approached one of the windows and peered out cautiously.

"It is an airplane, sir," he reported.

"We seldom have a plane around here," Doles replied.

"He is flying very low, sir, though the plane doesn't seem to be in trouble. Perhaps he is going to land."

"Land here? On my lawn?" Hiram cried. "I never heard of such a thing!"

"You don't suppose, sir—" Peters stopped his sentence abruptly as though embarrassed.

"Out with it!"

"Some of the modern criminals, so I've read, sir, do strange things. They have modern methods. Now, if this Rollicking

Rogue, as he calls himself—"

"Confound it, Peters, are you trying to intimate that he may come in an airplane?"

"If he dropped a few bombs, sir, or something of that nature—"

"Great heavens! Peters, did you put that gun into your pocket as I said? I have one, an automatic, in my pocket. The servants should be armed. If we are attacked, Peters, shoot to kill."

"The plane is circling and is going to land, sir," Peters reported.

"I wish Martin Shane was here! Oh, confound this business! It will wreck me for a month. What is the fellow doing now?"

"Going to land on the south stretch of lawn, sir, I'd say. Yes—they are landing."

"They?"

"There are two persons in the plane, sir. One of them is getting out."

"Am I not entitled to protection? It is a crime that a man of my standing—"

"I do believe that it is Mr. Shane, sir!" Peters interrupted.

"Shane?" Hiram Doles rushed to the window and peered out cautiously. "Yes, it is Shane!" he went on. "What did I tell you, Peters? There's a man—self-reliant and resourceful! He didn't wait for the afternoon train, or spend three or four hours getting here in motor car. He came in an airplane. I called for him, and he came to me in the quickest possible way."

"Yes, sir!"

"I feel better already. We'll have Shane right in here and turn this affair over to him. I'd like to see this Rollicking Rogue get at me now, with Shane here! He couldn't do it, could he, Peters?"

"It does seem impossible, sir."

"Confound it, it is impossible! How could he get at me, with all the doors and windows locked, the servants on guard, and Detective Martin Shane at my side to protect me? Laughs while he loots, does he? I'd like to see him get near enough to make me hear his laugh. I'd—"

Hiram Doles ceased speaking as though he had choked. Peters, who was turning away, turned back toward him quickly. Hiram Doles' eyes bulged, his face went white again, he seemed to be gasping for breath. Peters' eyes were bulging also.

To their ears had come a laugh—a low, mocking laugh. It was not from servant passing along the hall outside. It had seemed to be in this very room.

There was something in that laugh which sounded like a threat, something which seemed to indicate that all Hiram Doles' efforts to guard himself would be futile.

"Peters! What—?" Doles began.

"He—he laughs while he loots!" Peters quoted.

CHAPTER II

SHANE TAKES CHARGE

DETECTIVE MARTIN SHANE STALKED across the expanse of lawn to the bottom of the veranda steps, where he glanced up and beheld Sampson, the Doles' butler, waiting to greet him. Sampson was a bit annoyed because the landing of the airplane on the lawn was so unusual and irregular, and he disliked anything which upset the smooth-running menage.

"Take me to Mr. Doles!" Shane said.

"Pardon me, sir, but Mr. Doles is busy in his study with his confidential secretary, going over the books," Sampson replied. The butler knew Detective Shane, and did not like him.

"Take me to him, and be snappy about it!" Shane said. "He sent for me and told me to get here in a hurry. Going over his accounts, is he? He's locked in his library, scared half to death, and you know it!"

From a porch swing a few feet away, there came a little squeal of surprise. Miss Bernice Doles, the niece and ward of the financier, jumped out and hurried to them. "What's Uncle Hiram frightened about?" she demanded.

"Nothing for you to worry about, Miss Doles," Shane replied, quickly. "He's received some sort of threat in a letter. He's always getting them. All wealthy and important men do. Probably from some crank."

"I don't want any trouble to come to Uncle Hiram, but a little excitement wouldn't be so bad," she said, smiling at him.

"And, if you need help, Mr. Shane, Stanley Wayne will be here in time for luncheon."

"Who's Wayne?"

"The present boy friend," Bernice replied, continuing her smile.

"I don't doubt he'd be a great help," Shane said. "If I need him, I'll call."

He bowed to her and followed Sampson into the house, along a hall, and to the door of the library. Sampson knocked.

"Who's there?" the voice of Hiram Doles asked.

"It is Mr. Shane, sir. He says that you sent for him."

"Anybody there except you and Shane?"

"Nobody at all, sir."

A key was turned and a bolt was shot. The door was opened for a space of six inches, and they could see the white face of Hiram Doles.

"It's all right!" said he. "Come in, Shane! I'm glad to see you!"

The detective slipped into the room, and Sampson sniffed and went back to his duties with his nose in the air. Hiram Doles locked the door again.

"This affair is terrible, Shane," he said. "Peters and I have just had a distressing experience. I know that I am in danger. It is something unusual—"

"What happened?" Shane asked.

"We were talking about this thing, and I was commenting on your arrival, when we heard a terrible, mocking laugh. It seemed to be right in this room."

"He laughs while he loots!" Peters quoted, in sepulchral tones.

"Who laughed?" Shane demanded.

"There's nobody in the library but us. But the laugh sounded only a few feet away. It was terrible. It seemed to say that this Rollicking Rogue was going to get at me, no matter what precautions I took."

"Nonsense! We'll go into that later," Shane said.

"There, on the table, is the letter I got from the fellow," Doles said.

"I got one myself, at my office this morning," Shane replied. "Let me take a look at this one. Um! Mine was a lot longer and explained in detail. Mr. Doles, I don't know all about your business, but what I want to know now is this—who might feel that he had a right to collect from you in this manner?"

"Good heavens, man, how should I know? I have had a long and successful career in the business world. No doubt, I have made enemies."

"This is something, according to his letter to me, that happened ten years ago. He wrote me, and he was damned sarcastic about it, that he's going after you and a flock of others who were associated with you in some shady deal. You're the first. And he double-dared me, knowing I work for you and your friends, to stop him. Get that? He dared me, Martin Shane, to catch him."

"You must protect me. Shane! It may be some maniac, and he might harm me."

"In the pocketbook—that's where he aims to harm you," Shane replied. "He's going to loot you and some of your friends, one at a time. Now, give me a line on him, if you can."

"Ten years ago?" Hiram Doles said. "I remember the market was very active about then. Some of us formed a big pool and were quite successful."

"And how many men and firms did you smash?" Shane wanted to know.

"Several went down in the crash, but that's business. Why would a man want to wait ten years—"

"Whoever he is, he's the son of some man you ruined. And because of it, he was set back in life, couldn't go to college except by working his way through, and all that. Says his mother died of a broken heart and his father wasted away after the crash. He had the nerve to tell me that he's been watching you for several years now, getting in close touch with you and your friends, learning all your little habits, and all that. He thinks that he's well prepared now to collect."

"Great heavens! But, what can he do? You'll protect me, won't you, Shane?"

"That's my business," the detective said.

"Why, he may be somebody quite close to me. That terrible laugh—"

"Probably is somebody you know well. But, on the other hand, it may not be. He may have written some of that stuff just to throw me off the right track. How about your servants?"

"Been with me for years. Haven't a man on the place with courage enough to be a crook."

"Any new ones?" Shane addressed this remark to Peters.

"Only an assistant gardener, sir," the secretary replied. "But he is an old man, much older than Mr. Doles."

"Miss Doles mentioned a new boy friend, Stanley Wayne, as I came in," Shane continued. "What about him?"

"He's a splendid young man, of a good family," Doles explained. "I hope they make a match of it."

"His family got money?"

"Not very much. His father and uncle wrecked the family fortune some time ago. Good heavens, Shane! It—it was about ten years ago, if I remember correctly."

"So? What sort of lad is this Stanley Wayne?"

"He's an athlete—made quite a record in college."

"And did he have to work his way through college?"

"I believe he did at first. His uncle died, and then his father, but they had saved something from the wreckage, and the boy had a better chance his last two years at school. He's a bond salesman now, and doing well."

"So? We'll keep our eyes on young Mr. Wayne," the detective decided. "Athlete, huh? Probably loves adventure and excitement, too. Just the type to try such a thing as this Rollicking Rogue stunt! Anybody else we can suspect?"

"I know of nobody," Doles said. "And I'm not suspecting Stanley Wayne. He's a splendid—"

"Hope you're right," Shane interrupted. "But, if this thing isn't a joke, if the Rollicking Rogue is a real person and is in earnest about collecting, remember this—he'd have to get near you to collect, wouldn't he?"

"How could he do that when I am so well guarded and you are here?"

"He'd have to be somebody who could get close to you without arousing suspicion—that's my meaning," the detective said. "And what have you around here that he could steal, that would make the risk worth while?"

"Why, the usual things—some valuable art objects, silver plate—"

"If he's real, the Rollicking Rogue is going after heavier stuff than that. What's in the safe?"

"Documents, papers, some old articles of jewelry, nothing very valuable—a little money."

"You're talking to one of your confidential men," Shane hinted.

"I—I've got a considerable sum in the safe just now—fifty thousand dollars."

"What? Fifty thousand dollars up here in the woods, in a tin safe in your country place? Why so much? Won't the store-keepers in the village give you credit?"

"I—I have a little deal on," Doles said.

"And it may possibly be a deal where checks wouldn't look pretty, so you pay off in cash! Is that it? None of my business, however. Fifty thousand dollars in the safe, eh? That might be enough to attract this Rollicking Rogue."

"But we can guard it, can't we, Shane?"

"We'll do our best, keep our eyes on everybody, suspect everybody. If this is to be a real stunt, I want to land the Rollicking Rogue while he's trying to pull off his first trick! Double-dare me to catch him, will he!"

It was at this instant that the telephone bell rang, and Peters hurried to answer the call. He was back from the little office room immediately.

"Call for you from the city, Mr. Shane," he reported.

Shane hurried into the other room and sat down before the desk. "Hello! This is Shane!"

"National Airport calling you, Mr. Shane. Did you get out to the Doles place all right?"

"Since you've 'phoned me here, and I'm talking back at you, I must have done so," the detective answered. "What's the trouble? Wasn't it a good plane, and isn't this Bill Tharn who flew me out a good pilot?"

"That's the point, Mr. Shane—he isn't one of our pilots at all."

"How's that?"

"He's a flyer, but hasn't been flying for us. He's been working on the ground, and has been pestering us to put him in the flying end of the game, but we judged he did not have enough experience yet. We are very careful about our flyers."

"But he flew me out here!" Shane protested.

"Yes. When you telephoned we got the ship ready. Tharn was in charge of the ground crew. One of our best pilots was preparing to take you to the Doles place. Tharn passed himself off on you as the pilot and got off the ground before we knew what was up. Tell him to get that ship back here at once. When you're ready to return, we'll send for you."

"I may tell him a flock of things," Shane promised.

He hurried back into the library. "Please ring for the butler," he instructed Peters.

While Peters carried out the order, and Hiram Doles merely stood aside and watched, Detective Martin Shane began pacing back and forth across the room. He was doing considerable thinking.

The Rollicking Rogue! A potential crook who would select a working name like that evidently had original ideas. He could

THE ROLLICKING ROGUE   199

be expected to mix humor with his more serious work. And would it not be rare humor indeed to steal an airplane and fly to the scene of a planned crime the detective who expected to catch him? Sampson appeared. "You go get that aviator," Shane instructed him. "I want him right in here!"

Doles nodded in confirmation of the order, and the butler went on his mission. Detective Shane paced the floor some more, evidently working himself into a proper state of rage for snappy questioning.

But suddenly that pacing stopped, and Doles gave a little cry of fear, and Peters turned quickly toward them, his eyes bulging again.

Once more that mysterious laugh!

Not low and mocking this time, but a ringing laugh of derision that rang through the room and seemed to fill it.

Revolver out and ready, Martin Shane sprang to the hall door and jerked it open. There was nobody in the hall. He darted across to the nearest window and looked out. The nearest person was an old gardener working a hundred yards away.

That laugh had not come from the veranda, he knew.

"You see, Shane?" Doles whimpered. "The thing is getting on my nerves."

"It is terrible—uncanny," Peters offered.

Shane whirled to confront them. "It's a trick of some sort," he declared. "Nothing terrible about a laugh. Nothing uncanny! It's a human being making that laugh, and nobody else. And little Martin Shane is going to get him!"

THE ROGUE IN PERSON

THE INTERVIEW WITH BILL THARN was stormy but amounted to little. He told a straightforward story. He admitted that the airport official had told the truth. He wanted to fly, and they would not let him, and he had seen an opportunity and grasped it. The worst he could get for it, he thought, was being fired from his job.

He was a good flyer if he did say it himself, and there was no sense, said he, in flying back the plane and letting somebody else fly out another to pick up Shane. The detective agreed with him. Shane said that he would telephone later and fix it with the airport officials.

He wanted to keep Bill Tharn under observation. If Tharn was indeed the Rollicking Rogue, Shane wanted to let him get to work and catch him at it. So he dismissed the man with the injunction to keep close at hand where he could be reached speedily if needed.

Luncheon was passed and the afternoon wore away without incident except that Stanley Wayne arrived, and proved to be a breezy young man of evident athletic prowess. Shane observed his from the near distance and decided not to scratch his name off the list of suspects. He was inclined to suspect everybody. If this thing was not a hoax of some sort, and the Rollicking Rogue made an attempt to rob Hiram Doles, Shane wanted to catch him and remove the menace as far as his other clients were concerned.

As evening approached the nervousness of Hiram Doles increased. Shane could not prevent the fear that had seized upon the man. Peters, never noted for being courageous, seemed on the verge of collapse. The three had dinner in the library, on the pretense that important business was being discussed.

Then Martin Shane touched match to cigar, leaned back in his chair, and revealed his plans.

"If this Rollicking Rogue thing is on the level, he is expected to make a visit to-day, which means before midnight," Shane said. "Little Marty Shane will be on the job. If he comes to collect, you can make a bet that he'll try to collect from the safe in the office room."

"Perhaps, if we removed what is in the safe, and hid it away somewhere—" Doles began.

"Better leave it right where it is, with the safe locked," Shane interrupted. "And you gents go to bed."

"You mean you want to stay here alone?" Doles asked.

"I'll be right here on the job, with my eyes and ears open and a revolver handy. I know how to use one, too."

"I couldn't sleep," Doles said.

"I'll handle this down here, Mr. Doles. You needn't be afraid. You've got a valet, so just keep him near you. It's a risk to have you here. I'd be worrying too much about protecting you, and couldn't concentrate on the job of catching the Rollicking Rogue. And I sure intend to catch him! I want to make him eat that letter he sent me."

"As far as I am concerned, I—I shall be glad to retire," Peters put in.

"You go right ahead, Peters," the detective told him. "You'd only be a nuisance around here."

Five minutes later, Detective Martin Shane was alone in the library. He closed and locked the hall door, and inspected the windows to be sure that all of them were fastened. He drew the heavy shades, placed a chair just outside the entrance to the office room, and sat down to smoke and watch. He had turned off all the lights except two, one in the office room and one near the hall door. The remainder of the big library was a place of grotesque shadows.

It was ten-thirty when Peters and his employer left the library and ascended to the upper floor of the house. On the veranda, Stanley Wayne was taking leave of Bernice Doles. Bill Tharn, the aviator, had made the acquaintance of one of the gardeners, and they were out near the airplane, smoking and gossiping.

Hiram Doles prepared for bed, and finally retired. He left the lights in the bedchamber burning. He had no intention of going to sleep. The dread of the unknown was upon him. He felt that this Rollicking Rogue thing was no hoax. Deeds of his past that might call for vengeance came to haunt him.

A conscience accused him when he thought of that pool ten years before. He and some of his close associates had walked on thin ice. They had wrecked firms and individuals, had barely escaped a criminal investigation.

It was quite plausible that this Rollicking Rogue might be the son of one of his victims, as he had intimated in his letter to Detective Martin Shane, and had waited and prepared for ten years to take his revenge. Doles sensed that the revenge would be all the more terrible for this waiting.

And now Hiram Doles found himself growing sleepy, and fought against falling into a slumber. He kept telling himself that he must remain alert, in case anything happened in the library downstairs.

He propped himself up with pillows and tried to calm his jumping nerves. But his eyes finally closed, his head dropped forward. He was too exhausted by a day of fear to remain awake. Hiram Doles slept deeply, heavily.

As though from a far distance, he soon heard a voice:

"Careful! Get awake! Don't move! Don't make a sound!"

Doles was conscious also of somebody touching him on the shoulder. He fought to get back to complete consciousness, to shake off the heavy sleep. He opened his eyes.

"If you are thoroughly awake now, we'll talk. I am the Rollicking Rogue!" Hiram Doles sat up straight in bed, blinked and looked closer. "What do you want? What are you going to do with me?"

A hand dropped over his mouth to prevent the scream of fear he would have given. He was thrust back upon the bed again.

"Not a sound, unless you want to die!" There was a menace in the voice now.

Hiram Doles closed his eyes, opened them again when he sensed that the other had stepped back from the bed. At first he thought that what he saw before him was some monster from another world, some grotesque being called up from his sleep-drugged brain. And then he realized the meaning of it.

"If you are thoroughly awake now, we'll talk. I am the Rollicking Rogue!"

Hiram Doles sat up straight in bed, blinked, looked closer.

That this was a human being before him, he did not doubt, a man disguised in queer dress. On the head was a close-fitting helmet of red. Eyes glittered through tiny slits in it. The mouth was exposed, a mouth that could twist in a wry grin or voice a ringing laugh. On the top were horns, of yellow.

And beneath this was a shimmering bright yellow costume that enveloped the body and made disguise perfect. Around the robe was a sash of brilliant red. Over the shoulders was a cape.

The voice of the Rollicking Rogue was cold and hard. There could be no mistaking the threat offered by an automatic pistol which covered Hiram Doles effectively.

"Get up! Get into some of your clothes!" the Rollicking Rogue ordered. "Quick!"

Hiram Doles crept from the bed and started to dress. The Rogue did not speak again, and the silence was more terrible to Doles than the cold voice he had heard. He was trembling, the cold perspiration was popping out on his face and hands.

"That'll do! Clothes enough! We are not going to leave the house, as far as I know," the Rollicking Rogue explained. "Sit down on the edge of the bed again, Doles!"

Doles complied with this order gladly. He felt too weak to stand. But his fear gave him courage enough to ask the all-important question:

"What do you want? What are you going to do with me?"

"I should shoot you down like a dog, Hiram Doles! Ten years ago, you and your friends, through shady business methods, ruined men and women, even children. You wrecked families. I belong to one of those families. The future which had been outlined for me was wrecked. My whole outlook on life was changed. So I decided that I would prepare, and I have spent years doing so. Now, I am going to collect, from you, from some of the others. My plans have been perfected."

"It—it was business—" Doles mouthed.

"The old excuse! I know your guilt, and so do you and your

associates, so we'll waste no time going into that. The day of reckoning has come for you. When you hear the laugh of the Rollicking Rogue, you will know that vengeance is at hand!"

"You—they'll catch you—put you in jail—" Hiram Doles muttered, looking up timidly at the intruder.

From the Rollicking Rogue came a soft laugh that bespoke utter contempt. Doles shivered. And then he cringed and half lifted his hands as though to ward off a blow, when he saw the automatic held by the Rollicking Rogue being slowly lifted, so that the muzzle of it covered his heart. The Rogue took a step forward.

"No—no!" It was not a cry Hiram Doles gave, for he was incapable of a scream of terror. It was only a feeble moan.

"Silence!" the Rollicking Rogue commanded. "You owe a debt, and you must pay! You boast that you are a businessman, and a good businessman always pays his debts. Books must be balanced!"

"What are you—going to do with me?" Doles panted.

"You'll discover that in a very short time, Doles. When I think of all the misery you have caused, I feel like making an end of you without further delay. But I am in the collecting business just now—not killing. And it will take more than one of your private detectives, more than all your servants, to prevent me!"

Again, Hiram Doles heard that soft, menacing laugh. It seemed to him that the Rogue's eyes flamed through the mask.

"Get up, Doles!" the Rollicking Rogue ordered. "You're coming along with me!"

CHAPTER IV

TRAPPED

HIRAM DOLES LURCHED TO his feet, staggered, reeled, almost fell sprawling. The expression in his countenance was one of abject fear. He seemed to have aged during the few minutes he had been in the presence of the Rollicking Rogue.

But he had a faint hope. He remembered that Detective Martin Shane was supposed to be in the library, that possibly some of the servants were still up. It seemed impossible that this Rollicking Rogue could handle the master of the house as he pleased, without running afoul of somebody who could handle him.

This hope was not strong enough to give Hiram Doles much courage, however. When the Rollicking Rogue gestured with the hand which held the gun, Doles went ahead of him into the sitting room of his suite. At the hall door, the Rogue listened for a moment, and then returned to Doles.

"Talk in whispers!" he ordered. "Do you know how many servants are still up?"

"No," Doles replied. "I—I was asleep for a time. I've heard nothing."

"What have you in your library safe?"

"Not much of value," Doles replied. "A few old jewelry trinklets, and papers and documents that would be of no value at all to you."

"Any more lies, and this little gun of mine will do its work!"

the Rollicking Rogue snapped. "How about that fifty thousand?"

"How—how did you know that?" Doles gasped.

"I make it my business to know a lot of things. I told you that I have spent years preparing for what I am going to do. That fifty thousand of yours, Hiram Doles, is to be my first collection. There'll be others, and larger ones, from you and your associates. One by one, you'll be visited by me, until I have acquired a certain amount. When I have that, the Rollicking Rogue will cease to exist as such."

"That's a lot of money—fifty thousand," Doles whimpered.

"You've stolen a hundred times that in your career. It is only my first collection from you. Some day I'll be back for another fifty thousand. Now, we'll go downstairs."

"Downstairs?" Doles gasped.

"To get that fifty thousand out of the safe. Precisely, Mr. Doles. Oh, I know your pet private detective is waiting there! But that does not alarm me much."

"There—may be shooting."

"That is possible. If there is, watch out for yourself. The first shot may strike you."

"Don't—don't!" Doles whimpered.

"Not much of a man when somebody else has the upper hand, are you, Doles? Very much so when you are in your own office bellowing at your clerks! I may be one of those clerks, for all you know. I may be a man you know socially. We'll go downstairs now. And let me say that every move of yours should be a careful one."

The Rollicking Rogue listened at the hall door for an instant again, and then pulled it open. He glanced out, motioned Doles into the hall.

"Straight to the front stairs and down them," the Rogue ordered.

"They'll see you—there'll be fighting—"

"From now on, don't speak except to answer my questions," the Rogue said, "I'm the general in this campaign, and all my plans have been made. Here we are! Down the stairs slowly, and without making the slightest noise."

Down the stairs they went, with Hiram Doles a couple of steps in the lead. As they approached the bottom, the Rollicking Rogue stopped him, went ahead, scrutinized the living room and the long hall.

"Come ahead!" he whispered.

Now he directed Hiram Doles along the hall and toward the door of the library. But they did not go quite that far. Off the hall was a small room with portieres hanging across the entrance. The Rollicking Rogue thrust Doles through the door, gripped him by the arm, and dropped the portières into place.

"You are about to make a couple of wild calls for help, but not until I tell you to do so," the Rogue said. "And when you do call, be frightened about it. Put yourself into it, if you can catch my meaning. I want a call for help that will sound like the real thing. Wait a moment!"

Doles could feel the muzzle of the Rogue's automatic pressing against his side. And suddenly he felt it removed, there came a roar and a flash of flame, a cloud of pungent smoke. The Rogue had fired a shot into the floor.

"Yell!" he commanded, gripping Hiram Doles by the arm again.

Hiram Doles did not need the command. He had yelled already. The unexpected shot in that little room had been the last thing needed to wreck his nerves completely.

"Help! Help!" he shrieked. "Oh, help!"

"That's enough!" the Rollicking Rogue hissed in his ear. "Not another sound!"

Somewhere a door slammed. Pounding feet struck the stairs. Along the hallway came another who dashed madly toward the front of the house. The Rollicking Rogue peered through the portieres. A form flashed past the doorway.

"They've gone upstairs," the Rogue whispered. "Come along, now, and show us some speed, Doles. I want to get under cover."

He grasped his man by the arm again and hustled him into the hall and down it. The door of the library was standing wide open. That shot, those wild cries for help had brought instant action on the part of Detective Martin Shane. But Shane had made the very move the Rollicking Rogue had expected him to make, and which he most desired. He had deserted his post in the library, and now the Rollicking Rogue could get inside with Hiram Doles.

They darted through the door, and the Rogue closed the door, locked it, and shot a bolt into place. He whirled to Hiram Doles again. The Rogue seemed to have changed character in a measure. He had dropped his whimsical manner. He was all speed now, all earnestness, and Doles sensed it.

"To your safe—quick!" the Rogue ordered.

He rushed Doles down the length of the big library and into the little office room.

"Stop shaking like a leaf in the wind!" the Rogue hissed at him. "We've got business here! Work that combination and open the safe. Be quick about it! You'd better have a steady hand. If you don't work the combination right the first time—"

But Hiram Doles was kneeling in front of the safe already. His trembling hand went out to the combination knob. He brushed the other hand across his eyes, as though he scarcely could see and wished to clear his sight.

"Show me a little speed!" the Rollicking Rogue ordered. "I haven't any time to spare. They'll be after me in a moment. And, if they catch me, you're going to be the principal actor in a big funeral!"

"Please—please! I'm trying to hurry," Doles begged.

The Rollicking Rogue could hear persons rushing around the upper part of the house, men calling to one another. The servants had been aroused, he supposed. Detective Martin Shane was bellowing questions and orders. Somebody outside the house called to learn the trouble. That would be the night watchman, the Rogue supposed, or perhaps Bill Tharn, the aviator.

Hiram Doles pulled the door of the safe open.

"Get out that fifty thousand, and be quick about it!" the Rollicking Rogue said. "That's what I want—the first install-ment of what I am going to collect. After I attend to the others in your band of select thieves, I may return and give you another visit."

Doles had opened a drawer, and was getting out the cur-rency. There were two bundles of it. The Rogue reached over Doles' shoulder and snatched the bundles away. He stepped back a few feet and stuffed the money beneath his costume.

"The first installment!" he repeated. "I could almost shoot you down like a mad dog, Doles, when I remember how much this would have meant to certain persons ten years ago."

"Please—please!" Doles begged.

"Don't like to have it brought to your memory, eh? I don't blame you. Come along with me now! If we run into trouble, you're going to act as a body shield. So I hope, for your sake, that your pet detective isn't nervous when he handles a gun!"

He grasped Doles by an arm again, and started back through the library. They could hear persons rushing around the house, on both the upper and lower floors. The entire household was awake, searching frantically for Hiram Doles, seeking to learn where that shot had been fired, from whence had come those wild cries for help.

It was Sampson, the butler, who discovered where the shot had been fired, though the Rollicking Rogue never knew that. Sampson had looked into the little room off the hall, and had caught the odor of dead gunfire smoke. He called Shane.

They snapped on the lights.

"No blood, no sign of struggle," Shane said, quickly. "But here's the bullet hole in the floor. That shot was fired in here, all right!"

"But who fired it, and what has become of Mr. Doles?" the butler asked.

"That's what we're trying to find out, ass!" Shane snapped at him. "Ah—!"

Shane had glanced down the hall, and noticed that the door of the library was closed. And he knew that he had left it open when he had dashed out in answer to the alarm.

A horrible fear came to him—that he had made a serious blunder. He had deserted his post. He had left the safe and its burden of fifty thousand dollars unprotected.

Detective Martin Shane, revolver held ready for instant use, dashed madly down the hall with the butler at his heels. He reached out, tried the door, found it locked. His fear became a certainty now.

And so the Rollicking Rogue, rushing across the library with Hiram Doles, heard somebody pound suddenly upon the door, and heard the voice of Martin Shane:

"Open up in there! Be quick about it!"

CHAPTER V

INTO THE OPEN

THE ROLLICKING ROGUE STOPPED abruptly in his mad rush, brought Hiram Doles to a stop also. The pounding on the door continued.

"Open up, or we'll break in!" Shane howled. "Be quick about it! Who's in there?"

The Rogue whispered to Doles. "Is that your detective friend?"

"Yes."

"Call to him and tell him that you're all right."

The voice of Hiram Doles was thin and quavering as he called:

"I'm all right, Shane," he said.

"Then open the door! How'd you get in there? Anybody with you?" the detective howled.

"I—I'm all right!"

"Somebody's there and making you talk like that. Open the door, or we'll smash it down!"

The Rollicking Rogue could tell by the sounds he heard that Shane had assistance now. At least two more men were with him. And the Rogue did not doubt that he would call for more. To open that door, even with Hiram Doles as a body shield, might prove disastrous. He did not care to face such overwhelming odds at the outset of his career,

He made his decision quickly. He whispered into Doles' ear

again. "Do as I tell you!" he ended.

Once more the quavering voice of Doles was heard by those in the hall.

"The Rollicking Rogue is in here with me! He's robbed the safe!" he cried.

And the Rogue threw back his head and laughed—that taunting, derisive laugh that stung. Outside in the hall, they heard, and Detective Martin Shane gave a howl of rage. A body crashed against the door.

The Rollicking Rogue grasped Doles by the arm again and hurried him back into the office room. He snapped off the lights there, cautiously peered from behind a shade. There was nobody in sight on the moonlight-drenched lawn. And there were shadows cast by clumps of shrubs.

The Rollicking Rogue raised the window slowly and carefully, making scarcely any sound about it. Now those in the hall were pounding on the door, and the Rogue knew it would not withstand that onslaught long.

"Through that window with you, and be quiet about it!" the Rogue snapped at Hiram Doles.

He almost tossed the financier through, and Doles tumbled on the lawn. The Rogue was beside him instantly. He urged him on, darting from shadow to shadow and trying to get away from the house. Doles employed a night watchman, but the Rogue guessed he had gone to the assistance of Shane. But there were grooms, chauffeurs, gardeners who probably had been attracted by the din. They might be stumbled upon at any time.

"What are you going to do with me?" Doles was whimpering. "You've got the money. Let me go! I can't stand this. My—my heart is weak."

"Nobody ever granted that you have a heart," the Rollicking Rogue told him. "Come along!"

They had managed to get a hundred feet or so from the side of the house. But the hall door had been broken down, and Shane and the butler and night watchman had sprawled into the library to find it empty. Weapons held ready, they had dashed to the office room—and that open window told a story to Shane.

"Here's where they went out," he cried. "There goes somebody running across the lawn. Out and after them!"

There was no necessity for having a guard in the office now. Shane had caught a glimpse of the open safe, the open strong-box, and he knew that the Rollicking Rogue, whoever he was, had got what he had come to get.

Shane was a conscientious worker for his employers. He did not want this stain on his record. He had been decoyed from the safe by a ruse, and a robbery had occurred almost under his nose, so to speak.

Mingled determination and rage drove Martin Shane on. He threw up his gun and fired.

"Halt, there!" he cried.

At the orders of the Rollicking Rogue, the voice of Hiram Doles drifted back to Shane and the others:

"Don't shoot! You may hit me! This is Doles—don't shoot!"

"The cur is using Doles for a shield," Shane explained to the others. "Don't shoot, until we can see what we are doing—but keep after them."

But the Rollicking Rogue had no need to be afraid to shoot. His weapon spat flame and lead, and a bullet sang past the heads of his pursuers, uncomfortable close. They darted for cover.

"Scatter!" Shane ordered. "Don't bunch up! Right after them!"

Back to them came that mocking laugh, that taunting laugh that was enough to make a man's blood boil with rage. The Rogue fired again, purposely sending a wild shot meant to deter pursuit than to wound or kill.

Then he grasped the panting, almost exhausted Hiram Doles by the arm again and rushed him on. Doles stumbled, fell asprawl. The Rollicking Rogue yanked him to his feet.

"No tricks!" he warned. "Don't stumble again, to slow us up.

If I've got to make a stand, I'll shoot to kill!"

"I—I can't run any more."

"A man never knows how much he can run until he has to do it. Come along!"

For an instant they were out in the bright moonlight, the Rollicking Rogue and his prisoner, but those behind did not dare fire. The Rogue was keeping Hiram Doles close beside him. And now, in the darkness again, he hurled Doles from him, and ran on alone.

And he ran back toward the house.

Shane and his two men reached Doles, found that he had been abandoned, and while the butler remained to assist him, Shane and the night watchman rushed on. And now they emptied their guns at the flying, grotesque figure ahead of them, but the Rollicking Rogue did not do them the courtesy of replying to their fire. He was dodging from shadow to shadow, changing course often, making an elusive target for those behind.

Ahead of him loomed one of the gardeners. The Rollicking Rogue fired, and the man fell prone. The Rogue ran on. He knew he had not struck the gardener, and assumed the man had dropped because he had no weapon.

He was nearing the house now, and caution returned to him. He made straight for the window through which he had escaped from the office room. He had gained considerable distance on those who pursued.

Getting through the window was the work of only a moment. There was nobody in the office, nor in the library. The library door had been broken down.

The Rogue snapped off all the lights and darted across to the wrecked door. Nobody in the hall. He could hear somebody talking on the upper floor, and judged that they were in the hall. Like a shadow, he darted to the little room where he had fired the shot into the floor. The portières swayed as he disappeared.

CHAPTER VI

THE TAUNTING LAUGH

"**NOW WE'VE GOT HIM!**" Detective Martin Shane said, about ten minutes later. "We saw him get into the house. I've got men watching outside, to get him if he tries to get out again. And there are plenty of us to search this house from the roof down to the cellar. We'll get him! And when I lay my hands on him—"

Shane was standing in the living room as he spoke. Hiram Doles, panting and exhausted and the perfect picture of a physical wreck, had dropped into an easy chair.

And as Detective Shane concluded his little speech, they all heard it again—that taunting laugh of the Rollicking Rogue.

Shane's face turned purple. "Hear that?" he cried. "He's here! Playing a fancy game! Now, we'll get him! Mr. Doles will reward the first man to put hands on him. You know how he's dressed, unless he's managed to get rid of that costume."

He stopped speaking as another man came into the room. "Who are you?" he demanded.

"My name is Stanley Wayne."

"Yeah? What are you doing around here?"

"I was motoring by, and heard the shooting and noise. I'm a friend of Miss Doles, and wondered if something was happening, and whether I could be of assistance."

Stanley Wayne! The man Shane had suspected earlier in the day merely on what Doles had told him about Wayne's family history.

"Weren't you around here earlier in the night?" Shane asked.

"I was calling on Miss Doles. But what's the trouble? And who are you?" Wayne asked. He did not relish Shane's manner, evidently.

"I'm a detective. Mr. Doles' safe has been robbed. And we almost had the man who did it, and I think we're going to put our hands on him mighty quick. What time did you leave here?"

"Around ten-thirty, I believe. Am I under suspicion for something? I could use a little extra money myself, but I'd scarcely rob a safe to get it— and especially the uncle of my fiancé."

"What's that?" Doles cried.

"Yes, sir. Bernice and I came to an understanding this evening, sir."

"My boy, I'm glad! I certainly am—"

"Just a moment!" Shane interrupted. "We're not worrying any just now about people getting engaged and married. You've lost fifty thousand dollars, Mr. Doles, and I am trying to get it for you, and get the man who took it. Now, Wayne, how did you happen to return, and just when did you return?"

"I motored home from here when I said. I was rather elated because of my engagement, and did not go to bed. I pranced around my room for a time and then tried to settle down to read."

"And I suppose you got an idea to come back and see if the Doles residence was still here, and maybe throw rocks at the young lady's window," Shane suggested, sarcastically.

"I rather resent your attitude." Stanley Wayne told him.

"Isn't that too bad! I'm investigating a crime here."

"Go right ahead and investigate it. That's your business. I had nothing to do with it, I assure you. Continuing my story, let me say that I belong to the country club. A friend telephoned me a short time ago and wanted me to run over. A couple of the boys got a little wild and had a fight, and I'm sort of official peacemaker for our crowd."

"Of course, I can check up on all that," Shane said.

"Are you trying to call me a liar?"

Wayne cried at him, his face suddenly pale. "Step out on the lawn and we'll decide the thing."

"I've got something better to do than run around fighting college boys," the detective remarked.

He found, at that instant, a beautiful little fury in an ornate dressing gown standing before him, her eyes blazing. Miss Bernice Doles had overheard.

"How dare you?" she cried at Shane. "I shall have my uncle dismiss you from his service! How dare you think, for an instant, that Stanley could have anything to do with this miserable affair? You'd spend your time better trying to find the real criminal!"

Martin Shane did not know what to do, exactly, in the face of this. He had seen plenty of angry women in his career, but this was something different, this fine girl of excellent family defending the man she expected to marry.

"Just duty," Shane muttered. "We have to question everybody, you know. He went away, and he came back. It's possible he returned and played the part of the Rollicking Rogue, giving his nasty laughs and—"

The expression on Shane's face changed swiftly. Once more they heard the taunting laugh of the Rollicking Rogue, as though from a distance.

"That settles it! I apologize to you, Mr. Wayne," the detective said. "There's his laugh! Where is he? Search the house as I directed! Find him! I'll be in the library—want to have a look around the safe. He may have got careless and left a clue."

CHAPTER VII

WHAT HAPPENED TO SHANE

THEY SCATTERED AS SHANE had directed earlier, and Shane himself went down the hall to library. Stanley Wayne remained in the big living room with Doles and Bernice.

Since there were men on guard outside, the search was to start on the upper floor. Those designated hurried up the stairs, the butler leading the way to point out the nooks and corners of the house, any place where a man might be hiding.

Detective Martin Shane disappeared into the library, turned on all the lights again, and commenced his investigation there. He examined the rugs to see whether anything had been dropped by the intruder, and with no success. The highly-polished furniture could be examined for fingerprints later. But Shane had hope that it would not be necessary. The Rollicking Rogue was in the house, and probably would be caught, wearing his grotesque costume.

Shane went on into the little office room and inspected the desk. Evidently, nothing on it had been disturbed, nor were any of the drawers open. It was as the careful Peters, the almost perfect secretary, had left it.

Shane examined the rugs, and found no clue, and then he knelt in front of the safe. Some documents and papers had been spilled on the floor in front of it, but Shane guessed rightly that the highly nervous Hiram Doles had knocked them there.

He did find something, however—a tiny yellow tassel which,

it appeared, had caught on the corner of the safe door and been torn from some costume. A part of the costume of the Rollicking Rogue, undoubtedly. Shane put it into his pocket and began examining the rug in front of the safe again.

"I'll take that tassel, if you have no objections!"

The voice was almost in Shane's ear. He gasped his surprise and struggled to get to his feet. But a hand pressed him down again, and he felt, just behind his left ear, something that he knew to be the muzzle of a gun.

"Careful!" the voice warned. "I'd hate to remove an ornament to the detective service. Now get up slowly and sit in the desk chair, and put your hands flat on the desk in front of you. Let me warn you that I know all the tricks, and if you try one—oh, well! You probably know the answer."

The voice was sarcastic enough, but Martin Shane heard, as he started to get up, that nasty little laugh. The Rollicking Rogue! Here at his hand! He got up slowly, turned, dropped into the chair and put his hands on the desk as directed. Shane was in no hurry for a clash. He wanted to study his man.

The Rollicking Rogue had stepped back a few feet on the opposite side of the desk. Shane saw him well now—that shimmering yellow costume, the tight-fitting red hood that enveloped the head and left only two eyes glittering through slits and a mouth that curved in a sardonic grin. Shane knew that the lips had been made up, probably with a lipstick, to change their natural curve. It was a dark shade of red, too, almost running to a blue.

"The Rollicking Rogue, eh?" Shane said, "And how long do you think you're going to be rollicking around robbing people's safes?"

"Who knows? I didn't have much trouble to-night, did I?"

Shane's face purpled with wrath. "I'll be even with you before we're done," he said. "I've met you smart crooks before. Like the well-known sky rocket they start out in a blaze of glory and come down like a stick!"

"So I've heard," said the Rollicking Rogue. "I ran a little risk and hung around to give you a tip."

"Thanks!" Shane could be sarcastic himself. "What's the tip?"

"My next little affair, I thought possibly you'd like to know, will be concerned with a well-known financier of the shady variety."

"Maybe you'd like to give me his name and address?" Shane said.

"Surely! His name is Addison Swart. You know the address."

"I do, yes," Shane replied. "One thing more, my interesting young friend—"

"You don't know whether I'm young or not," the Rogue interrupted.

"All right! We'll let that pass for the moment. What I want to know is this—have you got the nerve to tell me just when you are going to call on Mr. Addison Swart?"

"Certainly! I'll be glad to meet you there, too. Let us say a week from Tuesday, sometime between the hours of eight and twelve in the evening. I'll drop Mr. Swart a note and try to make the engagement for us. Of course, if he gets frightened and runs out of town, we'll have to postpone the party."

"He'll be in town," Shane promised. "And I'll be at the party. But you may not be able to keep the engagement yourself. You may be in jail. You're not out of the Doles house yet, you know."

"Possibly I'll be soon."

"You have been so very much interested in baiting me, you Rollicking Rogue, that you've grown careless. A couple of very good friends of mine have approached you from behind. I believe one of them has a revolver trained on your back."

The Rollicking Rogue laughed again. "What a poor liar!" he said. "One of the oldest tricks in the world—to get me to turn so you can whip out a gun and have the advantage."

"You'll know in about two seconds."

"Stop clowning!" said the Rollicking Rogue. "There is a small

The Rogue jabbed the muzzle of his gun
into the detective's back. "I mean business!
Don't take a chance, Shane!" The other wrist
went back, and the handcuff was snapped.
Detective Martin Shane was wearing his own
handcuffs, with his wrists behind his back.

mirror on that wall, over the safe, and I can see what's going on at my back. That's why I am standing just here. I told you, my dear Mr. Shane, that I knew all the tricks!"

"If it takes me ten years, I'll get you!"

"Kindly keep down your voice, or I'll be compelled to silence you," the Rogue warned. "I do not care to have you attract your friends. And now, please, stand up and face the wall and lift your hands high—very high—in the air!"

Detective Martin Shane knew when he was at a disadvantage. Not knowing the identity of the Rollicking Rogue, he could not guess whether he might shoot or not. And Shane felt that the man would be caught when he tried to leave the house.

He got up and faced the wall, and lifted his hands high above his head, and the Rollicking Rogue deftly removed his gun. Stepping back, he broke the weapon, took out the cartridges, and tossed them through the open window.

"Put your hands behind your back, my dear Mr. Shane," the Rogue told him. "I am merely going to tie your wrists together. Ah, I have an idea! I was going to tie them with the cords which were around the two bundles of currency I got from Doles' safe. That would have been a deft touch. But I think I know even a better one. Stand perfectly still, please."

As he finished speaking, the Rogue acted, and in that instant Detective Martin Shane knew what he intended doing. He realized that he was to be made a laughing-stock for his friends and enemies, that ignominy had descended upon him. For the Rollicking Rogue had taken Shane's handcuffs from his hip pocket, and already had one wrist imprisoned.

"If you do this—" Shane threatened.

The Rogue jabbed the muzzle of his gun into Shane's back, and the bantering quality had left his voice when he spoke again: "I mean business! Don't take a chance, Shane!"

The other wrist went back, the handcuff was snapped. Detective Martin Shane was wearing his own handcuffs, with his wrists behind his back.

"And now what?" Shane demanded. "You're not out of this yet, Rogue! You can't handle all the men scattered around the place."

"Pardon me if I do not expose my plans at the moment," came the reply, the voice a bantering one again.

They were standing only about three feet from each other now, under the bright light, and Shane was watching that leering mouth. He thought that he might know it again.

The Rogue backed to the door and glanced out into the library, to find that there was nobody there. Upstairs the search of the house was being conducted. And suddenly the Rogue laughed, and turned and ran. Shane began bellowing for help.

Into the hall dashed the Rogue, and once more he disappeared through the swaying portières.

CHAPTER VIII

THE GUILTY MAN

HOWLING FOR HELP, SHANE attracted the attention of some of the men, and they came running to release him and allow him to dash violently into the hall, shouting for everybody to come to him.

In a few words he told of his experience with the Rogue.

"Line up everybody!" he cried. "We know he hasn't left the house! Everybody get here in the living room—quick! I want to take a look at some of you!"

It had occurred to Shane that he had rather neglected one person during all the excitement, and that person was Bill Tharn, the aviator. He remembered, now, that he had a reason for suspecting Tharn. The latter was supposed to be somewhere in the house, aiding in the search.

Tharn appeared with the others, and the eyes of Detective Shane glowed strangely when he regarded the aviator.

"Where have you been?" Shane demanded.

"Lookin' around for that guy with the trick suit on."

"With whom?"

"Well, I been alone the last half hour or so. I was goin' through some rooms upstairs, pokin' into closets."

"So nobody's seen you the last half hour, huh?" Shane said. "Ever use a lipstick?"

"You want me to paste you one?" Tharn cried.

"Let me tell you something. This Rollicking Rogue had his

lips made up, to change their lines. With a lipstick, I suppose. And what is that stuff on the corner of your mouth?" Shane demanded, bending forward. "Maybe you got out of that costume mighty quick, but you were careless cleaning off your lips!"

There was a moment of silence, and then Bill Tharn grinned.

"You're some dick," he declared. "I take off my hat to you. That Sherlock Holmes guy was an amateur. It just happens that I made a hit with the cook, waitin' around here for you to get ready to fly back to town, and I got me a big sledge of blueberry pie. Examine them lips well, you bozo!"

Shane almost choked. Somebody chuckled. And from the far distance there came, just once more, and for the last time that night, the taunting laugh of the Rollicking Rogue. It seemed to fade away and die in the distance, as though he meant he was leaving them in disgust.

"Go on searchin' this house!" Shane bellowed. "We've got to get him! He's in the house, all right! The men watchin' outside would have seen him if he'd gone out!"

They scattered again, and Martin Shane whirled around and bumped into another person.

"Get out of the way, Peters, you sleepy cuss!" he cried. "Where have you been, anyhow?"

"I—well, sir, I've been hiding in my room," Peters admitted. "I heard shooting and shouting—"

"Had your head under a pillow, I suppose. Peters, you're a total loss, except as a bookkeeper and secretary! Oh, well, a man can't be everything!"

Peters stepped back in a manner apologetic as Shane brushed past him. Peters allowed himself a faint smile. Peters knew where the costume of the Rollicking Rogue was hidden beneath a loose board in a certain room, and that fifty thousand in currency was hidden there also.

And Peters, who had troubles to avenge and had prepared for years to avenge them, was an expert ventriloquist, and could toss queer laughs around whenever it pleased him to do so.

II

THE ROLLICKING
ROGUE'S SECOND DEAL

CHAPTER I

THE SECOND SAFE

IN THE LAVISHLY-FURNISHED LIVING room of his elaborate apartment on the twelfth and top floor of the exclusive West-manor Arms, Mr. Addison Swart paced nervously back and forth from corner to corner. He was gesturing grandly, and delivering himself of sonorous words and high-sounding phrases.

Addison Swart was that sort of man—sonorous and high-sounding. In the offices of the important brokerage company of which he was the head, his clerks, stenographers and file girls quailed and shook before the menace of his stentorian tones. Like many other men, Addison Swart attempted to cover his shortcomings with pomposity and his lack of courage with loud talk.

But in his voice to-night there was an element of fear also. Addison Swart evidently was trying to convince himself that there was nothing of which to be afraid, trying to tell himself that here, in the seclusion of his own apartment, nobody could do him harm.

On this particular occasion, his audience consisted only of Detective Martin Shane, a private operative who served Mr. Swart and certain other financiers associated with him, the majority of whom were known to be ruthless and unscrupulous in their business lives.

Martin Shane sprawled on one of Addison Swart's expensive divans and puffed languidly on one of Addison Swart's expen-

sive imported cigars. It was a part of Shane's job to listen with
pretended interest and respect whenever one of his employers
blew off steam. He endured it because the pay was good and
the work generally light.

"It's ridiculous!" Addison Swart was saying, waving his arms
in eloquent gesture as he spoke. "It's ridiculous on the face of
it!"

"But it's a thing that's got to be considered carefully," Shane
told him.

"Ridiculous, I tell you! How could the fellow manage to get
into this apartment and rob me?"

"We're hoping that he can't," Shane replied. "I'm hoping that
he tries it! If I ever get my hands on him, there'll be one nuisance
less running around. But we'll take no chances. We'll be on
guard and ready for him."

"He'd never get past the desk downstairs, or up in the elevator. They are very particular about strangers in this building."

"He might manage to sneak in some way," Shane said.

"If he did, he couldn't get into this apartment either at the
front or the service door, for they've both been fitted with special
locks. And, even if he did get in here, he couldn't find my
safe—or make me open it for him. Moreover, Shane, *you* are
here!"

Detective Martin Shane removed the cigar from his mouth
and bowed slightly in acknowledgment of the compliment. He
was hoping that Addison Swart would get to the end of his
speech so that he, Martin Shane, could get down to business.
The time was growing short.

"He's only some wild crank, and the world is filled with
them," Swart continued, waving his arms again to give emphasis to his words. "He's trying to scare us."

"Oh, we'll nab him if he shows up around here!" Shane said,
confidentially. "But we don't want to be careless. Remember, he
robbed your friend, Hiram Doles, of a young fortune."

"Yes, out at Doles' country place, where there was not much

protection, where there are a hundred windows and half as many doors offering ways of escape, and acres of woods in which a man could hide. It's different here."

"Nevertheless, we'd better take some precautions, Mr. Swart. It'd be foolish not to do so."

"Certainly! We must take precautions. But I think that it's all nonsense! I don't believe the fellow will have the nerve to attempt it."

"Well, he's threatened to attempt it to-night between the hours of eight and twelve."

"And it is almost eight o'clock now," Addison Swart observed. "Confound it! This thing had wrecked my whole evening. I intended to witness a billiard match at the club. And here I am at home, prancing around like an ass and waiting for some fellow to come and try to rob me. Ridiculous!"

"You sent your daughter away?" Shane asked.

"Yes. I sent Molly away for the evening, as you suggested."

"I thought it best," Shane said. "No sense in frightening the young lady."

"You don't know her. Molly isn't so easily frightened," her father declared. "However, I sent her away. If she's suspicious that there's something unusual going on, she may come popping back at any moment."

"How about this Santiago, your Filipino house boy?"

"I didn't tell him anything about it. He's a good house boy, and if he knew about this he might get scared and walk out on me. And all because some nitwit who calls himself a fancy name goes around robbing people! I'd like to get my hands on him!"

"So would I!" Martin Shane said, in a burst of sincerity. "He made a fool of me out at the Doles place, and I want to get square for that. I'll get him this time, if he shows up. Made the mistake of underestimating him before. Didn't believe then was any such person. But this time—!"

"And that confounded card he had the nerve to send me through the mail!" Swart exploded. "It's almost insulting. Look at the thing, Shane!"

Detective Martin Shane accepted the card and looked at it, though he had done so half a dozen times already. It was quite an ordinary card, poorly printed, evidently the work of an amateur with a little hand press. It read:

THE ROLLICKING ROGUE
"He Laughs While He Loots!"
Will Call on You Tuesday Evening
Between Eight and Midnight.

Martin Shane chewed savagely at his cigar as though trying to work off a fit of rage. He turned the card over and read what had been written on the other side of it with a pen, the hand-writing obviously disguised:

Your sins have been found out! You must pay!
I am coming to collect!

Shane handed the card back to Addison Swart and lighted his cigar afresh.

"Speaking of collecting, Mr. Swart," the detective said, "just what could he collect?"

"How's that?"

"What have you in this apartment that might interest the Rollicking Rogue, and repay him for his time and trouble?"

"How do I know what the fellow might fancy?" Addison Swart asked. "There are a lot of things of value in the apartment."

"You mentioned a safe."

"A safe! Yes, I have a safe. Come along with me, Shane, and I'll show you something."

Addison Swart led the way through a short hall and to the library of the apartment. It was quite a large room for an apartment house. There were quantities of books in it, and a few good pictures. At one end of the room, beyond a curtained archway, was a smaller room which had been fitted up as a sort of glorified office.

Addison Swart crossed the library and pressed his hand against a certain panel in the wainscoting. The panel immediately slipped back.

"There's the safe," he pointed out.

"And what's in it?" Martin Shane wanted to know. "Anything that might attract the Rollicking Rogue? What do I have to guard?"

"What's in this safe? There are a few bonds of small denomination, but they're the sort a thief couldn't sell. Perhaps a couple of hundred in money, too. And some old pieces of jewelry that wouldn't bring much."

"And that's all he could hope to get out of the safe?" Shane asked.

"That's all."

"That wouldn't attract the Rollicking Rogue, if I've got him estimated right," Shane declared. "Isn't there anything else?"

Addison Swart grinned. "That's my little joke," he declared. "A burglar, a robber, a hold-up man, even this marvelous Rollicking Rogue who robbed that ass of a Hiram Doles—they might compel me to open that safe. With a gun pointed at me, no doubt I'd do so. They'd get that small amount of money, that old jewelry if they were silly enough to carry it away—and that'd be all. They'd miss the big haul."

"How's that?" Shane asked.

"The real stuff is in another safe. I've got a second safe in the apartment."

CHAPTER II

THE GRIP OF FEAR

MARTIN SHANE'S FACE BETRAYED his astonishment. "What?" he exclaimed.

"Watch me!" Addison Swart pressed his hand against another panel of the wainscoting, and it slipped back noiselessly. The front of a second safe was exposed, a wall safe of the latest pattern. Martin Shane knew the make of that safe at a glance. It was small, but almost burglar-proof. No cracksman could get into it without hours of work.

"What's the idea?" Shane asked.

"In here we have the real valuables," Addison Swart explained. "A criminal never would get to that. When he looted the first safe, he'd think that was all—that he'd dropped in on a bad night when I didn't happen to have much in it. He'd never suspect there was a second safe."

"That's not a bad idea," Martin Shane admitted. "You've got something valuable in this one?"

Addison Swart's eyes sparkled. "Jewels worth about fifty thousand dollars on the market," he admitted.

"What?" Shane exclaimed. "Pardon me for asking, Mr. Swart, but why do you keep such a fortune in jewels here in your apartment?"

"They're as well protected in that safe as they'd be anywhere else. I had a safe deposit box robbed once," Swart replied. "But that isn't the real reason. Shane, I'm a gem fiend. Most of those jewels are loose, unset. I like to get them out and roll them around the table, and watch them sparkle, play with them like a boy with marbles."

"Better close that panel," Shane suggested. "No sense in taking chances."

"But nobody could open that safe without the combination," Addison Swart declared, "and I'm the only person who has that. Ah, that reminds me!" He raised his voice and called: "Peters!" he snapped.

From the alcove at the end of the library there shuffled a man whose watery eyes blinked at them from behind thick spectacles. He was tall, thin, stoop-shouldered, and rather sickly-looking.

"You know Peters, don't you, Shane?" Addison Swart asked. "He's Hiram Doles' confidential secretary."

"Sure, I know him!" Shane replied. "Howdy, Peters! What are you doing here? Change jobs?"

"I borrowed him from Doles for a few hours, to make an audit of some of my books and compare them with Doles'," Swart explained. "We're in a little business deal together. Peters is the best auditor in six states. I had a couple of ledgers I didn't want my regular office force pawing over."

"I understand," Shane said.

"Pardon me a moment, Shane. Peters, come here!" Swart ordered. "You stand right here by this safe. I've got a bundle of negotiable bonds in here, and I'll give them to you now to check over. When you've made your notes about them, I'll put them back."

"You'd better let that go until later, Mr. Swart," Martin Shane suggested. "Suppose the Rollicking Rogue walked into the room while the safe was open?"

His words seemed to have an instant, terrifying effect on James Peters.

"What is that, Mr. Shane?" Peters cried. "Did you say the Rollicking Rogue, sir? Do you mean that he—" He ceased speaking, and seemed to be tongue-tied with fear.

"Don't collapse!" Shane said, with withering sarcasm. "You may be strong in the brains line, Peters, but you're pretty weak in courage."

"But, sir, when he robbed Mr. Doles, I was there—and it was terrible! I—I am frightened, sir!"

"We can see that," Shane replied, dryly.

"Do you mean that the Rollicking Rogue is coming here, sir?" Peters asked.

"He's threatened to come here between eight and midnight and rob Mr. Swart," Shane replied. He liked to see Peters squirm.

"Then I—I wish to go away, sir, immediately," Peters said. "Some other time, Mr. Swart, I'll be pleased to finish auditing your books."

Addison Swart whirled toward him. "Peters, I want those books finished this evening—got a certain reason for it," he said. "Mr. Doles will be angry if you don't help me out. It won't take you much longer. No nonsense, now! Stand there and take the bonds when I open the safe."

Deaf to the protests of Martin Shane, Swart worked the combination while Peters stood behind him, and pulled the door of the safe open. He removed a package of bonds and handed it to Peters.

"Hurry and check them, and then we'll put them back," Swart said. "Stop your shaking, Peters! You're not the man the Rollicking Rogue has threatened to rob."

Peters took the bonds and retired swiftly to the alcove with them. His manner was that of a man fleeing from a scene of danger.

"You'd better shut the door of that safe and give the combination knob a whirl," Martin Shane told Swart. "Close that panel, too. If the Rollicking Rogue happened to come into this room now, he'd learn the secret of that second safe."

"Shane, you pain and surprise me!" Swart declared. "How could the fellow get in here? The idea is ridiculous, as I said.

You'll see! He'll give it up as a bad job. Unless he invades this apartment house with a gang—"

"He worked alone at the Doles place," Shane said, "and I've an idea that he plans to work alone always. You know what he told Hiram Doles. He said that some of you financiers had wrecked his family's fortune years ago, that he'd been preparing for years to even the score, and now was going to collect with heavy interest."

"But, how could he do anything alone here?" Swart asked. "I'm here, and you're here! My Filipino house boy is in the kitchen. A touch on the button downstairs at the clerk's desk, if there was a disturbance, would bring the police in a hurry. If he did manage to get in here, he couldn't get out without being caught."

"He may have the nerve to try it," Shane said. "Hope he does! I haven't made an important arrest for a long time, and I'm getting stale."

Addison Swart started to make a reply, but he did not. There came an interruption which caused Martin Shanes' eyes to bulge and his lower jaw to sag in an expression of astonishment. Addison Swart himself gasped, and reeled back against the wall as though in sudden terror. Shane's hand darted swiftly toward the service revolver he wore in a shoulder holster.

To their ears had come a laugh!

It was a low and mocking laugh. From whence it had come, they were not able to determine. It seemed to fill the room, and it haunted them after it had died away.

"He—he laughs while he loots!" Addison Swart quoted.

CHAPTER III

DEVIL'S HEAD

DETECTIVE MARTIN SHANE RECOVERED from his moment of astonishment and sprang forward.

"Close that safe—quick!" he snapped at Addison Swart. "Shut the panel in front of it! And that other safe—shut the panel in front of that, too!"

Addison Swart was moved to sudden action. He locked the door of the little wall safe and closed the panel in front of it, and then darted across the room and closed the panel before the larger safe.

As he reeled back against the wall again, as though almost overcome with the effort, the cold perspiration of fear popping out on his forehead, there seemed to be an echo of that mocking laugh.

James Peters came rushing into the library from the alcove. Seemingly, he was upon the verge of panic. He dashed across the room to them.

"Did—did you hear it, gentlemen?" he stammered. "That terrible laugh! The same as we heard out to Mr. Doles' country place. There can be no mistake about it. That—that was the Rollicking Rogue!"

"Don't collapse!" Shane sneered at him.

"But it is so terrible! Why don't you do something about it, Mr. Shane? Why don't you catch him, and put him in jail? He may kill somebody next!"

"Let's pull ourselves together, now," Martin Shane begged.

"We heard a funny laugh—no doubt about that. And we don't know where it came from. But it surely didn't come from this apartment. There's nobody here but the three of us. There's some trick about that laugh."

"It sounded so near—right in this room," Addison Swart declared.

"Where's your house boy, Mr. Swart?" Shane asked.

"Santiago? He's probably in the kitchen. But he's beyond suspicion, Shane. He's been with me for years. And I happen to know that he was right here in this apartment the night the Rollicking Rogue robbed the Doles country place. So Santiago can't be the Rollicking Rogue."

"Never thought he was," Shane said. "He's scarcely the Rollicking Rogue type. Have Santiago hang around the living room."

"If I explain this affair to him, he may grow frightened and leave."

"Explain nothing to him. Just have him hang around. If the Rogue should appear while we're in some other part of the apartment, Santiago will yell and attract us. Peters, you got a gun?"

"No, sir! I—I dislike handling weapons, sir!"

"I don't doubt it," Shane replied. "How about you, Mr. Swart?"

"I have a pistol here in the library."

"Better get it," the detective suggested. "Come along with me. I'm going to search this apartment again, going to satisfy myself that there's nobody in it except the three of us and Santiago, and that the doors are locked securely."

"And what about me, sir?" Peters asked.

Addison Swart whirled to confront him. "You finish your work on those books, Peters," he directed. "It'll not take you very long."

"And those bonds, sir—?" Peters questioned.

"Check them over, as I said. I'll be back presently, and put

Santiago let out a piercing, blood-curdling scream.

them into the safe again."

Peters immediately retired to the alcove, as though glad to do so. Martin Shane followed him, to make a search of the alcove first. It took but a moment. There were only a few articles of furniture in the room, beyond or under any of which it was impossible for a person to hide. There was but one window, an art-glass affair high in the outside wall, which could not be opened. There was no door at all, only the archway opening into the library.

Leaving Peters working at his desk, Shane returned to the library and searched there with Swart, and then they passed through the hall and into the living room. Swart rang for the house boy.

"You remain here, Santiago," he instructed. "Miss Molly may return home. I'm going to show this gentleman through the apartment."

Santiago bowed and grinned. Addison Swart led Shane down

another hall, and they began exploring the bed chambers. Martin Shane overlooked nothing. He inspected closets and glanced under the beds. They finally emerged, and went into the kitchen.

The Swart apartment had large storage cupboards. Shane opened and searched them all. He missed nothing. Finally, he stopped with Swart at the service door, which was locked and bolted on the inside.

"There!" Shane said. "Now we're sure that there's nobody in this apartment in addition to ourselves, except Peters and your house boy. This service door is locked and bolted, and the front door is locked. We are on the twelfth floor, so we needn't fear that the Rollicking Rogue will come through a window, unless he lets himself down from the roof."

"He'll never try it!" Swart declared. "As I said before, the idea is ridiculous."

"How about that laugh we heard?" Shane asked.

"Some trick about it, as you said yourself. It certainly was not made by somebody in the apartment. We've searched, and there's nobody here."

"And the Rollicking Rogue can't get in except through one of the doors," Shane pointed out. "If he tries that, we'll nab him! How I wish he'd try it!"

"What shall we do now?" Swart asked.

"We'll go back to the library and sit there and smoke and talk. We'll sit there until after midnight, and make a liar out of the Rollicking Rogue."

It was then they heard the scream.

They both had heard plenty of screams before, but never anything like this. It rang through the apartment—a piercing screech. A second followed it, and after the echoes of that had died away there was an ominous silence.

Revolver held ready, Detective Martin Shane dashed back through the service hall and kitchen, through the dining room and into the living room, with Addison Swart right behind him.

They came to an abrupt stop. Standing in the middle of the big room was Santiago. He seemed rigid, paralyzed with fear. His eyes were bulging, his mouth was open, he was breathing heavily.

"What is it?" Shane cried. "Who let out that yell?"

As he spoke, he grasped Santiago by the arm. Santiago gave another screech at the touch. And then he seemed to recognize Shane and Swart.

He gulped, tried to speak.

James Peters came charging into the living room from the library hall. He, too, was the picture of fear.

"What is it?" he cried. "Who screamed? It sounded like a woman."

"It was the house boy," Shane explained. He shook Santiago and tried to make him come to his senses.

"What made you scream, Santiago?" Swart asked.

"Devil head!" Santiago informed them. "Saw devil head!"

"Talk sense," Swart implored.

"Saw devil head!" Santiago repeated.

"What did it look like? Where did you see it?" Martin Shane demanded.

Santiago gulped and managed to speak. "Through the curtains," he explained, pointing toward some portieres which masked a doorway. "Saw devil head! Red head—yellow horns! Funny mouth—little eyes!"

"Why, that—that's the Rollicking Rogue!" Peters cried. "He wore something like that over his head, out to the Doles place!"

"Devil head!" Santiago persisted. "I quit!"

"Now, Santiago—" Swart began.

"Just a minute before you quit!" Martin Shane snapped at the Filipino. "I want to hear more about this."

"Saw the devil head—through curtains," Santiago explained.

"Stay here with him, you two!" Shane told Swart and Peters.

He darted to the curtains and yanked them aside. He saw only the little hall. Running down the hall, he made a quick exploration of the library and alcove. Nobody was there. Back to the living room he charged.

"The boy must have been dreaming," Shane said. "Swart, we know that there's nobody else in the apartment!"

Santiago was himself now. To him there returned that grandiloquent form of speech so dear to his people.

"It is too much," he announced. "It is distressing to the nerves. I shall pack my suitcase and draw my wages and go. I cannot stand devil heads!"

"Don't be in a rush, Santiago," Swart said. "Somebody has been playing a joke on you. Go to your room and stay there until I come."

Santiago marched away. He was still trembling, but he was making an attempt at a dignified exit.

"Now, what—" Swart began.

"It certainly must have been the Rollicking Rogue," Peters put in. "The description fits the peculiar headpiece he wore out at the Doles place."

"Nonsense!" Martin Shane cried. "I tell you that there's nobody else in the apartment. Santiago merely thought that he saw something."

"Mr. Swart," Peters said, "I fear that I must stop work for this evening and go home. I find myself unable to concentrate. This sort of thing—"

"You go back into the alcove and stay there until you *can* concentrate," Swart interrupted.

"But, sir—"

"Finish those books!" Swart said. "I want to use them tomorrow."

"Don't collapse!" Shane shot at him.

James Peters sighed deeply, and turned away from them.

"We know that the Rollicking Rogue can't be in this apartment," Swart went on to say. "Santiago has been imagining things. Devil's head, indeed!"

Then they heard it again, low and soft, but yet mocking—that laugh!

CHAPTER IV

PRISONERS

DETECTIVE SHANE'S FACE TURNED purple with wrath. He did a deal of sputtering before he managed to speak.

"This is too much!" he declared. "Where did that laugh come from? There's nobody else in the apartment. Santiago didn't do that. And the other three of us—"

"I—I cannot endure much more of it," Peters said, as he turned toward them again.

"Go and finish your books," Shane told him. "Do as Mr. Swart tells you. We'll take care of this Rollicking Rogue affair. He isn't after you!"

Peters turned away again and went into the hall.

"How about it?" Swart asked, in a whisper, after Peters had gone.

"Well, the description Santiago gave fits the thing the Rollicking Rogue wears on his head," Shane admitted. "But he can't be in the apartment, confound it!"

"That laugh—" Swart hinted.

"Some trick about it—must be. It seemed to be all around the room," Shane said. "We'll light up cigars and sit right here in the living room, Mr. Swart. The Rogue couldn't tap either of your safes unless he made you open them for him. So, if he shows up, he'll have to come after you. And I'd like to seem him do that without us getting the drop on him!"

James Peters shuffled along the hall and entered the library. He passed on into the little alcove, stopped just inside the arch to listen for a moment And then his manner changed swiftly.

The sag was gone from his body. His shoulders straightened. The expression in his face changed. He became alert. Suddenly there was a snap to him. A ghost of a smile flashed across his face, and then the expression in his countenance was serious again.

On the end of the desk was a huge brief case wherein James Peters carried his books and documents. Peters opened it, the while listening to the distant voices of Addison Swart and Martin Shane.

From a double bottom cunningly contrived, James Peters drew forth—the devil's head Santiago had seen. He also took out garments of thin colored silk.

Again he listened for a moment, and then he got into the garments quickly, slipping them over his clothes. He presented a rather grotesque appearance. He wore a shimmering bright yellow costume which enveloped his body and made disguise perfect. Around the robe was a sash of brilliant red. Over the shoulders was a cape.

Now he drew on the red helmet with its yellow horns. His eyes glittered through tiny slits. The mouth was exposed, and he twisted it in a hideous grin.

James Peters, timid and retiring secretary for Hiram Doles, was the Rollicking Rogue!

He had spent years preparing for this affair. Doles, Swart and some others had swindled his family years before. James Peters, reared to be a rich man's heir, suddenly found that he was compelled to work his way through college. His mother and sister had been unable to survive under their changed conditions.

And so James Peters, as he now called himself, had made his plans. He had cultivated a false character. He became servile, cowardly to all outward appearances. He studied and became a good secretary, waited for his chance, and managed to get in the employ of one of the crowd that had ruined his family—

Hiram Doles.

Then he had his chance. He learned about Doles and his associates, their habits, their homes and offices. For James Peters had planned a systematic recovery of the funds he felt were due him. He would rob them one at a time, steal from the unscrupulous financiers as they had stolen from others.

He had thought out the Rollicking Rogue idea. And that mysterious laugh—well, Peters had drilled himself to be a wonderful ventriloquist.

Now, he went to the bottom of the big brief case again, and got out an automatic pistol. He slipped from the alcove and into the library, and out into the hall. The voices of Addison Swart and Martin Shane still came to him from the distance. They remained in the living room.

Along the hall the Rollicking Rogue went, slowly and cautiously, the automatic held ready for use. He did not go directly to the living room, but got into the side hall and approached the living room from the direction of the bedchambers.

Swart and Shane were sitting on a large divan, smoking, and from time to time glancing toward the front door of the apartment.

"It's past ten o'clock," Shane observed.

"And we'll be sitting here, just like this, when it's after twelve," Swart declared. "This Rollicking Rogue may have planned to rob me, but he probably found he couldn't get at me. I don't understand that laugh, though."

"Some trick," Shane said. "I was hoping that he'd try something. I can't nab him unless he shows up around where I am."

"You've got to get him, Shane. It's too bad we can't call in the police. But we don't want a lot of publicity. We don't want him to go howling around about his folks being robbed, and getting a lot of sympathy. The newspapers aren't any too friendly for some of us."

"I'll get him," said Martin Shane, "if I ever have the chance of putting eyes on him again."

That laugh again—the low, mocking laugh that seemed to be deriding them! They sat up straight, and Shane started to turn his head to look across the room.

"Hands up!" a stern voice snapped.

They sprang to their feet, whirling.

"Don't go for your guns!"

The warning stopped Shane. Addison Swart was too astonished and terrified to make an attempt to go for his gun. Shane sensed that the man before him meant business, that an attempt to reach his service revolver now would be equivalent to suicide.

Before them, they beheld the Rollicking Rogue. His mouth was twisted in a grotesque grin. But the eyes that glittered through the slits in his mask were far from being humorous. And the automatic he held was an evident menace.

"Ah, Mr. Shane, we meet again!" the Rollicking Rogue said. "Sorry to spoil your little smoke, Mr. Shane, but you may expect such rude interruptions when you are in bad company."

"You—you—!" Martin Shane sputtered. "How'd you get in here?"

"Pardon me, but I never disclose professional secrets," the Rollicking Rogue replied. "I may wish to use the same trick again sometime. You did not search the apartment thoroughly enough, my dear Mr. Shane."

"Can't you do something, Shane?" Swart wailed.

"He could be foolish," the Rollicking Rogue said, "and make a bad move. And then, naturally, you financiers would have to employ another operative. Now, gentlemen, march over to that wall. Stand about four feet out from it, and with your backs toward me. Keep your hands high above your heads. I may mention that this gun I am holding is an excellent weapon, and I am a crack shot with it."

He drove them over to the wall, got them into the positions he had indicated. Martin Shane was seething with rage. Addison Swart was trembling with fear.

"Stand steady!" the Rollicking Rogue commanded. From

beneath his robe he took two small coils of strong rope. Holding his automatic in his left hand, he ran a noose in one of the coils, and, with his right hand, manipulated it much as a cowboy might have done.

The noose sailed through the air, presently, and dropped over Martin Shane's hands, slipped down his arms, and was drawn taut around his middle.

"Steady!" the Rollicking Rogue warned him.

The second noose fell true, and Addison Swart felt the rope grow tight around his waist.

Now the Rollicking Rogue stepped forward briskly to Martin Shane's side. He jammed the muzzle of his automatic against Shane's back.

"Lower your hands carefully, and put them behind you," the Rogue commanded.

Shane muttered curses, but obeyed. Instantly, he felt the rope looped around his wrists, and drawn tight.

"I'm remembering this," Shane said.

"Do so," the Rollicking Rogue told him, as he gave his attention to Addison Swart. "It'll keep you from being proud. Pride is a bad trait in a detective."

Now he lashed them together, turned them around, stepped back and surveyed them. Again he laughed—that horrible laugh from the twisted mouth.

"Step out, gentlemen!" he said. "We'll march into the library, where we'll have the next scene of this very interesting drama!"

CHAPTER V

THE WAGER

THE ROLLICKING ROGUE COMPELLED them to march through the hall. Addison Swart staggered along, weak from fear. He was remembering what he had been told, that this Rogue had a grievance against certain financiers who had ruined his family years before. Detective Martin Shane was mouthing imprecations, profane and otherwise. Shane furtively tested the ropes, and discovered that the Rogue had done his work well.

In the library, the Rogue brought them to a stop in the middle of the room. He stood back some distance from them, keeping them covered with the automatic. Martin Shane surveyed him well, and told himself that identification was impossible. That Rogue costume was an effectual disguise.

"I presume you know, Mr. Swart, why I am here," the Rollicking Rogue said.

"I—I know nothing about it," Swart replied.

"Do not try to be nonchalant," the Rogue begged. "It doesn't become your present appearance. You're half scared to death, and you know it. And well you may be, Addison Swart! Many another man, standing in my place, having in his mind knowledge that I have, would simply make an easy end of it by shooting you down!"

"I—I—what do you want?" Swart stammered.

"As I told you on my card, I have come to collect a part of what is due me. Hiram Doles was the first on the list, and you are the second. We'll have a look into your safe, Mr. Swart."

"What safe?" Swart was bold enough to ask.

The Rollicking Rogue took one step toward him. "Let us have no levity," he warned. "I know that you have a safe in this room, a hidden safe. I want it opened. Get busy!"

"I—I can't, when I'm tied up like this," Swart said.

"Go where you please, and drag Shane along with you."

Addison Swart started across the room, and Martin Shane went along perforce. Swart was trying to keep a glow of triumph out his eyes. He was fighting to keep fear in his face, when hope was struggling to be mirrored there. For Addison Swart intended to expose and open his larger safe, the one which held very little of his worldly goods.

He managed to turn his back to the wall, fumbled with his bound hands, and touched the spring which released the sliding panel. The front of the safe was exposed.

"Very pretty," the Rollicking Rogue commented. "I notice that the safe is a good one, too."

"I—I can't open it with my hands tied like this," Swart told him.

"Who said anything about opening it?"

"You said that you'd come to collect. How can you get anything out of the safe if it isn't opened?"

"Is there anything in it worth my time and trouble?"

"Well—very little," Swart said. "A little money, not much, and some old pieces of jewelry. I never keep much in my safe."

The Rollicking Rogue gave that horrible grin. Addison Swart shivered.

"I've come to collect, and a little money and some pieces of old jewelry wouldn't be enough," the Rogue said.

"It's all there is. I—I'll open the safe and let you see."

"It'd only be a waste of time," said the Rogue. "And I do not care to remain around here all night. Let's get right down to business, Swart."

"What do you mean?"

"I mean—open the other safe!" the Rogue snapped at him.

"What other safe?" Swart cried. "Are you insane?"

"No levity, please!" the Rollicking Rogue begged. "Open your other safe!"

"No—no!" Swart cried.

"Keep your voice down, or I'll shoot! I know all about your other safe, Swart. Walk across the room and touch the hidden spring, move the panel back!"

Swart groaned, but started across the room, pulling the silent Martin Shane along with him. Once more Swart fumbled along the wall, found and touched a spring. The panel slipped back.

"A beauty!" the Rollicking Rogue paid tribute. "Now, that is a safe! I'd expect a safe like that to be stored with valuables."

"I'll not open it!" Swart cried. There was a new ring in his voice. Thought of losing his precious jewels had given him momentary courage.

"You'll not?" the Rogue said. "If you do not, Swart, your daughter will be an heiress to-morrow. I've come to collect, Swart, and I'm one of the best little collectors in the business. You'll open that safe!"

"I'll not!" Swart cried. "Can't you fight, Shane? Can't we get free?"

"No chance!" Martin Shane replied. "But you can bet one thing, Mr. Swart—I'll make this Rollicking Rogue pay for it!"

"Threats never did bother me much," the Rogue observed.

"Mine better bother you," Shane told him. "You've got me now, but I'll get you before we're done. And you're not out of this yet, Rogue! You haven't got away from the building yet."

"That isn't bothering me much, either," said the Rogue. "Swart, are you willing to open that safe?"

"I'll never open it for you!"

"Um! Your manner tells me, my dear Mr. Swart, that I'll make a rich haul from that safe. I hope I'll find enough to pay me for my trouble."

"You'll never get anything out of it!" Swart cried. "I'll not open it! You may kill me, but I'll not open it!"

"If you don't, I'll be compelled to open it myself."

Addison Swart laughed, almost hysterically. "You can't open it!" he said. "Even if you're an expert cracksman, it'd take you hours. It's one of the best safes made."

"I know all about it," the Rogue said. "I'll admit that it's a wonderful safe. I'll make a little bet with you, Swart. I'll try to open that safe. If I can't open it inside ten minutes, I'll go away without taking anything, and leave you alone hereafter. But, if I can open it, I'll take what I want from it—and then shoot you! What do you say, Swart?"

"Why—why—" Swart stammered.

"So you haven't much faith in your safe, after all? Are you afraid to make the deal?"

"You can't open it!" Swart declared, again. "But I—I won't make a bet."

"It's a bet, anyhow!" the Rollicking Rogue snapped at him. "Understand? If I can't open it inside ten minutes, I go away and leave you alone. If I can open it, I shoot you!"

He laughed again—that same low, mocking laugh. He stepped toward them.

"Be seated on that couch gentlemen, and make yourselves as comfortable as possible," the Rollicking Rogue ordered. "Be quick about it!"

They stumbled backward and sank upon the couch, almost back to back, but in such a position that both of them could see the safe. The Rollicking Rogue chuckled, and went across to the safe. He seemed to be inspecting the dial.

"Without doubt, a good safe," he reported. "An ordinary safe man couldn't open this, Swart. But I'm not an ordinary safe man."

He grasped the knob and started working the combination, turning his head frequently and twisting his mouth in that horrible grin.

"I anticipate a rich haul here," he said. "I have been told, Swart, that you collect fine jewels. Probably some of them are in this safe. I'll hurt you twice when I take them. You'll lose their value, and you'll also lose things you love."

"If—if you don't open the safe in ten minutes—" Swart began.

"If I do not, I'll go away and leave you alone, as I promised. But, if I do, Swart—I'll shoot you down! Remember the bet!"

He turned from them and bent over the dial. His fingers manipulated the knob. They could hear him chuckling as he worked.

The Rollicking Rogue was enjoying himself. As James Peters, he had expected to force Swart to open that safe. But Swart had opened it to get out those bonds, and James Peters had stood at his shoulder and watched. He had observed the combination—and his trained mind had retained it.

He was playing for suspense now, trying to torture Addison Swart mentally, as he believed Swart should be tortured. Once more he turned his head and regarded the two on the couch, his eyes glittering.

"Got a couple of minutes left," he told them. "If I can't open it very soon— Ah!"

Something clicked. Addison Swart gave a little cry of dismay. The Rollicking Rogue stood erect. He pulled the door of the safe open.

"You lose, Swart!" he said. "Better start remembering your prayers!"

CHAPTER VI

QUICK ACTION

ADDISON SWART GAVE A screech of mingled rage and fear. Martin Shane gasped his surprise.

"They don't make safes that I can't open," the Rollicking Rogue boasted. "Now, we'll investigate the contents of this one. And then, I'll attend to you, Swart!"

The Rogue turned from them slightly again, but Shane knew he was not off guard for a moment. He opened an inside box, and brought out a jewel case.

"No—no!" Swart cried.

"Think a lot of them, do you?" the Rogue asked. "I'm glad of that. I hope their loss means torture for you, Swart! I have a way of disposing of them."

He carried the case to the table, opened it, spilled the jewels out. They scintillated in the light, flashing a thousand rays from their facets. Addison Swart gave another cry of agony. The Rollicking Rogue laughed.

"Quite a haul," he observed. "I'll get top price for these, Swart. They'll liquidate your part of the debt owed me."

He tossed the jewel case aside. From beneath his costume he brought forth a handkerchief. He poured the jewels upon the handkerchief, made a neat little package. Swart watched him closely, in horror. A sudden realization came to him of what this meant. The jewels he loved were being stolen. This Rollicking Rogue thought only of their monetary value.

Swart gave another cry and tried to get up from the couch.

He started to get to his feet, and pulled Shane over against him.

"You can't make it," the Rollicking Rogue told him. "That is one reason why I tied you together. And now, Swart, we have a little settlement coming, I believe. You lost a bet!"

Swart dropped back upon the couch. Shane growled and fought to get his hands free. The Rollicking Rogue approached, the grin gone from his face now, his mouth a stern line, his eyes flashing through the holes in his mask.

"Say your prayers, Swart!" he snapped.

"Don't do it, Rogue!" Shane snapped at him. "Robbery means only prison, but murder means the hot chair!"

"If the murderer is caught!" the Rogue said.

"If you kill Swart, Rogue, you'd better kill me, too. For, if you don't, I'll get you if it takes me years!"

"Commendable ambition," the Rogue said. "How about it, Swart? Have you said your prayers?"

Swart recoiled before the Rogue's advance. Nearer and nearer he stepped, bending forward slightly. The muzzle of the automatic was lifted.

"No—no!" Addison Swart cried.

"You lost the bet! Losers must pay!"

"If you do it, Rogue—" Shane started again.

The Rogue ignored him. He bent closer to Addison Swart. Globules of perspiration popped out on Swart's forehead. His face turned green. His breath was coming in quick gasps. His eyes focused on the muzzle of that terrible weapon, bulged.

There was a moment of silence, of terrific tension. And then the Rollicking Rogue dropped the muzzle of his automatic and stepped back.

"Bah! I can't shoot a coward!" he said. "Look at him, Shane! He's fainted! He'll be conscious again in a moment, no doubt. And then, after I'm gone, you two can figure out some way of getting free."

The Rollicking Rogue chuckled again, twisted his mouth in

that hideous grin. But the grin was swept off his face as he heard a voice from the doorway:

"What's all this?"

The Rogue whirled swiftly, his automatic coming up. In the doorway stood Miss Molly Swart!...

SHE ADVANCED swiftly into the room, her eyes wide with wonder. Her father had told her nothing of the threat he had received from the Rollicking Rogue.

She did not know the meaning of this scene. But Martin Shane tried to inform her.

"Get back, Miss Swart!" Shane cried. "Run for help! This is the Rollicking Rogue! He's robbed the safe—"

Then she saw how her father and Shane were bound together, and that her father seemed to be unconscious. She gave another cry and rushed toward the couch. The Rollicking Rogue got around her, between her and the door.

"He'll be all right," the Rogue said. "He only fainted. Pardon me, Miss Swart, but—"

"You beast!" she flared at him.

"There are beasts and beasts," the Rogue observed. "Since my work here is done, and I have to make a getaway—"

"And do you think you'll get away?" she cried.

"I dislike to use violence toward a lady," he told her. "I sincerely hope I'll not have to do so in this case. But, if it proves necessary—"

She rushed at him suddenly, her eyes flaming, her hands going out like claws. The Rollicking Rogue, chuckling again, side-stepped neatly. But that was a slight error. For she did not turn and rush at him again. She ran out into the hall, sped down it toward the living room.

"Santiago!" she cried. "Santiago!"

She was shrieking for the house boy. And her cries might penetrate to another apartment and cause an investigation, the Rogue knew. He pursued at top speed, caught her just as she reached a telephone instrument and started to grasp the receiver.

She fought him like a mad woman, while the Rogue tried to get control of her wrists. She struck, kicked, tried to bite. The frightened Filipino house boy came hurrying into the room,

The Rollicking Rogue tossed the girl aside and threw up his automatic.

"You—Santiago!" he snapped. "Back against that wall! Hands up!"

The house boy obeyed the command instantly. Then Molly Swart was at the Rogue again, screaming, trying to fight, trying once more to reach the telephone. The Rogue got hold of her wrists, finally, held her comparatively quiet. But he could not stop her screams.

He picked her up, motioned Santiago to go ahead, and carried her rapidly through the hall. They went into her bedchamber, where the Rogue knew there was a large closet in a corner of the room. He tossed Molly Swart into the closet, slammed the door shut, locked it.

Once more he made a slight error. The Filipino had conquered his fear in a measure and the Rogue suddenly found another foe upon his back.

Santiago might not have fought for Addison Swart, holding to a belief that every man should fight his own battles, but he would fight for Molly Swart. He fought like a wildcat for a moment, until the Rogue got control of him. A short, sharp blow with the barrel of the automatic, and Santiago lapsed into momentary unconsciousness.

The Rogue carried him out into the hall, to another bedchamber, and there found another closet. He tossed Santiago in, and turned the key in the lock. Then he hurried back into the main hall.

Molly Swart was screaming in her closet. Martin Shane was bellowing in the library. In a moment, the Rogue supposed, Santiago would be conscious an adding his screams to the din.

And it was about eleven o'clock at night.

He heard the telephone bell jangle in the living room. The Rogue rushed toward it, lifted the receiver.

"Hello!" he called.

"Is this Mr. Swart?" a man's voice asked.

"What's wanted?"

"This is the night clerk, Mr. Swart. Some of the other tenants are telephoning the office—think there's something wrong in your apartment—say they are hearing screams."

The Rollicking Rogue laughed into the transmitter. "This is not Mr. Swart," he said. "This is the Rollicking Rogue! Those screams are being made by Miss Swart and the Filipino house boy. There's a private detective bellowing his head off, too. You see, I've been robbing the safe, and they don't like it!"

CHAPTER VII

THE WAY OUT

EPLACING THE RECEIVER ON its hook, the Rollicking Rogue dashed back through the hall to the library. He found that Addison Swart was conscious again, but still weak from fear.

"Shut up!" he commanded Shane. "You've howled enough! Keeping people awake. Get up, you two, and hustle along! If you don't I'll give you a couple of raps on the head and put you to sleep!"

He got them to their feet, hurried them along the hall and back to the kitchen. He knew that he had no time to spare. The night clerk would know there was something wrong. He would be up there soon, with the house detective and perhaps others.

The Rollicking Rogue stopped his victims in front of one of the big storage cupboards off the pantry, one which happened to be empty, and opened the door.

"In with you!" he snapped. "Somebody'll turn you loose before long. Got to make my getaway now."

"I'll get you—" Martin Shane began.

"I'll send you a notice, Shane, when I'm going to collect my next installment. That's a promise," said the Rollicking Rogue.

He thrust them inside, closed and locked the heavy door. Then he dashed down the hall toward the service entrance, making plenty of noise about it, knowing well that Shane was listening. He unbolted and unlocked the service door. It would look as though he had left the apartment that way.

263

The Rogue caught her just as she reached a telephone instrument....

Now he stripped off the Rogue costume and left it on the floor in a heap, in front of the door. More mute evidence that the Rollicking Rogue had shed his disguise and made a getaway from the service entrance.

It was James Peters who rushed back through the apartment to the living room. As he reached it, he heard voices in the corridor outside. Molly Swart was still screeching for help. Martin Shane had commenced again. Santiago was joining in the chorus.

Peters dashed into the library and through it and into the alcove. He stuffed the package of jewels into the secret compartment of his big brief case. He knocked a few books off the desk to the floor, and kicked them around.

From the brief case he took a gag, and effectually gagged himself. Next, he took out a length of rope, which was looped and knotted peculiarly. The loops went over his ankles and wrists. James Peters stretched himself on the floor, then drew up his knees. He gave a single jerk on a piece of the rope—and he was bound hand and foot, every knot tight....

THE NIGHT clerk pounded on the main door of the apartment. An assistant manager, the house detective, a janitor were with him. Nobody answered the ringing of the bell, nobody answered the knocking.

Screams and cries were still coming from the apartment. Other tenants were tumbling out into the corridor, in all stages of dress and undress.

"Smash in the door!" the assistant manager ordered.

The night clerk stepped aside. The house detective hurled his bulk against the door, backed away, hurled himself forward again. The heavy door held.

"Here!" the night clerk cried. "The service door's unlocked."

They rushed to the service door The house detective, revolver in hand, entered with the others close behind him. They heard the howls of Martin Shane, located him in the storage cupboard, opened the door to find Shane and Addison Swart lashed together.

"Get him!" Shane cried. "The Rollicking Rogue! He's somewhere in the building."

"The service door was unlocked," the house detective said.

"Then he got out that way," Shane declared. "Telephone downstairs and have everybody slopped leaving the house."

"He shed his funny clothes at the door," the night clerk said. "Who knows what he looks like? He may be a tenant in the house, or somebody visiting a tenant. We can't grab everybody and give him the third degree."

Shane darted toward the living room with Addison Swart at his heels. They could hear the cries of Molly Swart, and were trying to find her. They located her, released her, went in search of Santiago, whose shrill screams in two languages were still ringing through the apartment.

A door was unlocked, opened, and Santiago rushed forth. He darted up to Swart.

"I quit!" he cried. "Too much! I quit! Devil's head and devil's body! I get quiet job in insane house!"

Detective Martin Shane had a thought. "What became of Peters?" he asked Swart, whirling toward him. "He was in the alcove, wasn't he?"

"Yes. He had those bonds," Swart replied. "Maybe the Rogue killed Peters, the poor devil, and stole those bonds."

"We'll see," Shane said.

He led the rush to the library, through it, and to the alcove. There they found Peters. He was doubled upon the floor, bound and gagged. They worked feverishly getting the ropes off him. They tore away the gag, helped him to his feet.

"This is terrible—terrible!" Peters moaned. "Oh, Mr. Swart!"

"I'm sorry, Peters," Swart said. "The scoundrel got all my jewels."

"Look at my books all over the floor! Tut, tut!" Peters said.

"What happened to you?" Martin Shane asked.

"I do not know whether I can tell you," Peters replied. "I am rather confused, and might give you false information. I'd not like to do that."

"Out with it!" Martin Shane snapped impatiently.

"I—I must have been held up with a gun, commanded to keep silent, and bound and gagged," Peters said.

"Did the Rollicking Rogue bind and gag you?" Shane wanted to know.

"Yes, the Rollicking Rogue did it," Peters replied. They did not see the twinkle in his eyes.

"And the bonds—what about the bonds?" Addison Swart cried. "Did the fiend get the bonds?"

"They're safe," Peters replied. "I'd checked them, and I tossed them into a drawer of the desk. The Rollicking Rogue didn't ransack the desk. Here are your bonds, Mr. Swart."

Peters drew out a drawer of the desk, took the bonds from it, and handed them to Swart. It was a subtle touch. Had there been the faintest suspicion that Peters was the Rollicking Rogue, the return of those bonds would have lulled it.

Peters staggered and stumbled out into the library. He had his brief case with him. It was gaping open. Peters put it down on a table. As he talked and told of his experience, he arranged his books and documents in the big brief case.

Some half hour later, after the excitement had subsided, James Peters left the Westmanor Arms carrying that brief case in an ordinary manner, as though its contents had been of little value.

But, in the bottom of it, were Addison Swart's valuable jewels.

28630533R00160

Made in the USA
Lexington, KY
26 December 2013